Very truly yours
W. T. Thompson

New York, D. Appleton & Co.

MAJOR JONES'S COURTSHIP:

DETAILED, WITH OTHER

SCENES, INCIDENTS, AND ADVENTURES,

IN

A SERIES OF LETTERS BY HIMSELF.

REVISED AND ENLARGED.

TO WHICH ARE ADDED

THIRTEEN HUMOROUS SKETCHES.

WITH ILLUSTRATIONS BY CARY.

"A little nonsense, now and then,
Is relished by the wisest men."

NEW YORK:
D. APPLETON & COMPANY,
549 & 551 BROADWAY.
1872.

TO

MY WIFE,

THE DEAR COMPANION,

WHO BLESSED THE MORNING,

CHEERED THE NOON,

AND BRIGHTENS THE EVENING

OF MY LIFE,

I DEDICATE THIS VOLUME.

W. T. T

TO THE READER.

Twenty-eight years ago the sketches of rustic life and character comprised in the following pages —if so much may be claimed for them—were written to give variety and local interest to the columns of a Georgia country newspaper. In the composition of them, from week to week, the highest aim of the writer was to afford amusement to his readers, the thought that they would ever appear in any other form, or that they would have any other than a home circulation and an ephemeral existence, never having entered his mind; nor would his hastily-written letters ever have attained the dignity of a book, but for the importunities of a friend who insisted on giving them that form at his own expense. Inquiry as to the cost of a small edition brought a proposition from a publishing house in Philadelphia, which resulted in the issue of the first illustrated edition of "Major Jones's Courtship." In the first year of its publication, with no knowledge of its value, the copyright was, for a nominal consideration, assigned to the publishers; since which time till now the author has had no pecuniary interest in the book. The term of the original copyright, twenty-eight years, having expired, under the late just and beneficent law of Congress giving to living authors the exclusive right of renewal for a term of fourteen years, the copyright reverts to him.

The fact that the book has survived its copyright, and during more than a quarter of a century has maintained its place in public favor, must be accepted as a proof that popularity is not always the meed of merit, and that as reputation is "oft got without merit, and lost without deserving," so the humblest efforts sometimes achieve what genius cannot always command. With this fact in view, our maturer judgment distrusts itself, and in the revision of the crude production of youthful days, we hesitate to change expressions or re-dress thoughts which in their unstudied phrase have struck the chord of popular sympathy.

Nevertheless, in preparing this edition of the book for the press, much labor has been bestowed upon it. Puerilities have been eliminated, needed amplifications have been supplied, and many verbal and orthographic changes, not inconsistent with the general character of the story, have been made. The original design was to portray Southern rustic life and character, with no more of exaggeration than was necessary to give distinctiveness to the picture. For this purpose the local dialect or *patois* peculiar to the rural district of Georgia was employed, with the orthography necessary to convey the peculiar pronunciation of the word. Consistency, and not an effort at cheap wit, compelled the resort not only to incorrect grammar, but also to a mode of spelling many words, more simple than is found in our standard lexicons. Where this bad spelling was unnecessary to the "cracker" pronunciation, and the change did not involve too glaring an inconsistency with the style of the composition, it has been modified.

The series of sketches which have been added in this volume were written some time subsequently to the first publication of the "Courtship;" but as they are in the same style, describe the same localities, and comprise many of the same characters, they seem appropriate in the place which has been assigned them. If in their new dress they shall add interest to the volume, and serve the reader to beguile the tedium of a heavy hour, they will render him a cheerful debtor to

THE AUTHOR.

SAVANNAH, *March* 20, 1872.

PREFACE.

Sense my frend Mr. Thompson has made a book out of my letters, I spose I must put a preface to it; for that and the bindin and the title-page is the most important part of a book now-a-days—and one without a preface in frunt would be like a log cabin with no string hangin out at the dore. People can git along without the cider, if they can only git into the house—and so they can do without the sense in a book if they can only have some sort of a interduction to its contents.

Well, I do blieve if I was a author I would sooner write a dozen books nor one preface; it's a great deal easier to write a heap of nonsense than it is to put a good face on it after it's writ—and I don't know when I've had a job that's puzzled me so much how to begin it. I've looked over a whole heap of books to see how other writers done, but they all seem to be about the same thing. They all feel a monstrous desire to benefit the public one way or other—some is anxious to tell all they know about certain matters, jest for the good of the public—some wants to edify the public—some has been 'swaded by frends to give ther book to the public—and others has been induced to publish ther writins jest for the benefit of futer generations—but not one of 'em ever had a idee to make a cent for themselves!

Now, none of these excuses don't zactly meet my case. I don't suppose the public—'cept it is them as is courtin—will be much benefited by readin my letters—I'm sure Mr. Thompson wouldn't went to all the expense jest to please his frends, and for my part I'm perfectly willin to let posterity write ther own books. So I don't see any other way than to jest come right out with the naked truth—and that is, that *my book was made jest a purpose to sell and make money.* Ther aint a single lie in the book, and I'm termined ther shant be none in the preface.

When Mr. Thompson fust writ me word he was gwine to put my letters in a book, I felt sort o' skeered, for fear them bominable critics mought take hold of it and tear it all to flinders—as they always nabs a' most every thing that's got a kiver on; but when I come to think, I remembered ther was two ways of gittin into a field—under, as well as over the fence. Well, the critics is like a pretty considerable high fence round the public taste, and books gits into the world of letters jest as hogs does into a tater patch—some over and some under. Now and then one gits hung, and the way it gits peppered is distressin—but them that gits in under the fence is jest as safe as them that gits in over. Seein as I is perfectly satisfied with the under route, I dont think the critics will tackle my book. If they does all I can say is, I give 'em joy with ther small potaters.

JOSEPH JONES.

PINEVILLE (GA.), *April* 10, 1844.

CONTENTS.

MAJOR JONES'S COURTSHIP.

SKETCHES.

Characters who appear in this History.

MAJOR JONES'S LETTERS.

LETTER I.

PINEVILLE, *May* 28, 1842.

To MR. THOMPSON:—*Dear Sir*—Ever sense you was down to Pineville, it's been on my mind to write you a letter, but the boys lowed I'd better not, cause you mought take me off about my spellin and dictionary. But something happened to me tother night, so monstrous provoking, that I can't help tellin you about it, so you can put other young chaps on ther gard. It all come of chawing so much tobacker, and I reckon I've wished ther was no such plagy stuff, more'n five hundred times sense it happened.

You know the Stallinses lives on the plantation in the summer and goes to town in the winter. Well, Miss Mary Stallins, who you know is the darlinest gall in the county, come home tother day to see her folks. You know she's been to the Female College, down to Macon, for most a year now. Before she went, she used to be jest as plain as a old shoe, and used to go fishin and huckleberryin with us, with nothin but a calico sun-bonnet on, and was the wildest thing you ever seed. Well, I always used to have a sort of a sneakin notion after Mary Stallins, and so when she come, I brushed up, and was 'termined to have a right serious talk with her about old matters; not knowin but she mought be captivated by some of them Macon fellers.

So, shure enough, off I started, unbeknowin to anybody, and rode right over to the plantation—(you know ours is right jinin the widder Stallinses.) Well, when I got thar, I felt a little sort o' sheepish; but I soon got over that, when Miss Carline said, (but she didn't mean me to hear her,) "There, Pinny, (that's Miss Mary's nick-name, you know,) there's your bow come."

Miss Mary looked mighty sort o' redish when I shuck her hand and told her howdy; and she made a sort of stoop over and a dodge back, like the little galls does to the school-marm, and said "Good evenin, Mr. Jones," (she used to always call me jest Joe.)

"Take a chair, Joseph," said Miss Carline; and we sot down in the parlor, and I begun talkin to Miss Mary about Macon, and the long ride she had, and the bad roads, and the monstrous hot weather, and the like.

She didn't say much, but was in a mighty good humor and laughed a heap. I told her I never seed sich a change in anybody. Nor I never did. Why, she didn't look like the same gall. Good gracious! she looked so nice and trim—jest like some of them pictures what they have in APPLETONS' JOURNAL—with her hair all komed down longside of her face, as slick and shiny as a mahogany burow. When she laughed she didn't open her mouth like she used to; and she sot up straight and still in her chair, and looked so different, but so monstrous pretty! I ax'd her a heap of questions, about how she liked Macon, and the Female College, and so forth; and she told me a heap about 'em. But old Miss Stallins and Miss Carline and Miss Kesiah, and all of 'em, kep all the time interruptin us, axin about mother—if she was well, and if she was gwine to the Spring church next Sunday, and what luck she had with her soap, and all sich stuff—and I do believe I told the old woman more'n twenty times that mother's old turky-hen was settin on fourteen eggs.

Well, I wasn't to be backed out that-a-way—so I kep it a goin the best I could, till bimeby old Miss Stallins let her knitin drap three or four times, and then begun to nod.

I seed the galls lookin at oneanother and pinchin oneanother's elbows, and Miss Mary said she wondered what time it was, and said the College disciplines, or something like that, didn't low late hours. I seed how the game was gwine—but howsumever, I kep talkin to her like a cotton gin in packin time, as hard as I could clip it, till bimeby the old lady went to bed, and after a bit the galls all cleared, and left Miss Mary to herself. That was jest the thing I wanted.

Well, she sot on one side of the fire-place, and I sot on tother, so I could spit on the hath, whar ther was nothin but a lighterd chunk burnin to give light. Well, we talked and talked, and I know you would like to hear all we talked about, but that would be too long. When I'm very interested in any thing, or git bother'd about any thing, I can't help chawin a heap of tobacker, and then I spits uncontionable, specially if I'm talkin. Well, we sot thar and talked, and the way I spit, was larmin to the crickets! I axed Miss Mary if she had any bows down to Macon.

"Oh, yes," she said, and then she went on and named over Matthew Matix, Nat. Filosofy, Al. Geber, Retric Stronomy, and a whole heap of fellers, that she'd been keepin company with most all her time.

"Well," ses I, "I spose they're mazin poplar with you, aint they, Miss Mary?"—for I felt mighty oneasy, and begun to spit a good deal worse.

"Yes," ses she, "they're the most interestin companions I ever had, and I am anxious to resume their pleasant society."

I tell you what, that sort o' stumped me, and I spit right slap on the chunk and made it "flicker and flare" like the mischief. It was a good thing it did, for I blushed as blue as a Ginny squash.

I turned my tobacker round in my mouth, and spit two or three times, and the old chunk kep up a most bominable fryin.

"Then I spose your gwine to forgit old acquaintances," ses I, "sense you's been to Macon, among them lawyers and doctors, is you, Miss Mary? You thinks more of them than you does of anybody else, I spose."

"Oh," ses she, "I am devoted to them—I think of them day and night!"

That was *too* much—it shot me right up, and I

sot as still as could be for more'n a minute. I never felt so warm behind the ears afore in all my life. Thunder! how my blood did bile up all over me, and I felt like I could knock Matthew Matix into a greas-spot, if he'd only been thar.

Miss Mary sot with her handkercher up to her face, and I looked straight into the fire-place. The blue blazes was runnin round over the old chunk, ketchin hold here and lettin go thar, sometimes gwine most out, and then blazin up a little. I couldn't speak—I was makin up my mind for tellin her the sitewation of my hart—I was jest gwine to tell her my feelins, but my mouth was chock full of tobacker, so I had to spit—and slap it went, right on the light-wood chunk, and out *it* went, spang!

I swar, I never did feel so tuck aback in all my born days. I didn't know what to do.

"My lord, Miss Mary," ses I, "I didn't go to do it.—Jest tell me the way to the kitchen, and I'll go and git a light."

But she never said nothin, so I sot down agin, thinkin she'd gone to git one herself, for it was pitch dark, and I couldn't see my hand afore my face.

Well, I sot thar and ruminated, and waited a long time, but she didn't come; so I begun to think maybe she wasn't gone. I couldn't hear nothin, nor I couldn't see nothin; so bimeby ses I, very low, for I didn't want to wake up the family—ses I,

"Miss Mary! Miss Mary!" But nobody answered.

Thinks I, what's to be done? I tried agin.

"Miss Mary! Miss Mary!" ses I. But it was no use.

Then I heard the galls snickerin and laughin in the next room, and I begun to see how it was; Miss Mary was gone and left me thar alone.

"Whar's my hat?" ses I, pretty loud, so somebody mought tell me. But they only laughed worse.

I begun to feel about the room, and the first thing I know'd, spang! goes my head, agin the edge of the pantry dore what was standin open. The fire flew, and I couldn't help but swar a little. "D——n the dore," ses I—"whar's my hat?" But nobody said nothin, and I went gropin about in the dark, feelin round to find some way out, when I put my hand on the dore knob. All right, thinks I, as I pushed the dore open quick.——Ther was a scream!—heads poped under the bed kiver quicker'n lightnin—something white fluttered by the burow, and out went the candle. I was in the galls room! But there was no time for apologisin, even if they could stopped squealin long enough to hear me. I crawfished out of that place monstrous quick, you may depend. Hadn't I went and gone and done it sure enough! I know'd my cake was all dough then, and I jest determined to git out of them digins soon as possible, and never mind about my hat.

Well, I got through the parlor dore after rakin my shins three or four times agin the chairs, and was feelin along through the entry for the front dore; but somehow I was so flustrated that I tuck the wrong way, and bimeby kerslash I went, right over old Miss Stallinses spinnin-wheel, onto the floor! I

"I tuck the wrong way, and bimeby kerslosh I went, right over old Miss Stallinses spinnin-wheel." p. 22.

hurt myself a good deal; but that didn't make me half so mad as to hear them confounded galls a gigglin and laughin at me.

"Oh," said one of 'em, (it was Miss Kesiah, for I knowed her voice,) "there goes mother's wheel! my lord!"

I tried to set the cussed thing up agin, but it seemed to have more'n twenty legs, and wouldn't stand up no how.—Maybe it was broke. I went out of the dore, but I hadn't more'n got down the steps, when bow! wow! wow! comes four or five infernal grate big coon-dogs, rite at me. "Git out! git out! hellow, Cato! call off your dogs!" ses I, as loud as I could. But Cato was sound asleep, and if I hadn't a run back into the hall, and got out the front way as quick as I could, them devils would chawed my bones for true.

When I got to my hoss, I felt like a feller jest out of a hornet's nest; and I reckon I went home a little of the quickest.

Next mornin old Miss Stallins sent my hat by a little nigger; but I haint seed Mary Stallins sense. Now you see what comes of chawin tobacker! No more from

Your friend, till death, Jos. Jones.

P. S. I blieve Miss Mary's gone to the Female College agin. If you see her, I wish you would say a good word to her for me, and tell her I forgives her all, and I hope she will do the same by me. Don't you think I better write her a letter, and explain matters to her?

NOTABEMY.—This letter was writ to my perticke-ler frend Mr. Thompson, when he was editen the Family Companion magazine, down in Macon. I had no notion of turnin author then; but when it come out with my name to it, and ther wasn't no use of denyin it, and specially as he writ me a letter beggin I would go on and write for the Miscellany, I felt a obligation restin on me to continue my correspondence to that paper. All my other letters was writ to Mr. Thompson, in Madison. J. J.

LETTER II.

PINEVILLE, *August* 23, 1842.

TO MR. THOMPSON:—*Dear Sir*—The "Southern Miscellany," what you sent me, is received, and is jest the thing. It had that letter what I writ you down in Macon, only in larger letters, so our folks could read it a great deal better.

Miss Mary is home now, and things is tuck all sorts of a turn lately, sense I quit chawin tobacker and tuck to writin literature. I went down to Macon to the zamination, whar I got a heap of new kinks; but I havn't time to tell you nothin about that now, as our muster comes on next Friday. You know I's Majer, and things is in a most bominable snarl down here bout this time. I seed your piece to correspondents, whar you said you hoped Majer Jones would write for your colums, and I wanted to tell you that you mought spect to hear from me every now and then, if you like my writins. I felt a little sort o' scared at fust; but all my quaintances as had read my letter to you, advise me to go a-head and be a literary caracter, and as you want me to write for the "Miscellany," I'm termined to do what I kin to raise the literature of Pineville.

If nothin happens at the muster—for ther's some monstrous fractious caracters down in our beat, and they musn't come a cavortin bout me when I give orders, like they did round Samwell Cockrum, pullin him off his hoss and puttin him on the fence, and tyin things to his hosses tail, or I'll put every devil of 'em under the rest—if nothin don't turn up to pervent, you may expect a letter from me for your next paper. No more from

Your friend, till death, Jos. Jones.

LETTER III.

Pineville, *August* 29, 1842.

To Mr. Thompson:—*Dear Sir*—Jest as I expected, only a thunderin sight wurse! You know I said in my last that we was gwine to have a betallion muster in Pineville. Well, the muster has tuck place, and I reckon sich other doins you never hearn of afore.

I come in town the night before, with my regimentals in a bundle, so they couldn't be siled by ridin, and as soon as I got my breckfast, I begun rigin out for the muster. I had a bran new pair of boots, made jest a purpose, with long legs to 'em, and a cocked hat like a half moon, with one of the tallest kind of red fethers in it, a blue cloth regimental coat, all titivated off with gold and buttons, and a pair of yaller britches of the finest kind. Well, when I went to put 'em on, I couldn't help but cuss all the tailors and shoomakers in Georgia. In the fust place, my britches like to busted and wouldn't reach more'n half way to my jacket, then it tuck two niggers and a pint of soap to git my boots on; and my coat had tail enough for a bed-quilt, and stood straight out behind like a fan-tail pidgin.—It wouldn't hang right no how you could pull it. I never was so dratted mad, specially when ther was no time to fix things, for the fellers wer comin in town in gangs and beginin to call for me to come out and take the command. Expectation was ris considerable high, cause I was pledged to quip myself in uniformity to the law, if I was 'lected Majer.

Well, bimeby I went to the dore and told Bill Skinner and Tom Cullers to fix ther companys, and have 'em all ready when I made my 'pearance. Then the fuss commenced. Thar wasn't but one drum in town, and Bill Skinner swore that should drum for his company, cause it belonged to that beat; and Tom Cullers swore the nigger should drum for *his* company, cause he belonged to his crowd. Thar was the old harry to pay, and it was gittin wurse. I didn't know what to do, for they was all comin to me about it, and cussin and shinin and disputin so I couldn't hardly hear one from tother. Thinks I, I must show my authority in this bisness; so says I,

"I sot the niggers a drummin and fifin as hard as they could split."

p. 27

"In the name of the State of Georgia, I command the drum to drum for me. I's Majer of this betallion and I's commander of the musick too!" The thing tuck fust rate; ther was no more rumpus about it, and I sot the niggers a drummin and fifin as hard as they could split right afore the tavern dore.

It was monstrous diffikilt to git the men to fall in. Ther haint been none of them reformed drunkerds down here yit, and the way the fellers does love peach and hunny is mazin.

Bimeby Bill Skinner tuck a stick and made a long straight streak in the sand, and then hollered out, "Oh, yes! oh, yes! all you as belongs to Coon-holler beat is to git in a straight line on this trail!" Tom Cullers made a streak for his beat, and the fellers begun to string themselves along in a line, and in about a quarter of a ower they wer all settled like bees on a bean-pole, pretty considerable straight.

After a while they sent word to me that they was all ready, and I had my hoss fotched up to tother side of the tavern; but when I cum to him the bominable fool didn't know me sumhow, and begun kickin and prancin, and cavortin about like mad. I made the niggers hold him till I got on, then I sent word round to the drummer to drum like blazes as soon as he seed me turn the corner, and to the men to be ready to salute. My sword kep rattlin agin the side of my hoss, and the fool was skeered so he didn't know which eend he stood on, and kep dancin about and squattin and rarein, so I couldn't hardly hold on to him.

The nigger went and told the men what I sed;

and when I thought they was all ready, round I went in a canter, with my sash and regimentals a flyin and my red fether a wavin as graceful as a corn tossel in a whirlwind; but jest as I got to the corner ther was a fuss like heaven and yeath was comin together. Rattletebang, wher-r-r-r-r! went the drum, and the nigger blowed the fife right out straight, till his eyes was sot in his head—"harra! hey-y-y! hurra!" went all the niggers and everybody else—my hoss wheelin and pitchin worse than ever, right up to the muster—and, before I could draw my breth, bang! bang! bang de bang! bang! bang! went every gun in the crowd, and all I knowed was, I was whirlin, and pitchin, and swingin about in the smoke and fire till I cum full length right smack on the ground, "in all the pride, pomp, and circumstances of glorious war," as Mr. Shakspear ses.

Lucky enough I didn't git hurt; but my cote was split clean up to the coller, my yaller britches busted all to flinders, and my cocked hat and fether all nocked into a perfect mush. Thunder and lightnin! thinks I, what must be a man's feelins in a rale battle, whar they're shootin bullets in good yearnest!

Cum to find out, it was all a mistake; the men didn't know nothing about military ticktacks, and thought I meant a regular fourth of July salute.

I had to lay by my regimentals.—But I know'd my caracter was at stake as a officer, and I termined to go on with the muster. So I told Skinner and Cullers to git the men straight agin, and when they was all in a line I sorted 'em out. The fellers what had guns I put in front, them what had sticks in the rare,

Militia—The Parade.

p. 29.

and them what had no shoes, down to the bottom by themselves, so nobody couldn't tramp on ther toes. A good many of 'em begun to forgit which was ther right hand and which was ther left; and some of 'em begun to be very diffikilt to manage, so I termined to march 'em out to a old field, whar they couldn't git no more licker, specially sense I was bleeged to wear my tother clothes.

Well, after I got 'em all fixed, ses I, "Music! quick time! by the right flank, file left, march!" They stood for about a minit lookin at me. "By flank mar-r-r-ch!" ses I, as loud as I could holler. Then they begun lookin at oneanother and hunchin oneanother with ther elbows, and the fust thing I know'd they was all twisted up in a snarl, goin both ways at both eends, and all marchin through other in the middle, in all sorts of helter skelter fashion. "Halt!" ses I, "halt! Whar upon yeath is you all gwine!"—And thar they was, all in a huddle. They know'd better, but jest wanted to bother me, I do blieve.

"Never mind," ses I, "gentlemen, we'll try that revolution over agin." So when I got 'em all in line agin, I splained it to 'em, and gin 'em the word so they could understand it. "Forward march!" ses I —and away they went, not all together, but two by two, every feller waitin til his turn cum to step, so before the barefoot ones got started, I couldn't hardly see to tother eend of the betallion. I let 'em go ahead till we got to the old field, and then I tried to stop 'em; but I had 'em in gangs all over the field in less than no time. "Close up!" ses I, as loud as I could holler; but they only stood and looked at me like they didn't know what I meant. "Git into a straight line agin," ses I. That brung 'em all together, and I told 'em to rest a while, before I put 'em through the manuel.

Bout this time out come a whole heap of fellers with sum candidates, what was runnin for the Legislater, and wanted I should let 'em address the betallion. I told 'em I didn't care so long as they didn't kick up no row.

Well, the men wer all high up for hearin the speeches of the candidates, and got round 'em thick as flies around a fat gourd. Ben Ansley—he's the poplarest candidate down here—begun the show by gittin on a stump, and takin his hat off right in the brilin hot sun.

"Feller-citizens," ses he, "I spose you all know as how my friends is fotched me out to represent this county in the next Legislater, and I want to tell you what my principles is. I am posed to counterfit money and shinplasters; I am posed to abolition and free niggers, to the morus multicaulis and the Florida war, and all manner of shecoonery whatsumever! If I's lected your respectable representation, I shall go in for good money, twenty cents for cotton, and no taxes, and shall go for bolishin prisonment for debt and the Central Bank. I hope you'll all cum up to the poles of the lection, and vote like a patriot for your very humble servant—Amen."

Then he jumped down and went around shakin hands. "Hurra for Ben Ansley! Ansley for ever!" shouted every feller. "Down with the cussed bank—devil take the shinplasters and all the rale-roads!"

ses Captain Skinner. "Silence for a speech from Squire Pettybone!" "Hurra for Pettybone!"

Squire Pettybone was a little short fat man, what had run afore, and knowed how to talk to the boys.

"Friends and feller-citizens," ses he, "I's once more a candidate for your sufferins, and I want to splain my sentiments to you. You've jest hearn a grate deal about the Central Bank. I aint no bank man—I'm posed to all banks—but I is a friend to the pore man, and is always ready to stand up for his constitutional rights. When the Central Bank put out its money it was good, and rich men got it and made use of it when it was good; but now they want to buy it in for less nor what it's worth to pay ther dets to the bank, and they is tryin to put it down, and make the pore man lose by it. What does they want to put the bank down for, if it aint to cheat the pore man who's got sum of it? If I's lected, I shall go for makin the banks redeem ther bills in silver and gold, or put every devil of 'em into the penitentiary to makin nigger shoes. I's a hard money man and in favor of the vetos. I goes for the pore man agin the rich, and if you lect me that's what I mean to do."

Then *he* begun shakin hands all round.

"Hurra for Squire Pettybone! hurra for the bank and the veto!" shouted some of the men—"Hurra for Ansley! d—n the bank!" "Silence for Mr. Johnson's speech!" "Hurra for Harrison!" "Hurra for the vetos!" "Hurra for Jackson! I can lick any veto on the ground!" "Silence!" "Hurra for Ansley, d—n the bank!" "Whar's them vetos what's agin Ansley—let me at 'em!" "Fight! fight! make a ring! make a ring!"—"Whoop!" hollered Bill Sweeny, "I'm the blossom—go it shirt-tail!" "Hit 'em, Sweeny!"—

"'Tention, betallion!" ses I; but it wasn't no use—they was at it right in the middle and all round the edges, and I know'd the quicker I got out of that crowd the better for my wholesome.

Thar they was, up and down, five or six in a heap, rollin over and crawlin out from under, bitin and scratchin, gougin and strikin, kickin and cussin, head and heels, all through other, none of 'em knowin who they hurt or who hurt them—all the same whether they hit Ansley or veto, the blossom or Pettybone. The candidates was runnin about pullin and haulin, and tryin ther best to stop it; but you couldn't hear nothin but cussin, and "bank" and "veto," and "let me at 'em," "I'm your boy," "let go my eyes!" and sich talk for more'n twenty minits, and then they only kep 'em apart by holdin 'em off like dogs till they got done pantin.

It wasn't no use to try to git 'em into line agin. Some of 'em had got manuel exercise enough, and was knocked and twisted out of all caracter, and it would be no use to try to put 'em through the manuel in that situation. Lots of 'em had ther eyes bunged up so they couldn't "eyes right!" to save 'em. The whole betallion was completely demoralized—so I turned 'em over to ther captains, accordin to law, and aint 'sponsible for nothin that tuck place after I left. No more from

Your friend, till death, Jos. Jones.

P. S. I meant to tell you all about my visit to Macon in this letter, but I've been so flustrated about this blamed muster, that I haint had no time to think of nothing else. I'll give you that in my next. Miss Mary most fainted when she heard about my hoss throwin me. Don't you think that's a good sign?

LETTER IV.

PINEVILLE, *September* 5, 1842.

To MR. THOMPSON:—*Dear Sir*—I begin to think edecation is the most surprisinest thing in the world—specially female edecation. If things goes on the way they is now, Mr. Mountgomery ses we'll have a grate moral revolution—that the wimin will turn the world up-side down with ther smartness, and men what haint got no edecation wont stand no sort of chance with 'em. Sense I went to Macon to the zamination I've altered my notion about this matter. I used to think human nater was jest like the yeath about cultivation. Everybody knows ther's rich land, pore land what can be made tolerable good, and some bominable shaller, rollin truck what all the manure in creation wouldn't make grow cow peas. Well, there's some people whose nateral smartness helps 'em along first rate, some what takes a mighty sight of skoolin, and some that all the edecation in the world wouldn't do no manner of good—they'd be nateral fools any way you could fix 'em. Ther minds is too shaller and rollin; they haint got no foundation, and all the skoolin you could put into 'em wouldn't stay no longer nor so much manure on the side of a red sandhill. Now, I used to think all the galls, or most of 'em, was jest this sort, and that it was only throwin away money to try to educate 'em above readin, writin and ciferin and playin on the pianner; but if anybody wants to be convinced that it's all a mistake about galls not havin as good sense as anybody else, jest let 'em go to the Macon College. I haint altered my notion about the nater of the human mind, but I've cum to the conclusion that ther is jest as good intellectual soil among the galls as among the boys; and I wouldn't be supprised if we *was* to have a "moral revolution," shore enough; and if we was to have, Georgia Washingtons and Joana Adamses and Tobitha Jeffersons, what would do as much to 'mortalize ther sex and elevate the caracter of the female race, as the heroes of the revolution did in our glorious independence war.

I had hearn so much about the Female College, and Miss Mary seemed to be so entirely tuck up with it when she was home, that I termined to go to the zamination and see what kind of place it was. Well, bein as Miss Mary was thar, I put on my best clothes, and mounted Selim and set off for Macon. You know its a ding'd long ride from Pineville, and it tuck me most two days to git thar.

When I got thar I put up at the Washington Hall —a monstrous fine tavern—whar ther was lots of old chaps from all parts of the State, what had cum down after ther daughters to the College. They put me in a room to sleep whar ther was two old codgers who was talkin all night about animel magnetism—a new sort of ism what has jest broke out in the North, with which they sed they could carry a body all over the yeath, heaven and hell, if they could jest git him to go to sleep. They talked a mighty sight about what some fellers had done—how they tuck one feller to heaven whar he heard the angels singin camp-meetin tunes by the thousand, and how they tuck him to New York, whar he seed Fanny Elsler dance the *cracker-over-enny*, as they call it; then they tuck him to Constantinople, whar he seed lots of long-bearded chaps kissin the galls, and then down to the infernal regions, whar he seed the devils dancin jigs with pore sinners, and trippin 'em up into bilin hot brimstone, and drinkin nigger rum and smokin yankee cigars, and cussin like pipers. I never hearn of sich devlish doins afore, and I couldn't go to sleep for fear they mought try some of ther projects with me. I'd like well enough to go to New York and Constantinople, but I didn't keer about gwine to heaven before my time; and if they was to take me to tother place, I know'd I'd be so skeer'd that I'd wake up, and then I'd be in a monstrous pretty fix—wide awake in the infernal regions, and no way to git out. It was most day-light before them old chaps got still about edecation, modern science, and magnetism, and I didn't git more'n two hours sleep, if I did that.

After breckfast in the mornin, which was monstrous good, considerin they was town people, I tuck a walk up to the Female College on the Hill. I tell you what, it's a mighty stancheous lookin bildin, and looks far off at a distance when you're gwine up to it.

Well, when I got thar I found the zamination, and sich another lot of pretty galls aint to be seed often out of Georgia. Bless ther sweet little soles, thar they all sot on benches in one eend of the room, lookin as smilin and as innercent as if they was never agwine to brake nobody's heart; but I'm most certain, if I'd been in them old chap's magnetism, I could have seed little Coopid thar with his bow and arrow, poppin away like a Kentucky rifle-man, at a shootin match.

The room begun to git mighty full of people, and the president sed he hoped the gentlemen would make room on the front benches for the ladys; but thar wasn't one of 'em moved. Bimeby he cum back and sed he meant the *young* gentlemen, only the young gentlemen; then, if you could seed 'em scatter, you would thought ther wasn't no old men in the room. Two or three old codgers with wigs on like to brake ther necks tryin to jump over the backs of the benches, jest to be smart before the galls. Ther was plenty of room for the ladys after that.

I sot on a back seat in the fust place, and kep lookin out for Miss Mary; but ther was so many beautiful creters thar that it was like lookin for one perticeler star in the milkyway, or anywhar else, when they're all a shinin ther best.

Bimeby the bell rung and the zamination commenced—and sich larnin as we had thar don't grow in the piny-woods, I tell you. The master, a mighty sharp-lookin, hatchet-faced little man, with gold specks on, talked to 'em jest like he thought they knowed every thing, and he was termined to make 'em out with it. Some of the galls looked kind o' skeer'd and some of 'em cried a little, but you know galls cry so easy, it don't hurt 'em none.

After axin 'em a heap of questions about 'rithmetic and grammar and the like, ses he, "What's Mathew Matix?"

My heart begun to kick when he mentioned that feller's name. I ris up and looked over a tall feller's shoulder so I could see him if he was thar. Jest then I cotch'd Miss Mary's eye—she was lookin her prettyest. I felt kind of fainty—

"Mathewmatix," ses she, "is the science of quantity—magnitude—number——," and she went on with a heap of larnin. But I couldn't hear no more; my face got as red as fire, and Miss Mary kind of laughed, right in the middle of her speech.

"Go to the board," said the master—and maybe she didn't shine when she walked up to a grate black board, what stood in the corner, and tuck hold of a piece of chalk not half so white as her pretty little hand itself.

"Spose a cannon-ball is fired at the moon," ses the master, "how long would it take it to go thar?"

I reckon it would done you good to see her chalk slide over that board. She made figers faster than I could count, and the chalk rattled on the board like a flock of chickins pickin corn off a clap-board; the whole board was kivered over in no time. Bimeby ses she,

"One thousand one hundred and seventy-eight

years, five months, three weeks, four days, sixteen hours, twenty-three minutes and forty-two seconds and a half!"

My lord! thinks I, how could she tell it so zactly to half a second.

When Miss Mary tuck her seat, the master called 'em up, one after tother, and axed 'em the hardest questions he could find in the book, but he couldn't stump 'em no how he could fix it. Whenever one class was done, then one of the galls went to the pianner and played a tune or two—sumtimes they sung, and I never did hear sich good musick. If Miss Mary hadn't been thar, I would fell in love with every one what sung; bless 'em, ther sweet voices went right to my heart so.

The zamination went on for three or four days, and I don't believe the galls told more'n half ther larnin all the time. I never seed sich smart creeters; why, some of the little ones could tell how much three pounds and three-quarters of beef come to at three cents and three-quarters a pound, as quick as you could say Jack Robinson, and that's mor'n some grown folks kin do. I never could do it. At night they had a Sing. All the galls tuck a part, and I haint got some of them tunes out of my head yit. They sung the most diffikilt tunes jest like it come nateral to 'em.

The last day was the interestinest occasion of all. The graduation class read ther speeches and got ther Diplomas, as they call 'em. I spose they're a sort of certifikits of good behavior. Ther was twelve of 'em —all butiful as angels, and all dressed zactly alike in white. When they was done readin ther speeches, the President called 'em round him and made a speech to 'em. Pore dear creeters, they stood thar and trembled like they was gwine to be married right off; and when the old man told 'em they was now gwine to separate, and that they was like Tom Kimides—that love was like his lever, and the human heart was the fulcrum with which they could upset the world, they had to put ther handkerchers to ther faces to hide ther tears. A good many other folks was cryin, and I felt sort o' damp about the eyes myself.

After it was all over, I started down to the tavern to git my hoss, and was gwine along thinkin of Miss Mary and the Female College, and thankin my stars that Mathew Matix and Nat. Filosofy wasn't no body to be afeared of, when what should I hear but a band of music comin up the hill. Bein a military man myself, I was anxious to see that Macon company what fit the Ingins so, and I hurried round the corner, when —grate Laws-a-massy!—I never seed jest sich a sight in all my born days. Heavens and yeath! thinks I, whar could they come from?—they couldn't belong to no civilized nation, no how. Thar was Turks and Chinese, Arabs, Niggers, Hottentots, Ingins and Tartars. —Some had faces as big as a cow, painted and fixed off all sorts of fashions; one feller was ridin on the back of his grand-mammy, another feller had a nose made out of a powder-horn; one chap was ridin a big goose; all of 'em had weepons of all kinds and all shapes; some of 'em on hosses had everlastin grate long swords as much as they could tote, and one feller had cowcumbers, simblins, gourds, potaters, roastin-ears, pepper-pods, and every other kind of garden truck you could think of, all strung round him. They was marchin right up to the College, and I felt a leetle 'larmed for fear they was gwine to carry off the galls; so I turned back, and thinks I, I knows one leetle angel in perticular what you wont git till you kill Majer Jones fust. Jest as I got close up to 'em a hoss cum rearin up almost on top of me, and I never come so near drappin right in my tracks in all my life. I never was so skeered afore. Ther was a chap on the hoss with a grate long sharp-pinted dart in his hand, aimed straight at me!—he had horns on his head, and looked jest like death in the primer! I could see every bone in his body! I kind o' gasped for breath, and the outlandish cuss rode off without sayin a word.

Up to the College all the galls was out on the portico hollerin and shoutin like blazes, and I run like thunder; but when I got up to 'em I found they was only laughin.

"My lord!" ses I, "Miss Mary, aint you skeered?"

"Shaw, no, Majer," ses she, "its only the Fantastikils!"

"Fan-what-ikils?" ses I.

"The Fantastikils."

"Oh!" ses I, for jest then I saw a grate long-legged feller among 'em with a fan in his hand, fannin a nigger woman what had fainted. The chap with the fan had a dough face on, that looked as pitiful as if all his relations was ded; and every time the nigger fainted he would ketch her in his arms and fan her, and look so sorry at her.

The galls squeeled and laughed while the Fantastikils marched round the College and then marched down to town agin. I soon follered, but I kep away from that chap on the hoss. Down to the Hall, I paid my bill and cut out. No more from

Your friend, till death, JOS. JONES.

LETTER V.

PINEVILLE, *September* 27, 1842.

TO MR. THOMPSON:—*Dear Sir*—Some times I think I *is* the onluckiest man in the world. Everlastingly ther's some sarned thing happenin to me, in spite of all I kin do. Sense I come back from Macon, and my account of the zamination's ben read by most every body bout here, I blieve my popilarity's ris considerable. Miss Mary said she wouldn't be supprised much if I turned out a perfect Lord Birum, or Charles Dickens, and 'mortalized all the ladys of my acquaintance. She was mighty proud of what I said about her buty and larnin, but she ses I didn't give the right answer to the sum about the cannon ball and the moon. But that's no matter now.

I want to tell you about a scrape I got in tother day, as I know you never heard of jest sich a catasterfy before.

Last Sunday, Miss Mary and Miss Carline and Miss Kesiah and all of the Stallinses wer at church, and when it was out I jest rid right up to Miss Mary and 'lowed I'd see her home. She didn't say nothin, and I rid along side of her a little ways, and begun to feel mighty good; but before we got out of sight of the church ther was a whole gang of fellers, and a heap more young ladys, cum ridin up and reinin in, and prancin and cavortin about so that nobody could tell who was ridin with which: all jabberin and talkin and laughin, as if they'd been to a cornshuckin instead of a meetin-house. Of course cousin Pete was thar, on uncle Josh's old white-eyed hoss, with his saddle-bags on—for he always carrys 'em wherever he goes, to make folks blieve he's a doctor—and the way he tumbled the big words about was 'stonishin. I didn't say much, but rid monstrous close to one side of Miss Mary, so cousin Pete couldn't shine much thar.

Well, we all got to old Miss Stallinses without any perticeler accident happenin, though I spected every minit to see some of 'em histed rite in the mud, the way they kep whippin one another's hosses unawars, and playin all manner of pranks with one another. When we got thar the whole crowd stoped, and some one proposed a walk down to the branch to git some grapes. All hands was agreed 'cept old Miss Stallins, who sed the galls better stay home and read the bible. But you know it aint no use to talk about religion to young galls when they aint sick nor sorry bout nothin. So away we went—but I tuck monstrous good care to git long side of Miss Mary, and thar I stuck till we got down to the branch whar the grapes wer. You know the wild grapes is jest gittin good now—and I never seed a pretty young lady yet that didn't like something sour. Ther's lots of fox grapes all round the plantation, but the best ones is down on the branch. Cousin Pete and Ben Biers, and all the fellers, fell to gettin grapes for the ladys, but they all had ther Sunday fixins on and was fraid to go into the brush much.

"Oh, my! what pretty grapes is on that tree!" ses Miss Mary, lookin up half-way to the top of the grate big gum that stood right over the water—and her pretty bright eyes sparklin like dew-drops in the sunshine. "Oh, I wish I had some."

Cousin Pete had been tryin to make himself very poplar with Miss Mary, but he didn't seem to care about them high grapes more'n some that was lower down. But all the galls had got ther eyes on them high grapes.

"Them grapes is like the young ladys," ses cousin Pete.

"Why is they like the galls?" axed Miss Kesiah.

"Oh, cause—cause they's sweet," ses cousin Pete.

"I reckon it's cause they's hard to git," ses Bill Willson.

"It's cause they's more trouble to git than they's worth," ses Tom Stallins.

"Aint you shamed, brother Tom?" ses Miss Carline.

"What do you think, Majer?" ses Miss Mary—and she gin me one of them witchin side-looks of hers that almost made me jump rite out of my boots.

"Why," ses I, "I think they's like the young ladys, cause they's sour grapes to them as can't git 'em."

"Yes, Majer," ses she, "but you know they can git 'em that has the prowess to win 'em"—and then she gin me a look that made me feel prouder than I ever did afore in my life—"and *you* can git 'em if you try, Majer; I know you kin."

When she said that last part, I seed cousin Pete's lip sort o' drap. My heart liked to knock the buttons off my jacket, and I do blieve I'd had them grapes if I'd had to dig the tree up by the roots. My hat went off quicker than a flash, and up the old sweet-gum I went like a cat squirrel.

"Don't fall, Majer," ses Miss Mary. When she said that, I swar I like to let go, it made me feel so interestin. I wasn't no time gittin to the very tiptop branch, and the fust thing I done was to cut off the largest bunch, and throw it rite down to Miss Mary's feet.

"Thank you, Majer—thank you," ses she.

"Throw me some, Majer," ses Miss Carline, "and me too"—"and me too"—"thank you, Majer"—"throw me some, Majer"—"aint the Majer kind?"—"it takes him to climb trees," ses all the galls.

"He's good as a coon," ses Ben Biers.

"I can beat him any time," ses Tom Stallins.

"No y-o-u can't, brother Tom, no sich thing," ses Miss Mary, poutin out her pretty lips at him.

By this time I had gin 'em more grapes than they could all eat, and carry home to boot; and if I had jest come down then, I'd come out fust rate. But you know that's the nice pint—to know when to stop: ther is such a thing as bein a leetle *too* smart —and that's jest whar I mist the figure.

I was standin on one vine right over the branch, with my hands holt of one over my head, and thinks I to myself, how it would stonish 'em all now to see me skin the cat. My spunk was up, and thinks I, I'll jest show 'em what I kin do. So up I pulls my feet and twisted 'em round through my arms over backwards, and was lettin my body down tother side foremost, when they all hollered out,

"Oh, look at Majer Jones!"—"Oh, see what he's doin!"

"Oh, I'm so fraid," ses Miss Mary.

That made me want to do my best, so I let myself down slow and easy, and I begun to feel with my feet for the vine below.

"Oh, my gracious!" ses Miss Kesiah, "see how he is twisted his arms round."

Some how I couldn't find the vine, and my arms begun to hurt, but I didn't say nothin.

"A l-e-e-t-l-e further forward, Majer," ses Tom Stallins.

"No; more to the right," ses Ben Biers.

The galls wer all lookin and didn't know what to say. I kep tryin to touch both ways, but cuss the vine was thar. Then I tried to git back agin, but I couldn't raise myself some how, and I begun to feel monstrous dizzy; the water below looked sort o' yaller and green, and had sparks of fire runnin all through it, and my eyes begun to feel so tight, I thought they would bust. They was all hollerin something down below, but I couldn't hear nothin but a terrible roarin sound, and the fust thing I knowd something tuck me right under the chin, and before I had time to breathe, kerslash I went, right in the cold water, more'n six feet deep. I got my mouth chock full of muddy water, and how upon yeath I ever got out without droundin I can't see; for I was almost dead before I drapt, and when I come down I hit sumthing that like to broke my jaw-bone, and skinned my nose most bominable.

When I got out, the galls wer all screamin for life, and Miss Mary was pale as her pockethankercher.

"Oh, I'm so glad you aint hurt no wurse, Majer," ses she; "I thought you was killed."

But, lord! she didn't begin to know how bad I was hurt. I sot down on a log a little, and the fellers all come round laughin like they was almost tickeld to death.

"Wasn't I right, Majer—aint they more trouble to git than they's worth after you's got 'em?"

I didn't say nothin to Tom Stallins, cause he's Miss Mary's brother; but cousin Pete come up with his fine rigins on, laughing like a grate long-legged fool, as he is.—Says he,

"Aint you shamed to cut sich anticks as that—I'd have more sense—jest look at your nose—ha, ha! —Aint you got yourself in a nice fix with yer smartness?"

The galls was gitin ready to go home; Miss Mary was lookin monstrous serious.

"Don't you think he looks like a drounded rat, Miss Mary?" axed cousin Pete.

"I think he looks as good as you do any time," ses she, lookin as mad as she could.

Pete sort of looked a leetle sheapish, and turned round and tried to laugh.

"I wouldn't take sich a duckin as that not for all the sour grapes nor sour galls in Georgia," ses he.

Thinks I, that's sort of personally insultin to Miss Mary, and I seed her face grow sort o' red. It wouldn't never do to let cousin Pete hurt her feelins so right afore my face, so ses I—

"You wouldn't, wouldn't you?" and with that I jest tuck hold of the gentleman and pitched him neck and heels into the branch.

When he got out, he 'lowed he'd settle it with me some other time, when thar wasn't no ladys along to take my part. That's the way cousin Pete settles all his accounts—some other time.

Tom Stallins tuck his sisters home, and the rest of the galls and fellers went along; but cousin Pete and I didn't show ourselves no more that day. I haint seed him sense, tho' thars been all sorts of a muss 'tween mother and aunt Mahaly about that Sunday bisness. I don't think I'll ever skin the cat agin. No more from

Your friend, till death, Jos. Jones.

P. S. Miss Mary sent to inquire how my nose was, and told the nigger not to tell me who sent her. Don't you think she's comin too? Look out for a weddin about Crismus time. If things does work out rite, you may look for a cake as big as your head.

LETTER VI.

PINEVILLE, *October* 8, 1842.

TO MR. THOMPSON:—*Dear Sir*—That duckin what I got tother Sunday gin me a monstrous cold, and my nose feels jest about twice as big as it used to before. Colds is curious things any way; no wonder people always calls em *bad*, for I don't know nothin but a down right fever'n ager that makes me so out o' sorts. Why, I can't taste nothin nor smell nothin, and I do blieve I've sneezed more'n five thousand times in the last twenty-four owers. I'm all the time a hich-cheein! so, I can't do nothin, or I'd rit you before now about a coon hunt we had tother night, whar I cotched more cold than coons. But we had some rale fun, I tell you. It was the fust coon hunt we've had this season, and I reckon it tuck the starch out of sum of the boys, so they wont want to go agin in a hurry. Cousin Pete like to cotch'd his death.

You see, I's got two of the best coon dogs in the settlement, and the fellers can't never go without 'em. Well, jest after supper I heard 'em comin, blowin ther horns like they was gwine to tear down the walls of Jerico, and the dogs all howlin as if heaven and yeath was comin together. I'd been layin off to go to see Miss Mary, but my nose wasn't quite well whar I blazed it on that dratted grape-vine, and so I thought I mought as well go long with 'em; specially as they begged so hard for my company, (my patience, my nose feels jest like it was the spout of a bilin tea-kittle,) and Smart and Wise wouldn't trail good without me to make 'em. So I told nigger Jim to git some light-wood and the axe, and let the dogs out, and come along.

Well, cousin Pete—he's never said peas about the duckin I gin him, and I wish I hadn't done it now, for he's a rite clever-hearted feller after all, and, you know, it aint his fault cause he's got no better sense. Cousin Pete was along, with two hound pups, and Tom Stallins had three or four hounds, and one grate big yaller cur, what wasn't worth shucks to trail, but was bomination to fight. Ben Biers had more dogs than you could shake a stick at; and sich another hellabeloo as they all made! why, one couldn't hear himself think for 'em. It put me in mind of what Mr. Shakespear ses about dogs—

> "I never herd sich powerful discord,
> Sich sweet thunder."

Well, we soon tuck the woods down towards the branch, and ses I to Smart and Wise, "high on!" ses I, and away they went, snuffin and snortin like mad. The rest of the fellers hollered, "steboy! sick 'em, Tows! hunt 'em, Troup! high on! hey!" and part of 'em went tarein through the brush like they had a coon's tail within a inch of ther noses. But ther was two or three young hounds—and, you know, they's the biggest fools in the world—what wouldn't budge; and when anybody tried to encourage 'em to hunt, they'd begin to squall like all nater, and come jumpin about, and one of 'em licked Ben Biers rite in the face. "Cuss your imperence!" ses Ben, "I'll larn you how to tree coons better'n that," and spang he tuck him a side of the head with a lighterd-knot, and sich another ki-i! ki-i! ki-i-in! I never heard afore. Two or three of 'em tuck the hint and turned tail for home.

It was a bominable dark night, and every now and then it kep sprinklin a little. I and two or three more carried torches, but some of 'em had none, and was all the time gittin lost, or gittin hung in the bushes, and then they'd holler out, "hold the light sumbody, over here," till they got out of ther tanglement. It was a mighty sight of botherment, and we didn't go very fast, you may know.

Bimeby one of the dogs opened, and we all stoped to listen.

"Ough! ough-ough!" In about two minits more we heerd him agin: "Ough-ough! ough-ough! ough-ough!"

"That's Majer's Smart," ses Tom Stallins.

"He's treed," ses Ben Biers; "but he's way tother side of creation."

"No, he haint treed, but he's on a warm trail," ses I; for I know'd by the way he opened.

"I wouldn't go whar he is for all the coons in Georgia," ses cousin Pete.

"Stop," ses I, "maybe he'll bring the trail up this way."

Shore enough, he was comin like a steam-car, every now and then blowin off—"ough-ough! ough-ough! ough-ough!"—gittin faster and louder, as the track warmed. Then old Wise struck in, with his voice about three pitches higher than Smart's, and Troup and Touse, and the whole pack of 'em jined in, keepin up a most oudacious racket. On they come, and passed right by us, gwine up the branch towards old Mr. Myrick's corn field. We all turned and tuck after 'em, but they didn't go far before they all come to a stop, and old Smart gin out his loud bull-dog, "ough! —ough!—ough!" which is jest as much as to say, "here's yer coon!"

When we got up to 'em, thar they all was, friskin about one of the biggest kind of poplers, close to the branch; all barkin and pantin and lookin up into the tree like they seed the coon run up. Some times the young ones would git in the way of the old dogs, and the fust thing they'd know, they'd git slung more'n six foot into the bushes; but they'd give a yelp or so and come right back to git sarved the same way agin.

Well, I tell you what, it tuck a feller mighty wide between the eyes to tackle that tree, for it was a whopper; but off coats, and at it we went, and by the time nigger Jim got his fires kindled all round, so the coon couldn't run off without our seein him, the old tree begun to feel weak in the knees.

"Hold the dogs, boys, she's gwine to cave," ses Ben Biers.

The next minit, kerslash! went the old poplar, right into the branch, makin the muddy water fly in every direction, and before the limbs was all done fallin, in went the dogs. All was still for about two minits before any body sed a word.

"They've got him!" ses Ben Biers, who was standin with his mouth wide open all the while; "they've got him! hurra!"

Then ther was sich another rippin and tearin, and barkin and shoutin, and runnin among the dogs and fellers.

"Hurra! take him! bite him! sick him, Tows! lay hold of him, Wise! shake him, Smart!" and all kinds of encouragement was hollered to the dogs; but every now and then one of 'em would come out pantin and whinin and holdin his head a-one side, with his ears all slit to ribbins.

The coon had the advantage of the dogs, for he was down in the brush and water, so more'n one dog couldn't git to him at a time nohow, and if one of 'em happened to take hold of the bitin eend, in the dark, he was nearly licked to death before he could let loose.

Cousin Pete was on top of the log with a torch in his hand, coaxin on the dogs as hard as he could.

"Here, Wolf," ses he, "here, here, take hold of him, good feller,—shake him!"

Tom Stallinses big cur jumped onto the log, and the next thing I know'd cousin Pete's light was out, and the dogs had him down under the log with the coon.

"Oh, my lord! git out! call off the dogs! bring a light, fellers!" holler'd out cousin Pete; but before we could git thar the dogs like to used him up clean. The big dog he was callin knocked him off the log in his hurryment to git at the coon, and before the other dogs found out the mistake they like to tare all his clothes off his back, they and the brush together.

By this time the coon tuck the bank and tried to

make off, most of the dogs bein out of the notion of tryin him agin; but Tom Stallins' big cur, after a heap of coaxin, gin him one more hitch. The coon had no friends in the crowd, but the other dogs was perfectly willin to show him fair fight; and if any body don't blieve a coon's got natural pluck, he jest ought to seed that same old coon, the way he fit. Sometimes Wolf would gether holt of him like he was gwine to swoller him whole, and mash him all into a cocked hat, but it didn't seem to have no effect, for in less than no time he'd have the dog rite by the cheek or by the ear, and he wouldn't let go till the hide gin way. It was the hottest night's work ever old Wolf undertuck, and it tuck a mighty chance of hollerin to make him stand up to the rack as well as he did. The other dogs kept runnin round and whinin mighty anxious, but they tuck good care to keep out of reach of the coon. Bimeby I seed old Wolf drap his tail and kind o' wag it, when the coon had him by the jowl. I know'd it was all day with him then. "Shake him, Wolf! lay hold of him, old feller! bite him!" says Tom; but it want no use, the dog was clean licked, and the fust thing we knowd he was gone for home, kind o' whistlin to himself as he went—and if nigger Jim hadn't fotch'd my pistols along with him, the coon would got away after all.

Cousin Pete, who was terribly down in the mouth and as wet as a drounded rat, wanted to go, so we gin nigger Jim the coon and started for home. Some of the dogs was along, and they kep a mighty snortin like they'd cotch'd a monstrous bad cold, and every now and then they'd find sum new place about 'em what wanted lickin.

We was most up to the corner of our field when the dogs started up something, and run it a little ways and stopped. Tom Stallins and Ben Biers, and one or two more, run to 'em before I could git thar.

"Thar it is—that black and white thing—on that log," ses Tom. "Steboy; catch him!" ses he.

Ben run up with his light, and the fust thing I heerd him say was, "P-e-u-g-h! thunder an lightnin!—look out, fellers! its a pole-cat!"

But the warnin was too late for Ben Biers; he got scent enough on him to last him for a month. The dogs got chock full, and was rollin all about in the leaves, while Ben stood and cussed more'n would blow the roof off a meetin house.

It was most day before we got home. Cousin Pete and Ben Biers say they wont never go coon huntin any more down that way, any how. No more from

Your friend, till death, Jos. Jones.

P. S. I tell you what it is, old feller, I blieve all's right between me and Miss Mary now. She told a young lady tother day that I was the only real distinguished young gentleman in Pineville, and if my thografy was only as good as my reterick I'd do fust rate. Drat the larnin, say I—genus comes by natur, but everybody kin larn how to spell, you know. What knocks me all in a heap is, how upon yeath am

I gwine to "pop the question," as they call it, or ax old Miss Stallins for her daughter. Gracious! it makes me feel all over sort o' fainty to think of it. I'm a grate mind to come to Madison, and see you about it—as I know you're a pertickler friend of mine, and would tel me the best way to do.

LETTER VII.

PINEVILLE, *October* 27, 1842.

To MR. THOMPSON:—*Dear Sir*—I ariv here last night, all safe as a crate of warranted cups and sassers. My cold's got a good deal better sense I left Madison, and accordin to promis, I have tuck up my pen to give you a account of my trip to your town.

As I told you, I left my hoss in Warrenton and tuck the cars at Camack for Madison. It was bout leven o'clock fore the dratted thing come along, and when it got thar it made sich a bominable blowin and snortin that I was more'n half a mind not to venter in no sich outlandish sort of contrivance. I'd hearn a grate deal about steam ingins, but if the Semmynole ingins is any uglier, or frightfuller than they is, I don't wonder nobody wants to tack' em. Why, sich other cog-wheels, cranks, and conflutements I never did see —and then they's so spiteful, and makes the fire fly so. I couldn't help feelin sort o' skeered of it all the time, and I wouldn't been that feller what rid on top of the cussed critter, and fed and watered it, not for no considerashun. I was lookin round it a little, to try to git the hang of it, when the feller jest teched a little brass fixin, and feugh-h-h! it went right in my ear, and like to blowed my brains out with hot steam. "Hello!" ses I, "mister, what made it do that!" "Oh, it was jest blowin its nose," ses he, and he tuck hold of another thing, and the infernal critter sot up a yell like a panther with a grindstone on his tail. Thunderation, how the steam did fly! enough to blow all creation to Ballyhack.

"All aboard," ses the man—the bell tapped, and in about a minit everybody was stowed away and waitin. Chug, went something, and away I goes right over the back of the seat.—It jerked once more, and then it begun to go. Chow, chow, chow—chew, chew, chew—che, che, chit-tu, chit-to, fit-te, fit, fit, fit, cher-r-r-r; and the whole bilin of us was gwine a long with a perfect whiz, and the way the fire flew was miraculus—grate big sparks now and then dodgin all around a feller's face like a yaller-jacket, and then drappin right down into his busum. For some time it would tuck three men to watch the sparks off one, and they couldn't.

Well, we went hummin along jest like iled thunder, makin more noise nor a dozen cotton gins all gwine at once, only stoppin now and then to pile on lighterd and fill up the bilers, and to drap a passenger here and thar on the rode.

They was the sleepyest set of peeple aboard that I ever did see. Thar they was, all scattered about in the seats, heads and heels together; here a pair of boots stickin straight upwards, and thar a feller's face, opened wide enough to swaller a saw-mill. Some of 'em was monstrous troubled in ther dreams, and kep tossin and twistin about as bisy as bull yearlins in fly-time, while some big-footed fellers lay sprawl'd out on the benches, quiet as a midlin of meat, snorin a perfect harrycane.

The effect was unresistible, and the fust thing I knowd I didn't know any thing in pertickler, 'cept that my eyes felt monstrous gritty when I tried to open 'em wide——

"Look here; master—master!"

"Hello!" ses I, "Jim, what's the matter?"

"I isn't Jim, master," ses the nigger feller what was shakin me by the collar; "you better go to the Hotel, the passengers is all gone long time ago."

I soon seed how it was, and not havin no baggage but jest my saddel-bags, I tuck the road the feller pinted to, and went along down the hill, whar I like to fell over lots of cotton-bags, till I come to a place whar ther was more wagons than I could count in a hour. It was so dark I couldn't make out nothin but wagons and a lot of fellers settin round a fire. Thinks I, Madison aint sich a ding grate city as I thought it was, after all; and as I felt sort o' chilly, I jined the fellers round the fire.

"Whar's the hotel?" ses I.

"Thar aint no hotel here," ses one feller, wnat was singin,

"Drive my wagon long the rode:
Sorry team and a heavy load."

"Won't you take something?" ses he, drawin a old junk bottle of rum, that smelled strong enough of inguns to knock a man down, and pintin it right under my nose before I know'd what he was up to.

"No, I thank you," ses I, "I's a Washingtonian.'

"Who's they?" ses he; "sum of your d——n Flurnoy preachers, I spose?"

"No," ses I, "they's revolutioners."

"Revolutioners!" ses he, "why, my grandfather was a revolutioner, and fit agin the British at King's Mounting, and help'd to lick tyranny out of the country."

"Well, that was right," ses I; "hurra for the revolutioners."

"Come, take something," ses he, and he pinted the bottle at my nose agin.

"No," ses I, "I'm a revolutioner, and go agin King Alkohol tooth and toe nail."

"King who?" ses he.

"King Rum," ses I; "that very tyrant that's got you by the guzzle now, and he'll have you choked down on yer knees to him the fust thing you'll know, if you don't revolutionize on him and quit him."

The feller stopped and looked down in the fire—then at me—then at the bottle, and then he tuck another look at the fire.

"That's a fact," ses he, "it's had me on my back afore to-night; but somehow I can't—yes I kin—and here goes, mister—d——n all tyrants—I'm a revolutioner too, a Washington revolutioner, for ever!" and with that he throw'd the bottle of rum smack in the middle of the fire, and it blazed up blue and yaller like a hell-broth, as it is.

"Give me yer hand, mister!" ses I, "I don't

want no better proof of your manhood than that: stick to it like a true Washington revolutioner."

"Stick to it, mister?" ses he; "why, I never broke my word when I was sober in my life, and now I must tell a lie before I kin get drunk. Stick to it! I've been wantin to revolutionize long ago, and now I've done it, and I'll never knock under as long I live!" and he shuck my hand, and a tear shined in the fire-light. I don't blieve that wagoner 'll ever git stalled agin, on a good rode as long as he lives.

Well, after a while, before it was clear light, I started to find the town.

"Good mornin," ses one feller, comin out from among the wagons with a quare lookin gimlet and some tags of cotton in his hand. "Would you like a bid for your cotton this mornin?"

"I don't keer," ses I, "I'm always willin for a good trade.

"Whar is it?" ses he, and before I had time to answer him, another feller slapped me on the shoulder on tother side.

"Is it prime now, neighbor?" ses he; "I'll give you the top of the market. Is it prime now, eh?"

"Never mind," ses the fust, "it's as good as sold."

"Beg pardon," ses the other feller, "I won't interfere, then."

"Whar is it?" ses the fust chap, puttin his arm in mine, and walkin in among the wagons; "square or round bales, eh?"

"Stop, stop, mister," ses I, "your mistaken in the man; you——"

"Oh, let's have a sample, and we'll talk about the price; is this it?" and in goes his gimlet, "I always sample from both eends," ses he.

"But stop, mister," ses I, "I haint got no cotton here; my cotton is in Pineville, and aint more'n half ginned out yit. I haint got no——"

"Whar?" ses he.

"Way down in Pineville, in——"

"Pooh!" ses he, "beg yer pardon—thought you was in the market," and fore I could ax him about Madison or you, he was half a dozen wagons off, borin his gimlet into another bag of cotton.

The next feller I met was right at me to buy my cotton; but I tuck him a one side and splained things confidentially to him fore he went so far.

"Is this Madison," ses I, "whar the Southern Miscellany is printed?"

"Oh, no," ses he, "this is Beaver Tail."

"Beaver Tail!" ses I; "why, I never hearn of that place afore," and I jest begun to bile up a little. "I tuck my passage for Madison," ses I, "and paid the money, and they've gone and drapped me in Beaver Tail! Now that's a way to do bisness; that's the way travellers is tuck in, by these infernal corperashuns. If they don't fix it all to my satisfaction, I'll persecute the company as long as ther's any law in Georgia. Beaver Tail!" ses I.

"Yes," ses he, "this is Beaver Tail, which is to Madison as the 'Bay' is to Savannah, 'Wall-street' to New York, the 'Exchange' to Filadelfy, or the 'Rialto,' ('whar merchants most do congregate,') to

Venice. This is the bisness part of Madison, do you understand?" ses he.

"Yes, but I want to go to Madison, to see Mr. Thompson on pertickler bisness."

"This is Mr. Thompson's place of bisness; you'll find him thar," ses he, pintin to a big open brick house.

Well, I went thar, but he was the rale-rode agent, what keeps the books of the consarn. "Oh, no," ses I, "its the other Mr. Thompson what I want to see."

"Well, thar he is," ses he, "that's Mr. Thompson, jest come down from Covington."

When I went to the man he pinted to, he axed me if I wanted to take a contract on the rode? "Lord, no," ses I, "I want to see Mr. Thompson about a very different kind of a bisness."

"Perhaps you will find him over in that bildin," ses he.

Well, over I went.

"Kin we serve you this mornin, sir? Do you wish to store your cotton?" ses he.

"No, no," ses I, "I want to see Mr. Thompson what edits the Miscellany."

"Oh," ses he, "*that* Mr. Thompson—my name's Mr. Thom*a*son. You'll find him at the Planter's Hotel, the first good-lookin man you see with spectickles on."

Good gracious! thinks I, if the old Frenchman had lived in Beaver Tail he would have found monsieur Tonsons enough to kill him several times, as he says in the play.

Well, I put out for the Planter's as fast as I could —whar you know I found you at last—but (I hope you wont be riled at what I say) if it hadn't been for the specks I wouldn't a knowed you by Mr. Thomason's description.

I needn't tell you agin how much I is bleeged to you for yer kindness and advice in that pertickelerly delicate bisness on which we conversed. Takin every thing into consideration, I am very much pleased with my visit to Madison; and sense I went to Macon and your town I'm more'n ever in favor of travelin. I think the writer was about right, who said "The world is a monstrous big book, full of picters and good readin, but he that never travels only reads the title-page." I blieve I'll go to the city of Athens next.

You know I tuck dinner at the Planter's with you. Well, I was put a little to the onplush by that old nigger what waits on the table thar. I didn't know what to make of the old feller. He flew round me like I was Mr. Clay, or some other grate character.

"Will you have some of the Berkshire ham," ses he, "or some of the Durham beef—fust rate, stall-fed, sir, jest imported."

"Why, uncle, you aint got English beef here, is you?" ses I.

"Certain, master; we don't feed people on nothin else at the Planter's—pure English, in French style."

I tuck a piece of the Durham.

"Have a little of the essence?" ses he, puttin

some gravy on it. "Shall I have your plate splied with a piece of veal—real Durham—only twelve year old? Take some of the Irishmans, sir? A piece of the turky—wild turky, cotched wild in the Okefe noky—fust rate? Some peach sas, made out of the large English white reserve peaches, what grow big as your fist, sir?" and fore I knowed what to say, he had my plate piled up with good things, so I couldn't clear it in a hour, hard eatin at that.

"Have another plate, sir?" ses he. I had done eat more'n I wanted then, but everybody, as fur as I could see, on both sides, was gittin clean plates, so thinks I, here goes.

"Have some of the kramberry tarts," ses the old feller, "what grows on grape-vines, or some of the North Carolina black-berrys, second sister to the goosberry? Kustard, sir—tater kustard, made out of the biggest kind of yams? Here's a hot one, sir, right out of the mouth of a red hot oven? Have some milk, sir —Durham cow's milk; buttermilk, if you like, rich as cream?" And that's the way the old feller went on, never crackin a smile all the time; and I like to busted jest eatin to bleege him.

In the afternoon, I tuck a look at your town—and a mighty smart town it is—but I needn't tell you nothin about that. At supper, thar was that old feller agin, flyin round the long table, with his check apern on and a sarver in one hand.

"Will you have a hot biskit," ses he, "made out of the best Canal flower from imported wheat? Take a square-toed waffel, sir; here's swaller-tailed ones, if you like 'em better? Fust rate Rio coffee, sir; some

Muskevado sugar to give a pleasant taste to it? Cold ham! briled ditto! warm Durham stakes! briled fowl —English breed—so tender they wont bare bitin hard! Let me sply your plate with a very small piece of the busum of this pullit? Some of the reserves, sir? any kind—quince, pare, big English peaches. Take another hot biskit, sir——," and if I'd sot thar, he'd kep me eatin till this time. The cars was ready to start; I paid my bill at the Planter's, and was soon whirlin on the way home.

I've been thinkin ever sense of your advice, and I'm satisfied you was right. I shall ax Miss Mary fust, and by that time I'll be more used to it, and wont be so skeery of her mother. But it's the worst job I ever undertuck any way I can fix it. I'll tell you all about it. No more from

Your friend, till death, JOS. JONES.

LETTER VIII.

PINEVILLE, *November* 5, 1842.

TO MR. THOMPSON:—*Dear Sir*—Sense I writ you that last letter we've all been as busy as yaller jackets in a cotton blossom, movin over to town. It wasn't no great ways to haul things, but then you know it's sich a plagy job. I never thought ther was so much plunder about our house till we come to move. But it's jest so every year. Mother's always got more old washin-tubs, and fat-gourds, and spinnin-wheels, and quiltin frames, and sich fixins than would fill Noar's ark, big as it was; and she's got to have 'em all moved, lock, stock, and barrel, for she ses she can't trust nothin with niggers when she aint on the plantation. This movin into town every winter and out in the summer is all a fool quality notion any way, and I'm gittin right sick of it, and if it hadn't a been that the Stallinses was gone to town when I got back I blieve I'd coaxed the old woman out of it this time.

Well, now I've got a fair swing at Miss Mary, for she's so close I can jest call in any time; but 'tween you and me, I'm fraid I'm gwine to have some trouble bout this matter yit. Ther's a lot of fellers scootin round her that I don't more'n half like no how. One chap's jest come from the north, rigged out like a show monkey, with a little tag of hair hangin down under his chin jest like our old billy goat, that's a leetle too smart for this latitude, I think. He's got more brass in his face than ther is in mother's preservin kittle, and more gab than Mr. Mountgomery and our preacher together. He's a music teacher and I don't know what all, and makes himself jest as popler bout town as if he'd lived here all his life. All the town galls is gwine to take lessons from him on the pianer, 'cept Miss Mary, and old Miss Stallins ses she aint gwine to the expense of buyin a pianer these hard times, no how. She ses she's gwine to larn her galls to make good housekeepers and good wives, and when they git married, if ther husbands like musick, they can buy sich things for 'em if they've a mind to.

"Yes, madam, but though, you know"—ses the

imperent cuss, the very fust time he was interduced into the house by cousin Pete, who is jest as thick with him as two fools could be—"you know 'complishments is the best riches a young lady can have—'complishments last for ever, but riches don't."

"But nobody can't live on 'complishments," ses old Miss Stallins, "not these times they can't."

"Yes, but Miss Stallins," ses he, "you's rich enough to give your butiful daughters every gratification in the world. Now you hadn't ought to be so stingy with sich charmin daughters as you've got."

Well, cuss your imperence, thought I, for a stranger, right afore ther faces too; and I never wanted to settle my foot agin the seat of a feller's trowses so bad afore in my life. Old Miss Stallins didn't say much. I was settin pretty near Miss Mary, and when he begun to run on so, I sot in talkin with her, so she couldn't hear the dratted fool, but the fust thing I knowed Mr. Crotchet come and sot right down between us.

"Don't you think we can 'swade the old woman into it, Miss Mary, if we lay our heads together."

I gin Mary a look as much as to say, I think he's in a mighty grate hurry to lay your heds together; but she jest smiled, and put her hankercher up to her face and sed she didn't know.

"I say, Jones," ses he, "won't you be a spoke in my wheel, old feller? I'm dyin in love with this butiful young lady, and I can't bear to see her oppertunities neglected."

I looked at the feller rite in the face, and I jest had

it on the eend of my tongue to tell him cuss his insurance. But Miss Mary was thar and her mother, and I tried to turn it off the best way I could, without lettin my temper rise.

"I aint no wagon-maker, Crotchet," ses I, "but I've got a nigger feller that kin put a spoke in your wheel mighty quick, if that's all you want."

Miss Mary crammed her hankercher in her mouth.

"Oh," ses he, "you don't take—you don't take, Jones; I mean, can't you help me to court Miss Mary, here, and her mother."

I begun to feel sort 'o warm behind the ears, but I thought I'd jest give him a sort of a hint.

"I reckon you won't need no help," ses I, "you seem to git along pretty fast for a stranger."

"I think so too, Joseph," sed old Miss Stallins.

"Then you will give your consent, I spose, madam," ses he.

I didn't breath for more'n a minit, and tried to look at 'em all three at the same time.

"What, sir," axed the old woman, openin her eyes as wide as she could and drapin her ball of nittin yarn on the floor at the same time.

"You'll buy one, won't you?"

"Whew!" ses I, right out loud, for I felt so relieved.

Miss Mary laughed more'n I ever heard her afore in company.

"That's what I won't," ses old Miss Stallins, jerkin at the ball till she like to onwinded it all, tryin to pull it to her, "not these times, I'll asshore you, sir."

I jumped up and got the ball and wound all the yarn on it and handed it to her.

"Thank you, Joseph," ses she, "thank you, my son."

I kind o' cleared my throte, and my face burnt like fire when she sed that.

"Oh, ho!" ses he, lookin round to me, "I see how the wind blows, Jones, but you might as well give up the chase, for I don't think you can shine. I'm smitten myself. What say you, Miss Mary? The Majer haint got no morgage, has he?"

"Oh no, sir," said Miss Mary—"none at all."

"Any claim, Jones, eh?"

I tried to say something, but I couldn't git a word in edge-ways, and every time I looked at Miss Mary she kep laughin.

"Ther aint no morgage on nary nigger nor foot of ground, thank the Lord, these hard times," sed the old woman. She was drappin to sleep, and didn't know what she was talkin about.

It was Saturday night and time to go—but I wasn't gwine till Crotchett went, and he didn't seem like he was gwine at all.

"Wonder what time it is?" sed Miss Mary.

"Oh, taint late," ses he. "Is ther gwine to be any preachin here to-morrow?"

"Yes, sir," ses Miss Mary.

"Are you gwine?" axed Crotchett.

"I blieve mother intends to go."

"Very glad," ses he, "I'll be very much obliged to attend you."

"Mother is gwine, I blieve."

"But won't you go too—I'm certain to come after you—come, you must say——"

"It's most ten," ses I; but he didn't pay no tention to that.

"Shall I have the pleasure, Miss——"

"It's ten o'clock," ses I, agin, "and I'm a gwine"—and I looked at the feller and then shook my head at Miss Mary.

"I'll call for you, Miss Mary," sed Crotchett, pickin up his hat.

Miss Mary didn't say nothin, but kind o' smiled, I thought.

"Good evenin, Miss Mary," ses I.

"—That I won't, not these hard times"—ses old Miss Stallins, jest wakin up.

"Good evenin, ladies," ses Crotchett.

Well, next mornin don't you think Miss Mary went to meetin with that imperent cuss, and I had to take old Miss Stallins and Miss Carline, and Cousin Pete tuck Miss Kesiah. Thar he was, shore enough, and nobody couldn't git to say a word to Miss Mary, and before the galls was out of the dore he had her arm in his. I never felt jest zactly so cheap afore in my life, to see that journeyman fiddler, what nobody didn't know nothin about, walkin with Miss Mary to church, and stickin his big carroty whiskers right down under her bonnet, and talkin to her and grinnin like a baked possum. And what made me feel worse, was, she seemed to take it all so mighty fine.

Miss Carline ses I musn't mind it, cause Miss Mary couldn't help herself. But I mean to find out all about it, and if she is big enough fool to be tuck in by sich small taters as he is, I'll jest drap the whole bisness at once, for ther aint nothin in creation I hates wors'n a coquet. No more from

Your friend, till death, JOS. JONES.

P. S. I don't want you to think I'm jealous, caus I aint, not by no means. I don't zactly like the 'pearance of things—but I aint jealous of Crotchett. Only if Miss Mary Stallins goes to meetin any more with him, she don't never go thar with Joseph Jones—that's all.

LETTER IX.

PINEVILLE, *November* 23, 1842.

TO MR. THOMPSON: *Dear Sir*—If I didn't have some real fust rate news to tell you, I don't blieve I could find time to write now, I'm so monstrous bisy. It's hog-killin time now, you know, and the way we is into the hog-meat in Pineville is 'mazin. It seems to me that I haint seed nothin but hogs, and haint heard nothin but squealin, for more'n a week, and I know I haint eat nothin but back-bone and turnips, and spare-ribs, and sassingers, and cracklin-bread ever sense the killin commenced. But as for that part of it, I wouldn't care if hog-killin time lasted all the year. I go for hog meat myself, any way it can be fixed, notwithstandin old nick was turned into 'em once, and set a whole gang of 'em runin down a steep hill into the sea, whar they got drownded in the water.

Old Miss Stallins ses it's all a fact, and I don't never care about gitin into a argyment with her; but thar's one thing I'm certain of—if the old feller did git into the hogs then, he didn't spile the meat.

But that's not the pint. I want to tell you bout that little matter what I writ to you about last time. You know I told you I didn't zactly know how the cat was gwine to jump then. Well, ther's been a dredful climax among the galls in Pineville sense my last letter. Things has turned out jest as I spected, only a grate deal more so. They couldn't went more to my likin if they'd tried. That chap Crotchett, what I told you about, had all the galls in town crazy round him, in no time, and I do blieve they tried to see which could get the most 'tention out of him. The way the feller did shine for about a week beat any thing that was ever seed in Pineville; he was callin and takin tea here, and dinner thar, and ridin out with this young lady and walkin out and perminadin, as he called it, with that one, jest as if he was cousin or uncle, or some near kin to 'em all. Well, Miss Mary come in for her share, and I do blieve the cussed fool—it makes me so mad when I think of it—I do blieve he had a notion of marryin her; and what was a drated sight worse, she seemed to be bout as willin as he was. He sed his kin was all monstrous rich, and owned some mighty grate water-powers in the Jarseys. He told old Miss Stallins that he jest come out south to spend the winter, for his health, and he would like to 'stonish his people by takin a butiful wife to New York with him in the Spring.

He showed the old woman two or three maps of thunderin big towns that was all on his father's land; one was named Crotchettville, and had the greatest water-powers in it in the world, he sed, 'cept Niagara Falls, which he lowed was hard to beat. But old Miss Stallins wasn't to be tuck in so easy, and she gin her galls a good talkin to right afore me, about the way they was blievin every thing he told 'em.

"A track of land," ses she, "is worth more'n a bushel basket full of sich picter papers—and mind what I say galls, all aint gold as glitters. I haint lived my time for nothin, and I don't blieve in these Jarsey water-powers. Whar upon yeath is Jarsey, anyhow?" ses she.

"Why, mother, Jarsey's to the north," sed Miss Mary.

"Hush, child," ses the old woman, "your head's full of nothin but Crotchetts, and water-powers, and the north, and sich nonsense. I tell you I don't blieve in 'em."

"Thar aint no use of gittin mad at the gentleman, mother—I'm sure he's very polite to us all," sed Miss Mary.

"Perliteness aint every thing, my child, and 'pearances aint every thing nother. I don't blieve in these outlandish people, not till I know 'em good. If they's so monstrous well off, and sich big things whar they come from, what's the reason they don't stay thar and not be always travellin about for ther health, and tryin to marry every gall what's got a little property. Nobody that's any account don't never go to the north to git married, but whenever anybody gits found out in sum of ther meanness, they're shore to go to Texas or some whar else for ther health."

Them's my sentiments, thinks I, but I didn't say a word.

"Why, mother," ses Miss Mary, "anybody can see Mr. Crotchett's a gentleman of refinement and edecation."

Miss Kesiah and Miss Carline kep lookin at me and then at onenother and smilin; but Miss Mary looked as serious as a judge.

Old Miss Stallins was jest gwine to speak, when rap, rap, went somebody at the dore.

"Thar's that plagy Crotchett, I'll lay my life," ses she.

Miss Mary run to the dore as quick as she could.

"Ah, ha! Good evenin, Miss Stallins—ladies, good evenin. Ah, how are you, Jones—here agin, eh?"

I felt my dander risin when the imperent cus went and tuck a seat along side of Miss Mary, and she begun to smile and talk with him as pleasin as could be. I knowed it wouldn't do for me to stay thar, so I jest tuck my hat and went home.

"Good evenin, Jones," ses he.

I was in a ace of cussin him back.

"Oh, don't go, Majer," ses Miss Mary, "don't go yet, Majer."

I jest said, "Good evenin, ladies," without lookin at any one in pertickeler, and put out.

Well, the next mornin I went out to the plantation to tend to the hog-killin, and I was jest mad enough to kill all the hogs in Georgia. I couldn't git that imperent cuss out of my head all day, and as to Mary Stallins, I didn't hardly know what to think —sometimes I felt sort o' mad at her, but then agin I couldn't. The fact is, it aint sich a easy thing to feel mad at a right pretty gall, and the more a man feels mad at 'em, the more he's apt to feel sorry too. I tell you what, I was in a stew. I didn't know what to do.

It was after dark when I got home, and when I got thar, all Pineville was in a buz—everybody was talkin about Crotchett. Some said he was a bigamy, and some said he was a thief, and I don't know what all. Come to find out about it, what do you think? His name wasn't Crotchett, but Jackson alias Brown, and he was no more a music-teacher than I was, but a dandy barber, what had stole somebody's pocket-book with a heap of money, in New York, and then run away, and left his wife and two children, to keep from being sent to the Sing Song Penetentiary. He was gone, and nobody couldn't tell whar, and the man what come after him, stuck up some notices at the tavern and the post-office, offerin "$100 reward!" for anybody to ketch him.

Cousin Pete lowed he knowed he wasn't no grate shakes all the time, and was makin more noise than anybody else about gwine after him to ketch him; and all the fellers that was tryin to git into Mr. Crotchett's good graces, was tellin how they spected something, and how they had ther eyes on him—they was lookin out for him, and all that.

But Crotchett was gone, and that's what tuck my eye. I didn't care a tinker's cuss who he was, nor whar he was gone to—he couldn't shine bout Miss Mary no more, with his big whiskers and his water-powers in the Jarseys, and that's all I cared for. I don't know when I felt so good—not sense that time we went after grapes, and I had to go and "skin the cat" like a fool, and skinned my nose so oudaciously. I jest tuck one of the advertisements and writ on it, "this is a map of Mr. Crotchett's water-powers at the north, for Miss Mary Stallins," and sent it to her by one of the little niggers. When she read it she laughed right out, and sed she jest done so to try me. Maybe she did—but it's my turn to try her now, and I'm termined to do it. I'll let Miss Mary Stallins know that I've got a little spunk too, and I'll let her see that I can be as independent as she can. Don't you think it would be a good plan, if I don't carry the joke too far? I'll tell you how it works in my next. No more from

Your friend, till death, Jos. Jones.

P. S. I've jest heard that the galls is got it all over town that Miss Mary was gwine to marry Crotchett, and the way she is mad about it is larmin. "Lord knows," she ses, "she didn't never think of sich a thing." And old Miss Stallins seems like she'd have the hidrafoby or manupotu about it. She ses she's gwine to keep a tighter rein on her galls after this —and if givin 'em 'complishments is gwine to make 'em take up with every dandy barber what comes bout town, they won't get no more college larnin—

that they won't. I tell you what, the highfliers that's been tryin to be aristockrasy fokes has hawled in ther horns considerable sense Crotchett cut out. If the feller's ears don't burn then ther aint no truth in old sayins.

LETTER X.

PINEVILLE, *December* 5, 1842.

To Mr. THOMPSON:—*Dear Sir*—I do blieve last week was the longest one ever was. It seemed to me that the axeltree of the world wanted greasin or something or other was out of fix, for it didn't seem to turn round half so fast as it used to. The days was as long as the weeks ought to be, and the nights hadn't no eend to 'em. Somehow or other, I couldn't sleep o' nights nor eat nothin, and I don't know what upon yeath was the matter with me, 'thout it was the dispepsy, which, you know, makes people have mighty low sperits.

Cousin Pete thought he was monstrous smart, and went all around town and told everybody that my simptems was very bad, and sed he was gwine to put a strengthenin plaster, made out of Burgemy pitch, on my breast, to keep my heart from breakin. I know what he thought, but if he sposed I was gwine to make a fool of myself bout Mary Stallins, he's jest as much mistaken as he was when he tuck the show-man for Tom Peters, from Cracker's Neck. I did feel sort of vexed about the way she tuck up with that bominable scoundrel Crotchett, that's a fact; but then she was so disappinted when he turned out to be a run-away barber, that I couldn't help feelin sorry for her too. It's a monstrous curious feelin when anybody tries to hate somebody that they can't help likin. The more one tries to spite 'em the worse he feels himself. But I was termined to hold out, and if she hadn't come to, I——I——Well, the fact is I don't know what I should a' done, for it was monstrous tryin, you may depend.

But it's all over now, and every thing is jest as straight as a fish-hook. Old Miss Stallins was over to our house to take tea long of mother, one evenin last week. She and mother talked it all over about Crotchett and Miss Mary to themselves, and when I went to see her home, she didn't talk of nothin else all the way.

"Bomination take the retch," ses the old woman, "to run away from his wife and children, the fidlin wagabone, and come out here a tryin to ruinate some pore innocent gall by marryin her, when he's got a wife to home! He ought to be sent to the Peneten-tiary for life, so he ought."

"Zactly so, Miss Stallins," ses I; "but he was mighty popler 'mong the galls. Some of 'em was al-most crazy after him."

"I know they was, Joseph, I know they was; and now they want to turn it all on my pore daughter Mary, when, Laws knows, the child couldn't bear the creetur, only for perliteness."

"Yes, but," ses I, "she went to church with him, you know, and he was to your house every night when I was thar, talkin to her."

"That was only for perliteness, Joseph. That's what she larnt down to the Female College," ses she. "If a gentleman comes to see a lady, she must be perlite to him, whoever he is—"

Cuss sich perliteness as that, thinks I.

—"And it aint no matter if she despises him off the face of the yeath, she must talk and smile to him jest like she liked him ever so much."

"But Miss Mary looked like she thought a heap of Crotchett," ses I.

"It was all decate, Joseph, all decate and perliteness," ses she. "That's the way with the galls now-a-days, Joseph, and you musn't mind 'em. It didn't use to be so when I and your mother was galls. I'll warrant no Crotchetts didn't come bout us if we didn't like ther company, and we had to know all about 'em fore we kep company with anybody."

"It aint so now, though, Miss Stallins," ses I—and I blieve I sort o' drawed a long breath—"It's very different now. If a chap only comes from the North, or some place away out of creashun, and is got a crap of hair and whiskers that would make a saddle-pad, and is got a coat different from everybody else, and a thunderin grate big gold chain round his neck, no matter if he stole 'em, he's the poplerest man mong the ladys, and old acquaintances, whose been raised right along side of 'em, don't stand no sort of a chance."

"Not all the galls aint so, Joseph—my galls hasn't no sich fool notions in ther heds, I'll asshore you."

By this time we was right up to the door.

"Come in, Joseph," ses she.

"No thank you, Miss Stallins," ses I, "I blieve I'll go home."

"Oh, come in, child, and set a while with the galls—they's pullin lasses candy in the parlor."

I was kind of hesitatin, when I heard Miss Mary's voice say,

"Never mind, mother, I spose he's mad at me."

I couldn't stand that, no more'n a gum stump could stand a clap of thunder. I hadn't heard that voice for more'n a week, and it did sound so enticin. It made me feel sort of trembly all over. My face felt red as a pepper-pod, and my ears burnt like they was frostbit. When I went into the room, Miss Mary turned round with one of the wichinest smiles, with her hair all fallin over her rosy cheeks, lookin sweeter than the lasses candy what she had in her hand, and said.

"Are you mad at me, Majer?"

I never was so tuck all aback—my throte felt like I'd swallered a bundle of fodder, and I couldn't speak to save me. I don't know what would tuck place if it hadn't been for old Miss Stallins.

"Oh, no, Joseph ain't mad with you, child. Ther never was a quarrel 'tween the Stallinses and the Joneses, honey, and we've lived neighbors these twenty years!"

"What made you think I was mad with you, Miss Mary?" ses I. Then I kind o' stopped a little and cleared my throte. "You know I never *could* be mad with *you*."

"I thought you was," ses she, "cause you didn't come to see us any more sense that night that mean old Crotchett was here."

When she sed that, I do think she looked handsomer than ever she did in her life, and I couldn't have the heart to say any thing to make her feel bad. I felt that all was right agin and made up my mind to treat her jest like nothin unpleasant had ever happened, I was so happy.

We was all settin by the parlor fire, and the galls was pullin lasses candy. Miss Carline ax'd me if I wouldn't pull some. I felt so queer I didn't think about nothin but Miss Mary, who was pullin a grate big piece, right close to me.

"Take some, Majer," ses she, "and pull it for me, and I'll give you this when it's done," and she kind o' looked sideways at me.

"Well, I know it'll be mighty sweet," ses I, jest as I was gwine to take up some out of the dish.

"Take care, Majer," ses she, "it's dredful hot. Whar's the spoon, Cloe?" ses she, as she was pullin away as hard as she could at a grate big bright rope of lasses.

"O, never mind the spoon," ses I, and in goes my fingers right into the almost bilin hot lasses—

"Ugh!" ses I, and I pulled 'em out quicker'n lightnin.

"My lord!" ses Miss Kesiah, "if the Majer haint burnt his fingers dredful. That lasses is right out of the pot, I know. Haint you got no better sense, Cloe?"

I couldn't help dancin a little, and grindin my teeth, and slingin my fingers; but I didn't say nothin loud.

"Well, Miss Carline tole me bring some more from de kitchen," ses the cussed nigger.

"Oh, dear!" ses Miss Mary, "I'm so sorry. Did you git much on your fingers, Majer?"

The tears was runnin out of my eyes, but I didn't want to let on, for fear it would make her feel bad.

"Oh, no, not much. It aint *very* bad," ses I; and the fust thing I knowed my trousers was plastered all over with the cussed stuff whar I rubbed it off on 'em, it burnt so alfired bad.

They made old Cloe git a basin of water to wash the lasses off, and old Miss Stallins got some soft soap to draw the fire out, and after a while I sot down with the galls to eat candy and talk about Crotchett.

I tell you what, I had the game all my own way this time. I hinted to Miss Mary that I *was* sort of afraid Crotchett was gwine to cut me out, and that I was a leetle jealous at first; and she hinted to me that I ought to know'd better than that, and that I oughtn't to expect her to show her feelins for me no plainer than she had done before, and that she only tuck a little notice of Crotchett, jest to try me, to see if really I did think any thing of her.

My pen won't begin to tell my feelins. I never felt so full of talk before the galls in my life, and, I think, in one or two more heats (I don't mean the hot lasses) I'll be able to come up to the pint. I know I'm jest as good for old Miss Stallins's consent as a thrip is for a ginger cake; and if Miss Mary aint foolin (you know these galls is mighty uncertain) I think I wont have no difficulty in bringin all things round as I want 'em. No more from

Your friend, till death, JOS. JONES.

P. S. I wish you could come down to Pineville to Crismus. I don't think I will git married so soon as that, but we're gwine to have grand flower doins down here then. I've got some goblers so fat that the feathers won't hardly stick in 'em of a warm day. We're gwine to have one of 'em for dinner, and the Stallinses is all gwine to take dinner with us. My fingers is better, but they is bominable sore yit—so you must excuse bad spellin and bad writin this time.

LETTER XI.

PINEVILLE, *December* 20, 1842.

TO MR. THOMPSON:—*Dear Sir*—It seems our fokes always is in a fuss. First it was movin, then it was hog-killin, and now every thing is topsy-turvy makin ready for Crismus. I do blieve the niggers is skowered every spot from the garret to the dore-steps, and every time I come into the house they's all hollerin out, "thar, now, Mas Joe, jest look at your tracks!" and "don't you step on the heath, for it's jest redened," and "don't you spit agin the jam," and sich foolery, jest as if people's houses wasn't made for 'em to live in. It realy puts me out of all patience to see sich nonsensical doins. And mother, she's had all the niggers choppin sasage meat to make mince-pies, and poundin spice and ginger, and makin marvels and beatin egs to make pound-cake, and all sorts of sweet doins for Crismus; for when she takes any thing into her head, she aint a gwine to be outdone by nobody. She ses Crismus don't come but once a year now-a-days, and she's gwine to treat it hansum when it does cum—she's gwine to show the Stallinses that she's used to as good livin as most of fokes.

Well, I glory in her spunk, but it's monstrous expensive to go things on the big figer that she's on now; it never ought to be done only for weddins, and it wouldn't do then whar ther was to be many weddins in the same family.

I tell you what, I was monstrous riled tother day when I got a letter from Crotchett, callin me all sorts of hard names, and abusin me for every thing he could think of. I showed it to the Stallinses, and Miss Mary sed he was a good for nothing wicked retch, to go and run off and leave his wife and children, and then when he was found out, to dare to go and write about a respectable gentleman in that way.

"That's jest the way with the world, my child," ses old Miss Stallins, "the bigger rascal a man is the more insurance he's got. That's jest what put me agin him at fust. Whenever I see so much insurance I always suspect ther's some rascality with it."

And that's my blief, too, Mr. Thompson; I'll tell

you how I judge fokes what I don't know much about. When I see anybody tryin right off to show how smart they is, and takin all the conversation to themselves, I keep my eye on 'em. Cause when people is any account they's got sense enough to know that other people will soon find it out; but when they really aint nobody, and when they know they'd amount to less the more they's found out, then they try to make people blieve they's the mischief and all, before they can have a chance to see into 'em. Haint you never found it so? Insurance is like varnish; it makes the commonest kind of yaller pine look zactly like mahogany, and insurance covers all the rotten places in the character of the worst kind of rascals and makes 'em appear like gentlemen.

Do tell us what upon yeath all this talk means about the world comin to a eend next April. I've heard a great deal about Miller's doctrine, and bustles, and Dickens' Notes, lately in the papers. No other paper but the "Miscellany" haint got much else in 'em. Is it a April fool bisness, or is it a fact? If the world was to bust up bout that time, it would interfere with people's calculations monstrous, specially married fokes. Ther was a man here last week from Augusty, and he sed it was a fact, that he seed it all sifered out on a piece of paper, and ther was no mistake about it. He was collectin for a clock man in Boston, and he sed they was closin up bisness on that account. Now I don't like to blieve no sich nonsense; but if it was to come out true, I wouldn't like to be so tuck in.

Mother and old Miss Stallins and two or three

more old ladies is in a mighty fidget about it, and old Miss Stallins dreamed it was a fact, and mother dreamed she seed two moons tother night, and one of 'em was all blazin with fire and flyin about in the sky like all wrath. I don't 'zactly know what to think about it, but ther's one thing sartin, it's got to begin monstrous early in the mornin on the third day of April if I aint up to see it. If anybody was to set the woods afire bout Pineville, jest at that time, I wouldn't like to answer for the consequences among the old wimin.

But I'm not a gwine to let sich matters interfere with my marryin specelation. I call it specelation, for, you know, ther's no tellin how these things is gwine to turn out. In the fust place, it's a chance if a body gits the gall he's courtin, and after he's got her all to himself. for better or for worse, it's a chance again if she don't turn out a monstrous site worse nor he tuck her for. But I think mine's a pretty safe bisness, for Miss Mary is jest a leetle the smartest, and best, and the butifulest gall in Georgia. I've seed her two or three times sense the candy pullin, and I aint more'n half so fraid of her as I used to be. I told her tother night I had a Crismus gift for her which I hoped she would take and keep.

"What is it, Majer?" ses she.

"Oh," ses I, "it's something what I wouldn't give to nobody else in the world!"

"Well, but what is it?—*do* tell me."

"Something," ses I, "what you stole from me a long time ago, and sense you've got it I want you to keep it, and give me one like it in return."

"Well *do* tell me what it is, fust," ses she, and I seed her cut her eye at Miss Carline, and sort o' smile.

"But, will you give me one in return?" ses I.

"What, Majer—tell me what?"

"I'll tell you Crismus eve," ses I. "But will you give me *yours* in return?"

"*Yours!* eh, my——," then her face got as red as a poppy, and she looked down.

"You know what, Miss Mary," ses I—"will you?"

She didn't say nothin, but blushed worse and worse.

"Now, mind," ses I, "I must have a answer Crismus eve."

"Well," ses she—and then she looked up and laughed, and sed—"exchange is no robbery, is it, sister Carline?"

"No, sis," ses she, "but I reckon Joseph got his pay bout the same time you stole his——"

"Stop, stop, sister, Majer didn't say his heart—"

"There, there!" ses Miss Carline and Miss Kesiah, clappin ther hands, and laughin as loud as they could —"there, there, little innocent sister has let the cat out of the bag, at last. I told you so, Majer."

I never felt so good afore in all my born days, and Miss Mary, pore gall, hid her face in her hands and begun to cry, she felt so about it. That's the way with the galls, you know, they always cry when they feel the happyest. But I soon got her in a good humour, and then I went home.

I'm gwine to bring her right up to the scratch Crismus, or I aint here. It would take a barber's-shop full of Crotchetts to back me out now. I'll tell you how I come out in my next. No more from

Your friend, till death, JOS. JONES.

LETTER XII.

PINEVILLE, *December* 27, 1842.

To MR. THOMPSON:—*Dear Sir*—Crismus is over, and the thing is done did! You know I told you in my last letter I was gwine to bring Miss Mary up to the chalk on Crismus. Well, I done it, slick as a whistle, though it come mighty nigh bein a serious bisness. But I'll tell you all about the whole circumstance.

The fact is, I's made my mind up more'n twenty times to jest go and come right out with the whole bisness; but whenever I got whar she was, and whenever she looked at me with her witchin eyes, and kind o' blushed at me, I always felt sort o' skeered and fainty, and all what I made up to tell her was forgot, so I couldn't think of it to save me. But you's a married man, Mr. Thompson, so I couldn't tell you nothin about popin the question, as they call it. It's a mighty grate favour to ax of a pretty gall, and to people what aint used to it, it goes monstrous hard, don't it? They say widders don't mind it no more'n nothin. But I'm makin a transgression, as the preacher ses.

Crismus eve I put on my new suit, and shaved my face as slick as a smoothin iron, and after tea went over to old Miss Stallinses. As soon as I went into the parler whar they was all settin round the fire, Miss Carline and Miss Kesiah both laughed right out.

"There! there!" ses they, "I told you so! I know'd it would be Joseph."

"What's I done, Miss Carline?" ses I.

"You come under little sister's chicken bone, and I do believe she know'd you was comin when she put it over the dore."

"No I didn't—I didn't no such thing, now," ses Miss Mary, and her face blushed red all over.

"Oh, you needn't deny it," ses Miss Kesiah, "you belong to Joseph now, jest as sure as ther's any charm in chicken bones."

I know'd that was a first rate chance to say something, but the dear little creeter looked so sorry and kep blushin so, I couldn't say nothin zactly to the pint! so I tuck a chair and reached up and tuck down the bone and put it in my pocket.

"What are you gwine to do with that old chicken bone now, Majer?" ses Miss Mary.

"I'm gwine to keep it as long as I live," ses I, "as a Crismus present from the handsomest gall in Georgia."

When I sed that, she blushed worse and worse.

"Aint you shamed, Majer?" ses she.

"Now you ought to give *her* a Crismus gift, Joseph, to keep all *her* life," sed Miss Carline.

"Ah," ses old Miss Stallins, "when I was a gall we used to hang up our stockins——"

"Why, mother!" ses all of 'em, "to say stockins right before——"

Then I felt a little streaked too, cause they was all blushin as hard as they could.

"Highty-tity!" ses the old lady—"what monstrous 'finement to be shore! I'd like to know what harm ther is in stockins. People now-a-days is gittin so mealy-mouthed they can't call nothin by its right name, and I don't see as they's any better than the old time people was. When I was a gall like you, child, I use to hang up my stockins and git 'em full of presents."

The galls kep laughin and blushin.

"Never mind," ses Miss Mary, "Majer's got to give me a Crismus gift—won't you, Majer?"

"Oh, yes," ses I, "you know I promised you one."

"But I didn't mean *that*," ses she.

"I've got one for you, what I want you to keep all your life, but it would take a two bushel bag to hold it," ses I.

"Oh, that's the kind," ses she.

"But will you promise to keep it as long as you live?" ses I.

"Certainly I will, Majer."

—"Monstrous 'finement now-a-days—old people don't know nothin about perliteness," said old Miss Stallins, jest gwine to sleep with her nittin in her lap.

"Now you hear that, Miss Carline," ses I. "She ses she'll keep it all her life."

"Yes, I will," ses Miss Mary—"but what is it?"

"Never mind," ses I, "you hang up a bag big enough to hold it and you'll find out what it is, when you see it in the mornin."

Miss Carline winked at Miss Kesiah, and then whispered to her—then they both laughed and looked at me as mischievous as they could. They 'spicioned something.

"You'll be shore to give it to me now, if I hang up a bag," ses Miss Mary.

"And promise to keep it," ses I.

"Well, I will, cause I know that you wouldn't give me nothin that wasn't worth keepin."

They all agreed they would hang up a bag for me to put Miss Mary's Crismus present in, on the back porch, and about ten o'clock I told 'em good evenin and went home.

I sot up till mid-night, and when they was all gone to bed I went softly into the back gate, and went up to the porch, and thar, shore enough, was a great big meal-bag hangin to the jice. It was monstrous unhandy to git to it, but I was termined not to back out. So I sot some chairs on top of a bench and got hold of the rope and let myself down into the bag; but jest as I was gittin in, it swung agin the chairs, and down they went with a terrible racket; but nobody didn't wake up but Miss Stallinses old cur dog, and here he come rippin and tearin through the yard like rath, and round and round he went tryin to find what was the matter. I scrooch'd down in the bag and didn't breathe louder nor a kitten, for fear he'd find me out, and after a while he quit barkin.

The wind begun to blow bominable cold, and the old bag kep turnin round and swingin so it made me sea-sick as the mischief. I was afraid to move for fear the rope would break and let me fall, and thar I sot with my teeth rattlin like I had a ager. It seemed like it would never come daylight, and I do believe if I didn't love Miss Mary so powerful I would froze to death; for my heart was the only spot that felt warm, and it didn't beat more'n two licks a minit, only when I thought how she would be supprised in the mornin, and then it went in a canter. Bimeby the cussed old dog come up on the porch and begun to smell about the bag, and then he barked like he thought he'd treed something. "Bow! wow! wow!" ses he. Then he'd smell agin, and try to git up to the bag. "Git out!" ses I, very low, for fear the galls mought hear me. "Bow! wow!" ses he. "Be gone! you bominable fool," ses I, and I felt all over in spots, for I 'spected every minit he'd nip me, and what made it worse, I didn't know whar abouts he'd take hold. "Bow! wow! wow!" Then I tried coaxin—"Come here, good feller," ses I, and whistled a little to him, but it wasn't no use. Thar he stood and kep up his everlastin whinin and barkin, all night. I couldn't tell when daylight was breakin, only by the chickens crowin, and I was monstrous glad to hear 'em, for if I'd had to stay thar one hour more, I don't believe I'd ever got out of that bag alive.

Old Miss Stallins come out fust, and as soon as she seed the bag, ses she,

"What upon yeath has Joseph went and put in that bag for Mary? I'll lay its a yearlin or some live animal, or Bruin wouldn't bark at it so."

She went in to call the galls, and I sot thar, shiverin all over so I couldn't hardly speak if I tried to—but I didn't say nothin. Bimeby they all come running out on the porch.

"My goodness! what is it?" ses Miss Mary.

"Oh, it's alive!" ses Miss Kesiah, "I seed it move."

"Call Cato, and make him cut the rope," ses Miss Carline, "and lets see what it is. Come here, Cato, and git this bag down."

"Don't hurt it for the world," ses Miss Mary.

Cato untied the rope that was round the jice, and let the bag down easy on the floor, and I tumbled out all covered with corn meal, from head to foot.

"Goodness gracious!" ses Miss Mary, "if it aint the Majer himself!"

"Yes," ses I, "and you know you promised to keep my Crismus present as long as you lived."

The galls laughed themselves almiost to death, and went to brushin off the meal as fast as they could, sayin they was gwine to hang that bag up every Crismus till they got husbands too. Miss Mary—bless her bright eyes—she blushed as beautiful as a morning-glory, and sed she'd stick to her word. She was right out of bed, and her hair wasn't komed, and her dress wasn't fix'd at all, but the way she looked pretty was real distractin. I do believe if I was froze stiff, one look at her sweet face, as she stood thar lookin down to the floor with her roguish eyes, and her bright curls fallin all over her snowy neck, would have fotched me too. I tell you what, it was worth hangin in a meal bag from one Crismus to another to feel as happy as I have ever sense.

I went home after we had the laugh out, and sot by the fire till I got thawed. In the forenoon all the Stallinses come over to our house and we had one of

"Cato untied the rope that was round the jice, and let the bag down easy on the floor, and I tumbled out all covered with corn meal, from head to foot.

p. 92.

the greatest Crismus dinners that ever was seed in Georgia, and I don't believe a happier company ever sot down to the same table. Old Miss Stallins and mother settled the match, and talked over every thing that ever happened in ther families, and laughed at me and Mary, and cried about ther dead husbands, cause they wasn't alive to see ther children married.

It's all settled now, 'cept we haint sot the weddin day. I'd like to have it all over at once, but young galls always like to be engaged a while, you know, so I spose I must wait a month or so. Mary (she ses I mustn't call her Miss Mary now) has been a good deal of trouble and botheration to me; but if you could see her you wouldn't think I ought to grudge a little sufferin to git sich a sweet little wife.

You must come to the weddin if you possibly kin. I'll let you know when. No more from

Your friend, till death, JOS. JONES.

N. B. I like to forgot to tell you about cousin Pete. He got snapt on egnog when he heard of my ingagement, and he's been as meller as hoss-apple ever sense.

LETTER XIII.

PINEVILLE, *January* 5, 1842.

TO MR. THOMPSON:—*Dear Sir*—Ther's been a awful catasterfy in Pineville sense I writ my last letter to you. Little did I think then what was a comin, though I always thought some cussed thing would turn up jest to spile my happiness.

Last night I was over to old Miss Stallinses, talkin long with Mary and the galls, and makin calculations about the weddin and house-keepin, and sich things, when all at once ther was a terrible shakin and a rackin, like the house was gwine to tumble down on top of us. The galls all squalled out as loud as they could holler, and cotched right hold of me, and hugged close to me till they almost choked the breath out of me, and old Miss Stallins fainted away into a fit of the highstericks. The shakin didn't last more'n a minit, but it had a monstrous curious feelin while it did last.

When it was over the galls fell to rubbin the old woman's hands, and I poured a gourd of water in her face to bring her too, and bimeby she got better.

But all Pineville was shuck up as well as us, and every body was runnin in every direction to find out what was the matter. Some of the niggers tuck to the woods as hard as they could run, and some of the old ones got down on ther knees and went to prayin like they was at a campmeetin. For a while ther was a general panick, but when Mr. Mountgomery sed it was only a shock of a yeathquake, and the danger was all over, the people got over ther scare. Mary was frightened dreadful at fust, but she soon got over it, and so did Miss Kesiah, and Miss Carline. But pore old Miss Stallins—I do blieve the yeathquake has shuck all her senses out of her, for she hasn't talked about nothin else but the world comin to a eend ever sense. She ses she didn't dream about them two moons for nothin, and that the yeath shakin that-a-way is a shore sign that something terrible is gwine to happen. But that aint the worst of it. She says me and Mary mustn't git married not till after next April. She ses nobody ought to think nothin about any thing else but gittin ready to die, and that it's wicked to think about weddins and sich like, now. I told her, what if the world was to come to a eend, ses I, if we was married her daughter wouldn't be left a widder, and I never could die contented no way, without I was married fust.

But it aint no use to argy with her, for she blieves in parson Miller now like a book, and wont listen to no sort of reasonin. She ses it was jest so when old Mr. Noah built the ark—no body didn't blieve him till the water was up to ther chins, and then they couldn't help themselves.

So you see what a fix I'm in—after all my trouble, and jest when I thought I was gwine to be the happiest man in Georgia, a yeathquake must come jest to upset my calculations. I haint no notion of puttin off the weddin so long, but I spose I must wait if I can't do no better. I'm in hopes though, old Miss Stallins will git over her skeer, and come to her senses long afore April. I'll be shore to let you know. No more from

Your friend, till death, JOS. JONES.

P. S. You must excuse mistakes and bad writin this time, for I am in a great hurry to send you this, as I know your readers will be glad to hear the dredful news of a yeathquake, even if ther aint no lives lost. Everybody I've seed this mornin looks sort o' skeery 'cept cousin Pete, and he ses taint nothin to the shakin what they have in Egypt some times.

LETTER XIV.

PINEVILLE, *January* 18, 1842.

To MR. THOMPSON:—*Dear Sir*—When I writ my last letter to you I was in a peck of troubles, and it did seem to me like heaven and yeath was conspired agin me to prevent my marryin Mary Stallins. But things is tuck a turn agin, and now I can say with Mr. Mackbeth in Shakespere, "So foul, so fair a day I never seed afore, and all the clouds that lowered on my head, is in the deep busum of the ocean buried." You must excuse me for writin tragedy out of the book. I don't blieve in stickin in book larnin in every thing a body writes—but then ther is *some* times when jest common words won't express the full meanin, you know. That's the way with me now. But I'll tell you.

You must know the next day after the yeathquake what like to shuck old Miss Stallinses life out of her, nothin would do but she must move right back to the plantation, bag and baggage, galls and all. Mother and all of 'em tried ther best to swade her out of sich a foolish notion. But it wasn't no use. The old woman's head was sot, and you mought jest as well talk sense to a Georgia legislater, or try to build a mill-dam across the Mississippy river as to argy with her when she takes a notion. She sed she wasn't gwine to risk her life no longer in no sich place—ther was too many houses on the hill any way, for safety. She sed people had been comin in and buildin every year sense she settled in town, and she spected nothin else but the yeath would cave thar one of these days, if it didn't no whar else.

Well, shore enough, the Stallinses moved out that very day. Mary looked like she didn't like it, but never sed nothin, only that she hoped I'd come out to see 'em often. I was anxious to go and see Mary, but sense the old woman was so stubbern about it, I thought I wouldn't show too much hurry, so I waited till yesterday, when old uncle Cato brung me a letter from the old woman herself, which I can asshore you was as interestin to me as the Miscellany is when I fust git it out of the post-office. You may look out for a weddin before long. I'm 'termined to have the thing fixed 'thout waitin for enny more accidents. No more from

Your friend, till death, Jos. Jones.

P. S. I will fold her letter inside of this so you can read it.

My deer Joseph,—Arter my complyments, I want to say a word to you on the subjec of yourn an Mary's marryin. I've been a thinkin about it ever sense that nite when the yeathquake come along and like to swallered the whole of us up in the bowels of the yeath. Now you no, Joseph, that I consider you no more nor less than mi sun, perviden the world don't come to a eend, for I think Mary got sich a lessen from what turned up with that rascal Crotchit, that she'll mind how she projects with clever fokes what she's nown all her life, enny more. You no I aint gwine to oppose your marryin Mary for enny objectshun to you, for tho I say it to you when I oughtent to say it, I would ruther have you for a sun-in-law than enny young man I no of. But I did think it was no time to be thinkin about marryin when all nater was provin the truth of parson Miller's proffesyin. But Mary has tuck on so ever sense I opposed your marryin her right off, that it has worried me mazinly. She ses, ef the world does come to a eend she couldn't bare the site, no how ef you wasn't thar, right by her. She ses moren that, she ses—and I declare I'm shamed to rite it to you, and I no you'll blush to read it, jest to no how the child does love you—she ses she couldn't di no how, 'thout it was in your arms, and you no if you was to gratifi her when the catasterfy cum, and wasn't married, peple wood talk. And then agin, thar's that paper what Mary takes on your account has got them letters in it what you writ to your friend mister Tomson, whar you pored out your feelins on the subjec and let the whole cat out of the wallit; and Mary ses she spects that more'n five thousen peple has red all bout the whole bisness fore now, for she ses the editer ses his scripshun list is growin every day, and is most a thousen now, and you no more'n five borry it whar one scribes for it. That's one reason that Mary is so posed to your turnin editer—she ses it is hard work and pore pay, and five thousen borryers wouldn't support no paper. Mary is a mity spunky gal, and don't blieve in bein posed on by nobody, and ef the world don't come to a eend, I think you'll say in twelve months you've got the smartest wife in Pinevil, tho I say it hoo oughtent to. But I'm gwine off the subjec. I hav come to the conclusion that you and Mary may git married ef you say so, jest to save pearances, and you needent git no fixins for houskeepin till arter April, and when you is married I'll jest let you say whether we'll pitch a crap or no. No more but yourn till death,

POLLY STALLINS.

Perliteness of Cater.

LETTER XV.

PINEVILLE, *February* 2, 1843.

TO MR. THOMPSON:—*Dear Sir*—Ever sense I writ my last letter to you, things is gone on jest as straight as a shingle, and the only thing what troubles me is, I'm fraid it's all too good to last. It's always been the way with me ever sense I can remember, whenever I'm the happiest some cussed thing seems to turn up jest to upset all my calculations; and now, though the day is sot for the weddin, and the Stallinses is gettin every thing ready as fast as they can, I wouldn't be supprised much if some bominable thing was to happen, some yeathquake or something, jest to bust it all up agin, though I should hate it monstrous.

Old Miss Stallins read that piece in the Miscellany about the mistake in parson Miller's figers, and I do blieve she's as glad about it as if she was shore she would live a whole thousand years more herself. She ses she hain't got no objections to the weddin now, for me and Mary'll have plenty of time to make a fortin for our children and rais 'em up as they ought to be. She ses she always wondered how Mr. Miller could cifer the thing out so straight, to the very day, without a single mistake, but now he's made sich a terrible blunder of a whole thousand years, she ses she knows he aint no smarter nor other people, if he was raised at the north.

It's really surprisin how mazin poplar it does make a body to be engaged to be married to a butiful young lady. Sense the thing's leaked out, every body's my pertickeler friend, and I can't meet nobody wherever I go, but what wants to congratilate me on my good fortin, 'cept cousin Pete and two or three other fellers, who look sort o' like they wanted to laugh and couldn't. Almost every night Mary and me is invited to a party. Tother night we went to one to old Squire Rogerses, whar I got my dander up a little the worst I've had it for some time. I don't blieve you have ever hearn of jest sich a dingd fool trick as they played on me. Ther was a good many young people thar, and as the Squire don't allow dancin, they all played games and tricks, and sich foolishness to pass away the time, which to my notion is a bominable sight worse than dancin.

Cousin Pete was thar splurgin about in the biggest, with his dandy-cut trowsers and big whiskers, and tried to take the shine off everybody else, jest as he always does. Well, bimeby he ses,

"Spose we play brother Bob—lets play brother Bob."

"Yes, lets play that," ses all of 'em, "won't you be brother Bob, Majer?"

"Who's brother Bob?" ses I—for I didn't know nothin about it, and that's the way I come to be so bominably tuck in.

"I'll tell you," ses he, "you and somebody else must set down in the chairs and be blindfolded, and the rest must all walk round and round you, and keep tappin you on the head with something till you guess who bob'd you."

"But how bob me?" ses I.

"Why," ses he, "when any one taps you, you must say, 'Brother, I'm bob'd!' and then they'll ax, 'Who bob'd you?' and if you guess the right one, then they must take your place and be bob'd till they guess who bob'd 'em. If you'll be blindfolded I will," ses he, "jest for fun."

"Well," ses I, "any thing for fun."

Cousin Pete sot out two chairs into the middle of the room, back to back, and we sot down, and they tied a hankercher round my eyes tite as the mischief, so I couldn't see to guess no more'n if I had no eyes at all. Then the boys and galls commenced walkin round us in a circle all giglin and laughin.

I hadn't sot thar no time before cawhalux! some one tuck me right side of the head with a dratted big book. The fire flew out o' my eyes in big live coals, and I like to keeled over out of the chair. I felt my blood risin like a mill-tail, but they all laughed mightily at the fun, and after a while ses I,

"Brother, I'm bob'd."

"Who bob'd you?" ses they.

I guessed the biggest fisted feller in the room, but it wasn't him.

"No, no!" they all hollered, and round they went agin a rompin and laughin and enjoyin the fun all to themselves while my head was singin like a tea kettle.

The next minit, spang went the book agin cousin Pete's head.

"Whew!" ses he, "brother, I'm bob'd?"

"Who bob'd you?" ses they.

But cousin Pete didn't guess right nother, and the fust thing I know'd, whang they tuck me agin.

I was dredful anxious to guess right, but it was no use, I missed it every time, and so did cousin Pete, and the harder they hit the louder they laughed. One time they hit me a great deal softlier than the rest.

"Brother, I'm bob'd!" ses I.

"Who bob'd you?" ses they.

"Miss Mary Stallins," ses I.

"No, I never," ses she, and they all roared out worse than ever.

I begun to git monstrous tired of sich fun, which seemed so much like the boys and the frogs in the spellin book—for if it was fun to them it was death to me—and I don't know what I would done if Mary hadn't come up and untied the hankercher.

"Let's play something else," ses she, and her face was as red as fire, and she looked sort o' mad out of her eyes.

I seed ther was something wrong in a minit.

Well, they all went on playin "pawns," and "'pon honor," and "Here we go round the goose-berry bush," and "Oh, sister Feby, how merry we be," and sich tom fooleries till they played all they knowed, and while they was playin Mary told me all about the trick cousin Pete played on me.

It was the most oudacious take in I ever heard of. Do you think the cuss didn't set right down behind me, and never blindfolded himself at all, and hit me every lick himself, now and then hittin his knee with the book, to make me blieve he was bob'd too! My head was a buzzin with the licks when she told me how he done me, and I do blieve if it hadn't been for her I'd gin cousin Pete sich a lickin right thar in that room as he never had before in his born days. Blazes! but I was mad at fust. But Mary begged me not to raise no fuss about it, now it was all over, and she would fix him for his smartness. I hadn't no sort of a idee how she gwine to do it, but I know'd she was a match for cousin Pete any time, so I jest let her go ahed.

Well, she tuck the bominable fool off to one side and whispered to him like she was gwine to let him into a grate secret. She told him about a new play what she learned down to Macon when she was at the college, called "Interduction to the King and Queen," what she sed was a grate deal funnier than "Brother Bob," and got him to help to git 'em all to play it.

After she and him made it all up, cousin Pete put out three chairs close together in a row for a throne, and Mary she put a sheet over 'em to make 'em look a little grand. Bill Byers was to be King and Mary was to be Queen.

"Now, you must all come in tother room," ses cousin Pete, "only them what belongs to the court, and then you must come in and be interduced, one at a time.

"I aint gwine," ses Tom Stallins, "for ther's some trick in it."

"No ther aint," ses cousin Pete, "I'll give you my word ther aint no trick—only a little fun."

"Well," ses I, "I's had fun enough for one night."

Mary looked at me and kind o' winked, and ses she, "you're one of the court you know, Majer; but jest go out till the court is sumonsed before the throne."

Well, we all went out, and bimeby Bill Byers called out the names of all the lords and ladys what belonged to the court, and we all went in and tuck chairs on both sides of the throne.

Cousin Pete was to be the fust one interduced, and Sam Rogers was to be the usher, the feller what interduced the company. Well, bimeby the door opened and in come cousin Pete, bowin and scrapin, and twistin and rigglein and puttin on more dandy airs than a French dancin master—he beat Crotchett all to smash. The King sot on one side of the throne and the Queen on tother, leavin room in the middle for some one else. Sam was so full of laugh at cousin Pete's anticks that he couldn't hardly speak.

"Doctor Peter Jones," ses he, "I interduce you to ther Majestys the King and Queen."

"The fust thing he knowed, kersloch he went, rite into a big tub mor'n half full of cold water." p. 105.

Cousin Pete scraped about a while and then drapt on one knee, right before 'em.

"Rise, gallant knight," ses Bill Byers, "rise, we dub you knight of the royal bath."

Cousin Pete got up and bowed and scraped a few more times, and went to set down between 'em, but they ris up jest as he went to set down, and the fust thing he knowed, kerslosh he went, rite into a big tub mor'n half full of cold water, with nothing but his head and heels stickin out.

He tried to kiss Mary as he was takin his seat, and if you could jest seed him as he went into that tub with his arms reached out to her, and his mouth sot for a kiss, I do believe you'd laughed more'n you ever did before in your life. The fellers was all so 'spicious that some trick was gwine to be played, that they left the dore open, and when the thing tuck place they all run in shoutin and laughin like they would bust ther sides.

Pete got out as quick as he could, and I never seed a feller so wilted down in all my life. He was mad as a hornet, and sed it was a d—d mean trick to sarve enny body so, specially in cold weather. And he went right off home by himself to dry.

Mary made the niggers take out the middle chair what was covered by the sheet, and put the tub of water in its place when we was all in tother room. Pete didn't have no suspicion that the trick was gwine to turn out that way. He thought the queen was gwine to sentence every feller what didn't kiss her as he sot down, to do something that would make fun for the rest, and he was jest gwine to open the game.

I felt perfectly satisfied after that, and I don't think cousin Pete will be quite so fond of funny tricks the next time.

But I like to forgot to tell you, my weddin is to take place—perviden ther aint no more yeathquakes nor unaccountable things to prevent—on the 22d of this month, which you know is a famous day what ought to be celebrated by every genewine patriot in the world. I shall look for you to come, and I hope you will be shore to be thar, for I know you wouldn't grudge the ride jest to see Miss Mary Jones what is to be. We's gwine to have a considerable getherin, jest to please the old folks, and old Miss Stallins ses she's gwine to give us a real Georgia weddin of the old time fashion. No more from

Your friend, till death, Jos. Jones.

P. S. I went over tother night to see 'em all, and they was as bisy as bees in a tar-barrel sowin and makin up finery. Mary was sowin something mighty fine and white, with ruffles and jigamarees all round it. "What kind of a thing is that?" ses I. The galls looked at one another and laughed like they would die, and my poor little Mary (bless her soul) kep getherin it up in a heap and blushin dredful. "Tell him, sis," ses Miss Carline. But Mary looked right down and didn't say nothin. "I'll tell him," ses Miss Kesiah—"It's a——" "No, you shant now—stop, stop," ses Mary, and she put her pretty little hand right on Miss Kesiah's mouth, and looked like she'd cry for a little. I felt so sorry for her, I told 'em I didn't want to know, and they put the things away, and bimeby I went home, but I kep thinkin all the way what upon yeath it could be. I spose I'll find out some day.

LETTER XVI.

PINEVILLE, *February* 24, 1843.

TO MR. THOMPSON:—*Dear Sir*—I am too happy and no mistake—the twenty-second of February is over, and the "consumation so devotedly to be wished for" is tuck place. In other words, I's a married man!!

I aint in no situation to tell you all how the thing tuck place, not by no means, and if it wasn't for my promis, I don't blieve I could keep away from my wife long enough to write you a letter. Bless her little heart, I didn't think I loved her half so good as I do; but to tell you the real truth, I do blieve I've been almost out of my senses ever sense night before last. But I must be short this time while the galls is plaguein Mary in tother room. They is so full of ther mischief.

I had the license got mor'n a week ago, and old Mr. Eastman brung home my weddin suit jest in time. Mother would make me let cousin Pete wait on me, and Miss Kesiah was bride's maid. Mother and old Miss Stallins had every thing ranged in fust rate style long before the time ariv, and nothing was wantin but your company to make every thing complete.

Well, about sundown cousin Pete come round to my room whar we rigged out for the weddin, and I don't blieve I ever seed him look so good; but if he'd jest tuck off them bominable grate big sorrel whiskers of his, he'd looked a monstrous sight better. I put on my fawn-colored britches and blue cloth cote and white satin jacket, and my new beaver hat, and then we druv round to old Squire Rogerses and tuck him into the carriage and away we went out to Miss Stallinses plantation. When we got to the house ther was a most everlastin getherin thar waitin to see the ceremony before they eat ther supper. Everybody looked glad, and old Miss Stallins was flyin round like she didn't know which eend she stood on.

"Come in, Joseph," ses she, "the galls is in the other room."

But I couldn't begin to git in tother room for the fellers all pullin and haulin and shakin the life out of me to tell me how glad they was.

"Howdy, Majer, howdy," ses old Mr. Byers, "I give you joy," ses he—"yer gwine to marry the flower of the county, as I always sed. She's a monstrous nice gall, Majer."

"That's a fact," ses old Mr. Skinner, "that's a fact, and I hope you'll be a good husband to her, Joseph, and that you'll have good luck with your little——"

"Thank you, thank you, gentlemen—come along, cousin Pete," ses I, as quick as I could git away from 'em.

The dore to tother room was opened and in we went. I never was so struck all up in a heap. Thar sot Mary with three or four more galls, butiful as a angel and blushin like a rose. When she seed me she kind o' looked down and sort o' smiled, and sed "good evenin, Joseph."

I couldn't say a word for my life, for more'n a minit. Thar she sot, the dear gall of my heart—and I couldn't help but think to myself what a infernel cuss a man must be that could marry her and then make her unhappy by treatin her mean; and I determined in my sole, to stand between her and the storms of the world, and to love her, and take care of her, and make her happy, as long as I lived. If you could jest seen her as she was dressed then, and you wasn't a married man, you couldn't help but envy my luck, after all the trouble I've had to git her. She was dressed jest to my likin, in a fine white muslin frock, with short sleeves, and white satin slippers, with her hair all hangin over her snow-white neck and shoulders in butiful curls, without a single breastpin or any kind of jewelry or ornament, 'cept a little white satin bow on the side of her head. Bimeby Miss Carline come in the room.

"Come, sis, they's all ready," ses she, and ther was grate big tears in her eyes, and she went and gave Mary a kiss right in her mouth, and hugged her a time or two.

We all got up to go. Mary trembled monstrous, and I felt sort o' fainty myself, but I didn't feel nothin like cryin.

When we got in the room whar the company was, old Squire Rogers stopt us right in the middle of the floor and axed us for the license. Cousin Pete handed 'em to him and he read 'em out loud to the people, who was all as still as death. After talkin a little he went on——

"If enny body's got enny thing to say why this couple shouldn't be united in the holy bands of wedlock," ses he, "let 'em now speak or always afterwards hold ther peace——"

"Oh, my lord! oh, my darlin daughter! oh, dear laws a massy!" ses old Miss Stallins as loud as she could squall—a clappin her hands and cryin and shoutin like she was at a camp meetin.

Thunder and lightnin! thinks I, here's another yeathquake. But I held on to Mary, and was termined that nothin short of a real bust up of all creation should git her away from me.

"Go ahed, Squire," ses cousin Pete. "It aint nothin."

Mary blushed dredful, and seemed like she would drap on the floor.

Miss Carline come and whispered something to her, and mother and two or three more old wimmin got old Miss Stallins to go in tother room.

The Squire went through the rest of the bisness in a hurry, and me and Mary was made flesh of one bone and bone of one flesh before the old woman got over her highstericks. When she got better she come to me and hugged and kissed me as hard as she could right afore 'em all, while all the old codgers in the room was salutin the bride as they called it. I didn't like that part of the ceremony at all, and wanted to change with 'em monstrous bad; but I reckon I've made up for it sense.

After the marryin was over we all tuck supper, and the way old Miss Stallinses table was kivered over with good things was uncommon. After playin and frolickin till bout ten o'clock, the bride's cake was cut, and sich a cake was never baked in Georgia before. The Stallinses bein Washingtonians, ther wasn't no wine, but the cake wasn't bad to take jest dry so. About twelve o'clock the company begun to leave for home, all of 'em jest as sober as when they come.

I had to shake hands again with 'em all, and tell 'em all good night.

"Good night, cousin Mary," ses Pete—"good night, Majer," ses he, "I spose you aint gwine back to town to night," and then bust right out in a big laugh, and away he went.

That's jest the way with Pete; he's a good feller enough, but he aint got no better sense.

Mary ses she's sorry she couldn't send you no more cake, but Mr. Mountgomery's saddlebags wouldn't hold half she wraped up for you. Don't forgit to put our marriage in the Miscellany. No more from

Your friend, till death, JOS. JONES.

LETTER XVII.

PINEVILLE, *March* 28, 1843.

TO MR. THOMPSON:—*Dear Sir*—I really owe you a apology for not writin to you so long; but the fact is, I've been too happy ever sense I was married, to think about writin or enny thing else much. Besides I use to have time to write nights; but now my time is tuck up with so many things, receivin company and payin visits, and goin to quiltens and partys of one kind and another, that I haint no time for nothing; and as for writin letters, when my wife's all the time lookin over my shoulder, pullin my ears, and tickelin me, and disputin about my spellin, it aint no kind of use to try. She's gone over to mother's this afternoon with her sisters, and her mother's out in the garden, lookin if the frost is killed the peas, so I thought I'd write you a few lines jest to let you know how we is all comin on.

We's all pretty well, 'cept the old woman, who's been in a monstrous flustration about the comet, and the yeathquakes, and the harrycanes, and snowstorms, and sich things, for more'n a month, and I've had a most bominable sore throat, which I got lookin at the comet jest to please her; but Mary soon cured that with some sage tea and turpentine. I'm livin with Mary's mother for the present; but that makes mother monstrous jealous, and to satisfy both the old wimin, Mary and me is gwine to housekeepin next fall to ourselves.

I don't know what to make of the weather. The months is either got mixed up and January's swaped places with March this time, or that bominable grate big comet is got between our yeath and the sun, and is soakin all the sunshine up in its everlastin tail, which the newspapers say is more'n two thousand miles long. We planted some corn most a month ago, but it's all rotten or froze to death; and if the weather don't git no better I don't know when we'll plant enny more; and if cotton's gwine clean down to nothin, I don't mean to put a seed in the ground this year.

Old Miss Stallins reads the Bible most all the time, and ses she's jest as shore as she wants to be that something's gwine to turn up. She ses that comet is sent to let us know the judgment day's a comin, and these yeathquakes and harrycanes is signs that it aint far off. She's all the time lookin out, and she's got a grate big cow-bell fixed right by her bed, so the least touch will make it ring, so she can tell when the yeathquake comes next time. Tother night old Sookey, the cook, who's about as big as a cow, slipped up in the snow on the porch, and shuck the whole house and made the bell ring. The old woman jumped out of bed and lit a candle in a minit, and had us all up with her hollerin about the yeathquake; and last night, when it lightened so, I thought she'd die shore enough. She sed tother eend of the world was a fire, and we'd all be burnt into cracklins before mornin. She shouted and clapped her hands, and prayed, and bid good-by to us all; and I do blieve if it hadn't thundered as soon and as loud as it did, she would kick'd the bucket shore enough. Jest hearin so much about that dratted old Miller, has played the wild with the old woman's senses. It's a grate pity ther aint some way to put a stop to that old feller's bominable nonsence. He ought to be put in the penetentiary for tryin to make people blieve he's sich a monstrous sight smarter than the Lord ever intended him to be, that he can tell when the world's gwine to come to a eend. The Bible ses that thing was to be kep a grate secret and nobody in heaven or yeath should know any thing about it. Well, aint it most oudacious insurance, then, for him to come and say he's found it out—that he knows all about it? And if he did know it, he ought to have principle and good breedin enough not to go and blab it all about, jest to scare fokes to death. The old cuss ought to be brought to the eend of a rope jest for his meanness.

For my part I haint no notion of the world bustin up yit, though things does look kind of skeery jest now. It would jest be my luck if some bominable thing like a war or a coleramorbus, or a famin was to come along now that I've got the handsomest and smartest gall in Georgia for a wife. They say ther is no sich thing as complete happiness on this yeath, and that makes me think so more, for nothing short of some monstrous grate calamity could rumple my feathers now. But I do hope it will all blow over. I do blieve Mary grows handsomer every day, and if things could stay jest as they is now, I'd like to live till I was old enough to be grandaddy to Methusla. But it's time I was gwine over to mother's to bring Mary home. So no more from

Your friend, till death, Jos. Jones.

P. S. At first I didn't hardly know what to say about your printin my letters in a book, but I was talkin to Mr. Mountgomery about it tother day, and I told him I was afraid people would laugh at it. Ses he, "That's jest the very thing you ought to want 'em to do. You couldn't do 'em no greater favor than to make 'em laugh a little these hard times, and the more you make 'em laugh they'll like you all the better for it." Well, I know the old man knows a heap about these things and is a first rate friend of mine, and wouldn't give me no bad advice. So I have come to the conclusion that you may go ahead, and have rit a preface for you to put in frunt of the book. Now do be careful about the spellin, cause you know ther's some people what's jest got sense enough to find out mistakes, and they's the very ones that allways makes the biggest fuss over 'em.

LETTER XVIII.

PINEVILLE, *May* 20, 1843.

To MR. THOMPSON:—*Dear Sir*—The last mail brung the Miscellany and a big yaller package, marked on the outside "six pamphlets for Major Joseph Jones, Pineville, Georgia." As soon as the post-office was open I got 'em out and looked over the Miscellany like I always do afore I let ennybody take it, and what should I see but that piece of Mr. Holmeses, praisin up my book, and that all sorts of a puff what you tuck from the "Georgia Courier." I read along down, and the further I went the reder my face got, till it burned so I could feel my beard singin and curlin like burnt bristles. The fellers all begun to look at me, and old Mr. Rogers, seshe,

"What upon yeath's the matter with the Major?"

"Why, he looks like he was sent for and don't want to go," ses cousin Pete.

"What is you tuck up with so in that paper?" ses Mr. Mountgomery, the schoolmaster, who was waitin to git his papers—"let me see what it is," ses he.

Well, I couldn't refuse Mr. Mountgomery, so I let him look at it. He tuck out his specks and rubbed 'em, and then I watched him. He looked a little while, and then ses he,

"Oh ho! I see, I see—it's a piece about the Major's book. I spose somebody's been blowin him up, and he aint used to it."

"Ha, ha!" ses cousin Pete, "jest as I spected—I know'd it would be so whenever them ritins was printed in a book. Read it out, Mr. Mountgomery."

"Yes, read it out, read it out, so we all can hear it," sed the fellers.

I felt monstrous shamed, and was gwine to walk away out of the crowd, when cousin Pete, ses he, "Don't let him go, fellers, less have our fun out of the auther," and they all got round me and wouldn't let me budge a peg.

Well, when they all got still, old Mr. Mountgomery got up on the steps and read the whole piece right out, loud as he could. Cousin Pete had got his mouth sot for sich a big horse-laugh at me that he couldn't git it back agin right away, so after he saw the turn the thing had tuck he jest stood with his mouth open, and drawed up at the corners like he was laughin, and his eyes starin open and sot in his head like he seed a ghost. His mouth was pretendin to laugh while his eyes didn't seem to have any notion of what it was laughin at.

"Hurra! hurra!" ses all the fellers—"hurra for Majer Jones, the Pineville auther!—Hurra for Pineville literature!—Hurra for Majer Jones."

Cousin Pete got his mouth shut, but he didn't open it agin. Old Mr. Mountgomery stood on the steps wavin the Miscellany over his head, while the boys was shoutin, and as soon as they was done he come down and held out his hand to me and ses he—

"Majer, allow me to congratulate you on the success of your first literary enterprize. Your book is a very original perduction, and though it don't belong to the more useful and elvated branches of literary composition, I think it's equally as good as one half the foreign matter what is published in this country, and not half so pernicious as some of it."

And then he smiled and shuck my hand agin.

"Hurra!" ses the fellers—"hurra for Pineville—hurra for Jones!"

"Allow me to congratulate you," ses the old man, after the fellers was done hollerin—"you have married a wife and writ a book, and only one thing more is wantin to make you a man of standin in society."

The fellers all hollered and shouted agin, but I couldn't hear 'em.

"Majer, see if them aint some of your books in that bundle," ses Squire Rogers.

Well, I tore it open and shore enough thar they was, six blue books, with the title-page on the outside. Then the fuss commenced—every feller wanted one right off, and I wanted to save one to show it to Mary. I let 'em have five of 'em, and away I went for home to show the other one to the wimin.

As soon as I got home I showed it to Mary, and what do you think? the very fust thing she sed was that it was all spilt, and wasn't worth a cent, and she pouted out her pretty mouth and looked as mad as she could. I never was so surprised at her in my life—

"Why," ses I, "Mary, what makes you say that —jest hear what the papers ses. Now listen," ses I, and I begun to read that piece.

"Oh, shaw," ses she, "I don't mean the book ain't good enough, but jest look what a ugly old fright the printer has went and put on the cover. Jest look at the mean old thing with his big whiskers, and his mouth screwed up like he had been eatin a peck of green simmons. It don't look no more like you, Joseph, than you does like a cow. I declare if anybody would go and make a picter like that for me, I'd prosecute 'em for it, so I would."

I couldn't help laughin at her when she sed that—jest to see how proud she is of my good looks.

"Oh, you musn't think nothing of that," ses I, "picters don't mean nothin, and it aint one time in a hundred you can find one that looks like anybody. I spose it's so long since Mr. Thompson seed me that he's forgot how I looked, and he's done the best he could from recollection."

But it wasn't no use to try to talk her out of her notion about that picter, so I let her paste a pretty one she got out of some picter-book over the place.

The boys has read the letters over and over, and they was monstrous glad cause I put in that piece about cousin Pete's interduction to the King and Queen, what wasn't in the paper, and they plague him so much about it, that he stays in his room in the daytime like a possum in a gum. He's mad as the mischief about it, and ses if ther was any good law in Georgia, he would sue me for a liebill. But I don't care three straws for cousin Pete.

I owe you a apology for not writin before. But the fact is, I've had so much to tend to—crapin and fixin for a settlement to myself next fall, that I haint had no time for nothin. We all gits on smooth as glass, 'cept Mary has queer ways now and then. The fact is, her sisters, and old Miss Stallins, and mother, and all of 'em, spile her too much, and she's as notionate as a child here lately. Sometimes she cries, and ses I don't love her like she does me, and sich nonsense; and then agin she's as bright and happy as a lark. The fact is, Mr. Thompson, these wimin's curious things, and it takes a long time to understand 'em. Mr. Weller was about right when he told his son Samivel that when he was married he'd know somethings as he didn't know then; but he showed his want of sense when he said he didn't know whether it would be worth while to go to so much trouble to learn so little. A man aint more'n half a right sort of a man until he's married, and if he ain't willin to swaller the few little bitter things for the thousand sweet things of a married life, he better jest commit dogacide at once, for sich a man aint much better nor a dog at best. But I must bring this letter to a close. So no more from

Your friend, till death, JOS. JONES.

LETTER XIX.

PINEVILLE, *June* 7, 1843.

TO MR. THOMPSON:—*Dear Sir*—Pineville has been in a perfect harrycane of excitement for more'n a week past, and the thing hain't died away yet. The fact is, my book has turned some people's heads, and ther's some down in these parts that is so pisen mad at my popilarity that I'll jest have to weed 'em out a few before they's satisfied. I've always noticed it to be the case, that whenever a man begins to rise a little in the world, everybody that knows him is shore to try to set him back; but if he's got real genus he's shore to succeed in spite of all his *old friends*, and then ther's nobody hurras for him louder than they does. It's the way with human nater—envy won't let 'em give a man popilarity, but when he gits it in spite of 'em, and is independent of 'em, then they feel like the boot was on tother leg, and is monstrous glad to git any notice from him. They all likes to be considered a grate man's friend, whenever he gits poplar enough to be independent of ther influence. But I want to tell you how the thing has worked down here.

Sense you sent me them copies of my book, and everybody's read 'em and talked about 'em all over the whole settlement, I've felt so sort o' shamed, that I hain't went no whar, not even to church on Sunday, so nobody couldn't have a chance to talk to me about it. Well, tother day I was out on the plantation overseein the niggers that was cuttin my wheat. I was away over in the field, bisy as I could be shockin it up, when I seed nigger Tom comin ridin into the field as hard as he could gallop on my hoss, all saddled and bridled. Before I had time to ax him any questions, he rid right up and pulled a paper out of his hat and handed it to me, with his eyes stickin out of his head like he'd been crakin walnuts with his teeth for a month. I tuck the paper and read it, and it was a letter from Mary.

"Oh, my dear Joseph, what have you done? Fly for you life. My hand trembles so I can hardly write. Oh dear, what shall I do when you are gone? Mother is almost crazy. I have sent your horse, so you can make your escape immediately. I have just heard that there is a man in town who has come to take you prisoner, and carry you to Augusta for $1000 reward. His name is Mr. Holmes. Don't let them take my dear Joseph from me. Oh, I should die if you were to be taken to prison. Fly with the speed of the wind. My love will bear you from harm, and follow you to the remotest part of the earth. Write to me when you are in safety, and I will soon be with you. Adieu. May heaven protect you.

"Your affectionate MARY."

Heavens and yeath! thinks I, what does all this mean? what is the matter with Mary? I know'd I hadn't done nothing to be put in prison for, and I never was so stumped.

"What's the matter of your young misses, Tom?" ses I.

"Don't know, massa Joe," ses he, "only they is all cryin, and Miss Mary's layin on the bed and Miss Carline and Miss Kesiah is rubbin her hands and puttin campfire on her face. Old Missus ses you musn't stop to read the letter, but must git on Selim and run as hard as you kin."

I was satisfied something was broke loose, but what upon yeath it could be I couldn't think. It must be some other Jones, ses I to myself. Ther's a good many Joneses in Georgia, and I know some myself that ain't no great scratches. They must mistuck me for some feller what's been robbin the bank or killin somebody. I had no notion of runnin, so I determined to go right over to the house and have a full understandin of the matter, and try to quiet Mary's fears, for I was worse scared about her than I was about the $1000 reward.

Well, when I got to the house, sich a fuss I never did see. Thar was old Miss Stallins walkin up and down the floor, ringin her hands and cryin and talkin.

"Oh dear, oh dear!" ses she, "we's ruin'd, our family is disgraced! what is you done, Joseph, my child—what is they gwine to take you to prisen for? It will be the death of Mary, pore thing, she will never git over it."

"Why mother, don't take on so," ses I; "it's all a mistake—I hain't done nothin agin the law. It's some other Jones."

"Oh, no, they said it was you—something about your ruinin some butiful young ladys down in Augusta, and twistin ther mouths all out of shape and a whole heap o' things."

"Lord," ses I, "I never teched one of 'em in my life."

"Kiss me, Joseph, and then go"—ses pore Mary, bustin out into a hearty cry.—"Do go, Joseph, for my sake, for I shall die if they carry you to jail."

"Why, Mary," ses I, "it's all a mistake as shore as I live. I never tetched a young lady's mouth in Augusta in my life."

But it was all no use; nothing would do but I must go.—So I gave the pore gall a good fashioned hug and bid 'em all good by and got on Selim, but not to run away. I was determined to see the upshot of the whole bisness, and away I went right down to town.

Some how I mistrusted cousin Pete was at the bottom of the whole fuss. I know'd he felt monstrous sore about the popilarity of my book, and he haint got no more sense than jest to go and make a fool of himself to try to spite me. Shore enough, as soon as I got in town, I met a crowd of fellers with cousin Pete and a constable at ther head.

"There he is! ketch him, fellers! take hold of him!" ses he; and they all come getherin round me like they was gwine to surround some wild animal.

"Now jest stop," ses I—for I begun to feel my blood bile when I seed Pete, and thought what a infernel fuss he had kicked up, and how he had skared Mary almost to death.—"Now jest stop, and tell me what you want of me before you put your fingers on me."

"Take hold of him, fellers, before he cuts out.—Pull him off his hoss!"

"I've got a warrant for you, Majer," ses Mr. Snipe, a little thick-lipped, blinky-eyed, snaggle-toothed, sandy-haired, man what looks zactly like Bullfrog in the play, and kills the dogs and ketches the runaway niggers, and does all the little jobs about Pineville what a decent white man is too good to do, and the law wont low a nigger to do.

"A warrant for what?" ses I.

"Oh, you'll find out soon enough," ses all of 'em—"a thousand dollars reward aint offered for a man now-a-days not for nothing."

I was jest gwine to git off my hoss and go with 'em to old Squire Rogerses, when cousin Pete hollers out,

"Lay hold of him, fellers! secure the prisoner!" And with that he pulled out a rope and made a grab at my leg.

That was more'n I could stand from him, and I jest brung my hand round and tuck him spang in the mouth. I spose it must have been pretty much of a lick, for it sounded jest like hittin a piece of raw beef with the flat side of a meat-axe, and it drawed considerable blood and a tooth or two. Pete kivered his mouth with his hand and sort o' backed out of the crowd. But little Snipe stood off and hollered "help! rescue! help!" as loud as he could, and the fellers grabbled hold of me like they was gwine to tear me to pieces. My dander was up and I couldn't help slingen 'em a little; and after I piled five or six of 'em on top of one another and put two or three of ther noses out of jint, I told Snipe I was ready to go with him.

Well, before we got to Squire Rogerses thar was the biggest sort of a crowd gethered thar to hear the trial. The old Squire looked monstrous solemn, and everybody was bisy talkin about it, but all I could hear 'em say was something about $1000 reward!

"Silence," ses Squire Rogers. "Call Dr. Peter Jones, Mr. Baliff."

In come Pete with his white ruffles all bloody and his lips stickin out like a link of green sassengers.

"You have been arrested and fotched before me, Mr. Jones, on the following warrant," ses the Squire; and then he axed Squire Jinkins, who was thar, to read it out. Squire Jinkins tuck the paper and commenced.

State of Georgia, Pineville Dist.	By W. B. Rogers, a Justice of the Peace for said District.

Whereas, complaint hath been made before me on the oath of Peter Jones, that on or about the 20th day of May, in the year of our Lord one thousand eight hundred and forty-three, one Joseph Jones, of the town of Pineville aforesaid, instigated by the devil and not having the fear of God before his eyes, did with wicked and malicious intent write, and caused to be published, a certain ludicrous book of letters, by which means he, the said Jones, wrought and effected an almost total destruction of the personal beauty of all the young ladies of the city of Augusta and surrounding country, convulsing their delicate systems and contorting their lovely faces out of all due shape, in such a manner as to excite the fears of their friends for their recovery, by reason of which most wanton outrage upon the risibility of the literary community of said city, one Silas A. Holmes, proprietor of the Literary Depot, has been constrained to declare and offer a reward, and by his proclamation, dated at Augusta, on 20th day of May, 1843, does offer a reward of one thousand dollars, for the discovery and apprehension of the said Jones: These are therefore to command you forthwith to bring the said Joseph Jones before me or some other justice of the peace of said town, to answer to the said complaint, and further to be dealt with according to law.

Given under my hand and seal the 1st day of June, in the year of our Lord one thousand eight hundred and forty-three. W. B. Rogers, J. P.

"What do you answer to that, Mr. Jones? Have you any thing to say agin these charges?"

Squire Jinkins laughed right out, and the people begun to giggle all over the room; but old Squire Rogers looked as solemn as a toom-stone.

"Why," ses I, "I say I never done no sich thing. —Its all a pack of Dr. Sweetlips nonsense there. I never convulsed nor contorted no Augusta gall in my life, nor I never spilt nobody's beauty."

"You deny it, do you?" ses cousin Pete, pullin a newspaper out of his pocket.

"I mought swelled *your* lips a little," ses I, "but I don't think ther was much beauty to spile in the fust place."

Cousin Pete looked monstrous mad, and axed Squire Rogers to read the piece what he pinted out in the paper.

He hadn't got half done before the people laughed so loud that you couldn't hear a word. It was a advertisement of Mr. Holmes, the great book-man in Augusta, who sells my books in that city, and was nothing more nor a downright crow over the book, offerin $1000 reward jest to make people take notice.

"Is that all the proof you've got?" ses Squire Jinkins. "Ha, ha, this beats all the cases I ever seed in a court of justice. It is a perfect piece of foolery, Squire Rogers, and I think the least you can do is to dismiss it at once."

Cousin Pete looked like he was gwine to bust with rage, and sed he wanted a warrant for me for salt and batter with intent to kill.

"Very well," ses Squire Jinkins, "very well, go ahead, and my friend will have his remedy for false imprisonment."

Cousin Pete's eyes watered, and he blowed his nose two or three times, like he couldn't breathe fast enough through his mouth.

Squire Rogers talked with Squire Jinkins a little

while, but nobody couldn't hear what they sed for the laughin, and bimeby the old man sed as loud as he could—

"I reckon, boys, takin all things in consideration, we better drap this bisness."

Then all the fellers—among 'em the very chaps what wanted to help cousin Pete to ketch me—hollered, "Hurra for Major Jones! the greatest man in Pineville,—hurra! hurra!" and before I knowed any thing about it, they had me upon ther heads carryin me through the streets hollerin and shoutin like they was all crazy, and if I hadn't been a Washingtonian I'd had to treat the whole bilin of 'em.

I hain't seed nothin more of cousin Pete sense, but I think he'll take care how he goes about takin people up for thousand dollar rewards in futer.

We had a perfect frolic when I got home and told 'em all about it. But plague take that fool, Pete; it makes me sort o' mad now, when I think what a skare he gin Mary. I wouldn't a had it tuck place not for the best nigger on the plantation. You know sich things is dangerous sometimes. But no more from

Your friend, till death, Jos. Jones.

P. S. Come to find out, the warrant was writ by a young chap what's readin law with Mr. Jinkins, jest for devilment, and cousin Pete, the bominable fool, got Squire Rogers to sign it, thinkin he was gwine to make a thousand dollars on the job.

LETTER XX.

PINEVILLE, *June* 19, 1843.

To MR. THOMPSON:—*Dear Sir*—Every thing has went on pretty smooth sense I writ my last letter to you. Mary soon got over her skare, but the way she's mad at cousin Pete won't wear off in a coon's age. She ses he musen't never put his foot in our house, if he don't want to git his old red whiskers scalded off his fool face. She ses she always thought Pete had *some sense*, but now, she ses, she don't know whether he's a bigger rascal than he is a fool.

Wimmin is monstrous curious creeters, now 'tween you and me, and it takes more head than I've got to manage 'em without some diffikilties now and then. It seems to me, Mary is gittin curiouser every day. I don't know what upon yeath to make of her sometimes, she acts so quare. Lord knows, I does every thing in my power to please her—I gits every thing she wants—I always lets her have her own way in every thing, and I stays home with her more'n half my time.—But every now and then she takes a cryin spell, jest for nothin. Now, I'll jest tell you one little circumstance, jest to let you see how curious she does do me sometimes.

Two or three months ago little Sally Rogers gin her one of the smallest dogs I reckon you ever did see. It's a little white curly thing about as big as my fist, with red eyes and a little bushy tail screwed up over its back so tight that it can't hardly touch its hind legs to the floor; and when it barks its got a the sharpest voice, that goes right through a body's head like a cotton gimblet. And then Mary and the galls is all the time washin it, and combin it, and fixin it off with ribbons on its neck and on its tail, and nursin it in ther laps, till they've got the dratted thing so sassy that ther aint no gittin along with it. Whenever I go about Mary it's a snarlin and snappin at me, and when anybody comes in the house, it flies at 'em like it was gwine to tare 'em all to pieces, and makes more racket than all the dogs on the place. It's bit my fingers two or three times; and if I jest tetch it, it'll squall out like its back was broke, and run right to the wimmin and git under ther chairs, and then the very old harry's to pay. If ever I say anything about it, then they all say I'm "jealous of pore little Tip," and that I ought to be ashamed of myself to be mad at "the dear little feller." I always laugh it off the best way I can—but I reckon I've wished some rat would catch "pore little Tip" more'n a thousand times; and I wouldn't be surprised if it was to be tuck suddenly sick and die some of these days, 'thout anybody knowin the cause. But I jest want to tell a instance of the devilment he kicks up sometimes.

Last night we was all settin in the parlor—the galls was sowin, and Mary and me was playin a game of drafts, and I was jest about to pen her with three kings, when one of the checks happened to drap off the board right down by Mary's foot. I stooped over to pick it up, when the fust thing I know'd, snap the little devil of a dog tuck me right by the finger, and then sot up a terrible barkin and run behind Mary's foot. I never wanted to hit nothin so bad in my life, and I leaned over to tap him on the head, but Mary put her little foot out before him, and I missed Tip's nose about a quarter of a inch, and he snapped agin. I leaned over further and further, and tried to hit him, but Mary's foot was always in the way every time, and the last time when I was reachin jest as far as I could, and her foot was in the way, and the little cuss was squallin and snappin as hard as he could, I got sort o' out of patience tryin to hit him, and ses I, "*Don't* put your foot in the way!" Jest then down went the "History of England" and all the checks on the floor, and Tip run under Mary's chair, clear out of sight, squallin like he was killed, when ther wasn't a hair of him tetched.

When I ris up my face was a little red, and I would gin a five dollar bill jest to tramp that infernal dog out of his hide. Well, what do you think? The fust thing I knowed Mary was cryin like her heart was gwine to brake.

"Why," ses I, "Mary what's the matter with you? I didn't hurt Tip."

She didn't say nothin, but jest went on cryin worse and worse, and told Miss Carline to hand her the colone bottle; and thar she sot and cried and snuffed the colone and sighed, and nobody didn't know what the matter was.

"Why, Mary," ses I, "what upon yeath ails you? I didn't hurt you, did I?"

"Y-e-s, you-oo did. I didn't think you-oo would speak so to-oo me, Joseph. I didn't think you'd git mad at me-e-e, so I didn't."

"Why, lord bless your dear soul, I aint mad at you, Mary," ses I. "What makes you think I could git mad at you?"

"Cause I didn't want you to hurt pore little Tip. Pore little feller—he didn't know no better."

"But, Mary, I wasn't mad at you at all," ses I. "What makes you think so?"

"Cause you never said *don't* so cross to me before. You said it jest as cross as you could."

"But I wasn't mad, honey.—It was reachin over so far made me speak sort o' quick," ses I. "I never was mad at you in my life."

But in spite of all I could say or do I couldn't git her in a good humor the whole evenin, jest because I said "don't" to her, when she kep puttin her foot in my way. It's all over now, but I dasn't look sideways at Tip for fear he'll kick up another fuss.

Its monstrous curious. I know Mary loves me, and ther aint a sweeter tempered nor a better gall in Georgia; but they all have such curious ways some times. Old Miss Stallins says its always so at first, but she ses Mary'll git over all them little childish notions one of these days. Ther's one thing certain, I wish ther was no little dogs in our family.

I never was so surprised in my life as when I heard about them oudacious bank robbers. I think they better alter the law about jurys, so that when they want to try criminal cases hereafter, they can jest send to the Penitentiary and git twelve fellers at once to come and be jurymen. They'd answer the purpose jest as well, and then honest men wouldn't be put to no trouble to go to court jest to be objected to by the lawyers on account of ther good characters. Besides, it's a insult to a decent man to be put on a jury now-a-days, in a criminal case.

Ther was a trial in our county not long ago of a feller what had killed a man and robbed him of a heap of money. Ther was lots of lawyers here in his favor, and when they come to pick out the jury ther was hardly twelve men in the county that the lawyers thought mean enough to set on the case. They was two days a gittin a jury, and every time they called up a decent lookin man, the prisoner's lawyers would look at him and say "give him the book," and if he sed he hadn't formed and expressed no opinion as to the gilt of the prisoner, (which most every man that cared anything about law or justice had done,) they'd look at him close, and then whisper to one another, and if they hadn't never heard of his robbin anybody's hen-roost nor stealin anything, they'd say, "object." Mose Sanders was called up, and Mose aint a very good lookin feller, though he's a honest man as ever lived. They looked at Mose awhile, and he felt sort o' bashful I spose, and looked sort o' mean, and they said "content." Well, the case was tried, and it was such a perfect open and shut bisness that they couldn't help bringin the feller in guilty in spite of the lawyers. But ther aint a man in the county that's got any confidence in Mose Sanders after that. His character is completely ruined; cause everybody thinks the lawyers wouldn't tuck him on that jury if they didn't know he was a rascal. For my own part I would jest as leav be spicioned of stealin a sheep, as to be put upon a criminal jury by the lawyers now-a-days. No more from

Your friend, till death, Jos. Jones.

P. S. The boys is pitch'd on me to make a oration on the fourth of July. I tried to git out of the scrape every way I could, but they wouldn't hear to none of my objections, so I jest had to turn in and make up the best speech I could. I've got it most all by heart, but Mary's at me all the time to put more dictionary words in it. I've almost spilt it now jest to humor her.

LETTER XXI.

Pineville, *July* 8, 1843.

To Mr. Thompson:—*Dear Sir*—I expect you have begun to think I wasn't never gwine to write to you agin, but the fact is I haint had time to tend to nothin but the fourth of July ever sense I writ my last letter to you. But ther aint no use of apologys tween old friends. I always take a long apology as the very best evidence that the writer don't mean what he ses.—It shows that he knows ther's something wrong at the bottom, and he's tryin to throw dust in a body's eyes.

Well, to proceed without no apology.—We had the most gloriousest fourth of July this year that ever tuck place in Pineville. It was one of them memoriable occasions which don't happen more than once or twice in a man's lifetime, even in this country; and I spose don't never happen in any other. We had a real temperance celebration, and though ther wasn't no licker on the ground, I never seed the people in better spirits in my life. Ther wasn't no cussin and swearin and fightin like ther used to be, and ther wasn't no noses nor heads, nor bottles and glasses, nor dishes broke, and ther wasn't no fellers left under the tables for the hogs to root about till they got sober. But I must give you a reguler account of our proceedins, accordin to the request of the "Pineville Temperance Club."

Well, it had been gin out all over the county that I was gwine to deliver the oration, and I do blieve every man, woman, and child for more'n ten miles round was thar to hear it, affordin a very strong evidence of my grate literary popilarity, sense my book has been printed. It wouldn't be worth while for me to tell you about the shootin in the mornin. You know the boys always keeps up a most alfired racket on sich occasions, till ther powder gives out, and then they used to git drunk and fight, but this time they was all as quiet and friendly as you please, flyin round 'mong the galls, till the persession was formed and marched down to the spring, whar the dinner was to take place.

The crowd was so large they couldn't all begin to git in the church, so seats was fixed all along the side of the hill under the trees, and the proceedins tuck place out thar, while the niggers was settin the tables for the barbycue down in the holler. I wanted to go with Mary to keep her from gittin skeered, but bein orator of the day they wouldn't hear to no sich 'rangement, and I had to walk in the persession, with Mr. Mountgomery, who read the Declaration of Independence.

Mary and mother and all of 'em was in a terrible swivet all the time, for fear I'd git cowed and wouldn't succeed in my oration; and I felt a little jubus myself, for I never seed so many people together before in my life. But I was 'termined to sustain my repetation, and while parson Storrs was prayin and Mr. Mountgomery was readin the Declaration, I sot thar and screwed up my spunk to the very highest notch.

As soon as the readin and prayin was done, the boys raised a thunderin shout, and the old gentleman come to me and ses he, "Majer, do your best." I felt kind o' choky, but after they was all done hollerin and was as still as mice, I tuck a gourd of water and cleared my throte two or three times, and stepped out onto the platform and begun my

Oration.

"Friends and feller citizens!"—hem, ses I—[and I never felt sich a roarin sound in my ears, and my heart seemed like it was gwine to jump right out of my mouth. I couldn't think of the fust word to begin with, and I hem'd three or four times, and looked down to my feet and then up to the trees. I didn't know what upon yeath to do. Jest then I happened to see Mary. Her face was as pale as a sheet and her bright blue eyes was filled with tears, and she looked like she was jest gwine to fly away. Ther was 'lectricity, or mesmerism, or something in her looks, for I never felt so brave and so determined to do or dye tryin in my life, and I jest gin the croud a bold look all round and stood like I was waitin a purpose for bout half a minit.] "My feelins on a occasion like this can't find words fit to speak 'em in—[the idea tuck fust rate,—'Hurra for Majer Jones!' ses all of 'em.]—and my tongue has done silent homage to the sublime emotions of my heart!—[then I laid my hand on my busum and gin 'em another look,—'Hurra!' ses they.]

What is this occasion? what day is this upon which we is assembled! It is the Sabbath day of freedom! the day upon which a glad nation of freemen worship at the alter of liberty. While we is assembled here, millions is getherin from the great cities and towns of the north and east, from the broad valleys of the west, and the homesteds of the sunny south, to celebrate the declaration you have jest herd—that great and glorious resolution in support of which was pledged the 'lives, fortunes, and sacred honors' of our gallant fathers—and to offer up thanks for the blessed privileges they bequeathed to us. Who then can think of this occasion with feelins of a ordinary character?—[Nobody, hurra, hurra!] Feller citizens, I feel my unqualification for the task you have honored me with. I know I can't begin to do justice to this occasion, but I will do the best I can. [Go ahead! hurra for Majer Jones!]

I needn't tell you any thing about the Revolution—I needn't tell you how our fore-fathers fit, bled, and died for ther country!—you all know that as well as I do. We haint got nothin to do with the past—the present and future is what consarns us; and if we does our duty to our country, if we performs our part as well as our great-grand-fathers did theirs, we'll all come out straight in the eend. But that's the rub, as Mr. Shakspear ses. Is we carryin out the great principles of our ansisters? Is we actin like worthy children of sich worthy parents? Is we exertin ourselves as we should do to keep pure, and clean, and spotless, and untainted, the free institutions and glorious republican principles handed down to us by the heroes that won our independence? Can any man look over our country, and see the pride, the meanery, the rascality, the corruption, the foppery, the monkeyism, the treachery, the dissipation, and the tetotal disregard for morality, religion, and virtuous principles, that characterizes the people of our day, and say Yes to these questions? No, feller citizens, he cannot. The truth can't be disguised—we is gwine down hill in the scale of human advancement.—[That's a fact! hurra!]—Our boasted republicanism is fast fadin away—our free and glorious institutions is fast sinkin into contempt—our laws is set at defiance by bad men of every grade, and instead of givin evidence to the world of man's fitness for self government, we is exhibiting the most melancholy proofs of his weakness, corruption, and perfidy. We have gone far away from the bright example set us by our fathers, and if we don't look to it, and retrace our steps before we go much further, like the children of Israel in the wilderness, we will be paid off for our meaness and never be 'lowed to enjoy the promised blessins which the wisdom of our patriotic ansisters beheld in reserve for the faithful.—[Amen! ses old Deacon Rogers.]

The past and present generations is gilty of a great fallin off, and the only amends we can make is, to try to improve the succeedin one. Livin as we is in these degenerated times, it aint so easy to see the difference between the people of this day and them of '76, as we call it, without we take the trouble to consider into the matter. Well then, feller citizens, spose General Washington could come back and go into the White-House at Washington now. What would he think to find John Tyler and John Jones, and Bob Tyler settin round the President's table, schemin and planin, turnin out post-masters and appintin collectors and marshels, and makin new cabinets, and appintin new ministers, as often as the wind changes the political weathercock? Would he not like Cæsar's ghost, when he seed his degenerated countrymen dancin monkeys and playin on a hand organ in the streets of Rome, vanish in a fury of shame and indignation? Suppose the ghost of Henry, or Hancock, or Franklin could go into the House of Representatives in the middle of a debate and hear the vulgarity and blackgardism of them fellers, and witness the confusion and the rowdyism that disgraces that house. Wouldn't he think he was in a Georgia rum-grocery instead of the American Congress, whar they used to make laws to govern the nation? [To be sure he would—give it to 'em, Majer!] What would sich sperits as Joneses and Preble's and Bainbridge's think, if they was 'lowed to see the little navy, for which they won sich everlastin glory, wastin all its time in petty court-marshals of its officers, and rottin upon the seas in inglorious inactivity? What would sich ghosts as Marion's, and Sumpter's, and Greene's think if they was 'lowed to review the army of the present day, or to read the disgraceful history of the Semminole war, with all its extravagance and rascality? What would the honest men of the old time, who managed the money affairs of our government, say of the thousands of defaulters that have plundered the treasury within the past ten years? What would the people of them days think if they could read the newspapers now and see all the murders, and robberies, and all manner of rascalities that they's filled with every week? Do you think, if one of them plain old broad-brimed, straight-collared, knee-buckled republicans was to come back, he could recognise his countrymen in the starched up, soap-locked, high-heeled, sickly-lookin dandys of the present day? No, no, feller citizens, they would be jest as apt to claim kin with the Hottentots or Malays. They wouldn't know us, neither by the spirit of our government, by the characters of our public men, nor by our dress, sentiments, or habits—certainly not by our veneration for the laws or the verdicts of our juries. [That's a fact!] A little reflection on this subject, feller citizens, will convince you of the importance of political as well as social reform; and I hope that the genius that presides over the destinies of our country will this day inspire every citizen of the Republic with a firm resolution to bring back both the government and the people to their original purity. [Hurra! hurra!]

"Ladies, I must say a few words to you before I'm done. Your country expects much from you. You exerts a most powerful influence in the world, and we looks to you for a futer generation [some of 'em put ther fans and hankerchers to ther faces] of men and wimmin fit to inherit this glorious government, and to bring it back to its orignal purity and beauty. Your's is the power of influence, which, says a beautiful writer, 'has its source in human sympathy, and is as boundless in its operation.' I glorys in the thought that the day is come when that power is beginin to be felt in this country, and when men no longer look upon women as mere creatures of moonshine, but give to 'em ther full importance in society. Owing to past neglect, female influence has not been directed as it ought to be, and it is to this cause that much of our degeneracy as a people is owin. Let the ladys but take the right stand and they can bring every thing straight in no time. If they won't marry a drunkard, who's gwine to drink licker? If *they* won't keep company with fops, who's gwine to make a monkey of himself? If *they* is republican in ther principles and sentiments, who's gwine to put on airs and try to be aristocrats? If *they* thinks more of a good character than they does of riches, who's gwine to sell his character for money? If *they* upholds virtue, who's gwine to practice vice? If *they* is pious, who's gwine to dare to make game of religion? This is the proper field for the exercise of wimmin's influence. Directed in this way it will not only secure the permanent prosperity of ther country, but ther own happiness in ther domestic relations in this life, and everlastin blessins in the world to come."

"Hurra! Amen! Glory! Hurra! Hurra!" shouted all the fellers, and the galls waved ther parasols and hankerchers like a perfect harrycane, and old Mr. Mountgomery shook me by the hand for more'n a minit—"Why, Joseph," ses he, "you have excelled yourself."

The fellers all crowded round me, and the galls all got round Mary, congratilatin her, and I couldn't git a chance to say a word to her till the drum beat for us to go to the table. Ther was lots of every thing that was good to eat thar, but my appetite was all gone, and Mary couldn't eat for talkin about my speech. She sed she was half scared to death when I fust commenced, and if I hadn't got started when I did she was jest gwine to go right straight home. I can't tell you half what mother sed, and old Miss Stallins.

After the dinner was over, Squire Rogers and Mr. Mountgomery read the toasts, but they would be so long I spose you wouldn't like to put 'em in the "Miscellany." It was particularly understood ther was to be no political toasts, and nobody was fool enough but cousin Pete to brake the rule. He was dyin to make himself conspicuous, and the first chance he got he jumped upon the table and hollered out as loud as he could, "The honourable Mr. Martin Van——" "Stop," ses Squire Rogers, "we don't have no political toasts here, Dr. Jones." "No! no!" ses the fellers, "git down, git down, if that's yer game." I thought Pete would faint before he could git off the table. I didn't see him no more that day. Every thing went off perfectly smooth and quiet, and the day was very pleasant. No more from

Your friend, till death, JOS. JONES.

P. S. I see some feller in Charleston is advertisin for sale, "Majer Jones's Courtship, by Judge Longstreet." That's a most bominable mistake, for the Judge never writ a line of my book. I don't know whether he feels flattered by havin my writins attributed to him, but if he does, I am even with him, for I take it as a very grate compliment to myself.

I wish you would tell Mr. Holmes of Augusta that I aint no candidate for President, and if he's got enny friendship for me he won't put me in the papers for President any more. I hain't got no very grate opinion of myself, but I've always tried to live a honest man and what little character I is got I want to keep.

LETTER XXII.

PINEVILLE, *August* 8, 1843.

TO MR. THOMPSON:—*Dear Sir*—You know I promised you, when I saw you up in Athens, to give you a account of the Commencement and other matters and things as soon as I got home. Well, if ther's any thing I do bominate, it's a man what brakes his promise to a printer, or don't pay him for his paper when he ought to—so the fust thing I done when I got home was to write a letter to you.

Ever sense I went to the Commencement of the Female college down to Macon, I've had a monstrous curiosity to see how they done things at a reglar boy college, and as soon as I found out the time it was gwine to take place, I told Mary I was gwine to Athens. Her lip drapt in a minit.

"Oh, yes," ses she, "you don't care nothin for me now—you'd jest as leav be away from home now as not.—I didn't think you'd git tired of me so soon. But it's always the way with the men."

I told her I wasn't tired of her at all, but jest wanted to go up to Athens, and she could go along with me in the buggy.

"Yes," ses old Miss Stallins, "you can go along with Joseph, and it'll be good for yer health."

"But, mother," says Mary, "you know I ain't well enough to travel."

"Oh, yes you is, child, and it'll do you good," ses the old woman.

The galls all 'lowed it would be the very best thing for her, and I promised I would drive as careful as I could, and after a while she consented to go; but I blieve it was more because she didn't want to be away from me than for the good of her health.

Well, it tuck 'em about a half a day to fix, and when we got loaded up, I was afraid old Bosen was gwine to have more'n his match to pull us, they'd put in so much plunder. We had two trunks, and a banbox of course, and lots of provisions, and more vials of medicine than would fill a piny woods doctor's shop, and hartshorn and assafedity enough to kill all the vermin in Georgia.

Nothin serious didn't hapen on the road, only Mary was monstrous skeery every now and then when we come to a bad place, and like to make me upset three or four times by catchin hold of the lines when I was doin my very best drivin to git round the holes.

We got to Athens a little before dark, and I tell you what, I was a good deal disappinted in the place. It's a monstrous hilly and hollery place, but it's a right smart sort of a town, and has got some pretty conspicuous bildins in it. I hadn't no idee it was any thing like so large nor so handsome. But I needn't tell you nothin about that. I stopped at the Planter's Hotel, whar we got a first rate supper, and whar I never seed so many people at one table afore in my life. At first I ate rather sparin, thinkin ther wouldn't begin to be enough for 'em all, but the niggers was all the time bringin in new dishes, right hot out of the kitchen, and I believe ther was as many baskets full of scraps left when we was all done as would feed all the people in Pineville. After supper, Mary found some of her old acquaintances from the Female College, and I left her in the parlor to talk with 'em, and went out on the porch and smoked a segar and talked politics with the gentlemen till bedtime.

The next day was Tuesday, and after breckfast I tuck a walk down to the College Avenue to see the crowd, and sich a crowd I never met before. Thar was people of every sort, size, condition and circumstance, from the Governor of the State down to free niggers and dandies. Thar was members of Congress and judges and big lawyers from every part of the State, and some from Carolina, and Seinors, and Juniors Freshmen and Softmores enough to keep Georgia in a stew for a century to come.

About ten o'clock the bell rung for the Junior exercises, and I went and got Mary and went to the chapel as soon as I could, to git a good seat. The house was full, but the crowd kep comin from all quarters, and whar I sot I had a perfect view of 'em as they marched up the passage ways lookin round for seats.

I tell you what, it was a live animal show for true. I never could blieved ther was so many different tastes, so many outlandish notions in human natur. Ther was fellers with ther britches stickin to 'em as tight as if they'd been melted and poured into 'em, and some with trowsers all puckered round the waist like a lady's work-bag; but ther clothes was nothin to compare to ther hair and whiskers. Some had grate long frizzled locks that almost kivered ther faces, and looked like they hadn't been combed in a month, and some had long straight greasy hair that hung down in clumps like taller candles. Some had whiskers that hid all but two little openings right round ther eyes, and some was shaved clean all over except right on the tip eend of ther chins, whar a little nasty-lookin tag of hair stuck out like a billy-gote's beard; and it was really amusin to see some young chaps with soap-locks of some six months' standin, but who hadn't been long enough away from the breast to raise a goat-knot—jest to see the little pin-feathers, as you mought call 'em, on ther chins, how proud they was of 'em, and how they would stick 'em out towards the galls.

I was settin lookin at the natural curiosities as they passed, when I seed a sort of a stir down to wards the dore, and some old gentleman behind me sed, "What upon yeath is that comin yonder?" I looked, and shore enough ther was a climax of hairy wonders comin up the aisle. I never was so put to to make any thing out afore. I couldn't tell whether it was a man, woman, or monkey. It had grate long thin silky hair hangin all down over its neck and shoulders, and sich a pair of whiskers as no human ever wore before. They kivered all the sides of its face and run clear round its chin, and hung way down on its breast. Its complexion was light, and its face looked sort o' pale and sheepy, and its hair and whiskers, close up to its chin, was tween a sorrel and a drab color, but down towards the eend the whiskers was colored as black as a bareskin. Everybody was gazin at it and wonderin whar it come from, and some of 'em was laughin right in its face.

I was monstrous glad Mary was settin right behind a big tall woman what had a great big conestoga bonnet on, so she couldn't see the outlandish thing, for I know'd it would skeer her almost to death if she was to see it walkin towards her. It got a seat after a while, and I thought the galls would die laughin at it. But, good lord, some of 'em had no bisness to laugh, for they had bustles on that would have litterally throwed the whiskers and the thing that wore 'em entirely in the shade. I never knowed what a bustle was afore. Would you blieve it, Mr. Thompson, that I saw bustles up to Athens that, if they'd been real flesh and blood, would broke the back of any gall in Georgia to carry 'em? It's a fact, as shore as I'm sittin here. Why, some of 'em looked out of proportion, like a bundle of fodder tied to the handle of a pitchfork. It is really oudacious to see to what monstrous extremities they carry them things. I'm a married man, and I blieve I love my wife as well as the next man, but I do think if any thing would make me sue for a divorce, it would be to see my wife toatin about sich a monstrous pack on her back as some of them I saw up to Athens.—But shaw, Mary aint sich a fool.

After they all got pretty well settled, the young gentlemen commenced ther speeches, and I don't think any body could want any better evidence that Georgia boys is got some smartness. Mary liked 'em all first rate, except one feller who spoke last. He gin the galls all sorts of a rakin, and I could see some of ther eyes shinin like they didn't thank him for it. He run 'em down for every thing he could think of, and sed if one of 'em had made her appearance to old father Adam in the garden, with sich a huge bustle on as they wear now a days, the old feller would tuck fright and never stopped till he scaled the walls of Paradise. Mary sed she didn't blieve in bustles, but she thought he had a great deal of insurance to talk that-a-way about the ladys.

After the speeches was over I tuck Mary to the hotel, and after dinner I perswaded her to go and take a little walk. I was gwine down to the river to show her the cotton factory, and was walkin along College

Avenue, talkin to her about the fine stores and handsome houses, when, jest as we got opposite to a watermelon cart, she gin a loud scream, and if I hadn't grabed hold of her like a steel trap, she'd drapt right down in the street.—"Oh, oh, my Lord," ses she, "what's that?" I looked up and what should I see but that infernal hairy thing jest comin out from behind the cart. I never had a better mind to spile any thing all to pieces in my life.—To think the bominble creeter should come and skare Mary almost out of her senses. But I had to take care of her, and so I had to let it go on.

Mary was so overcome I had to take her right back to the hotel and stay with her all the evenin, and give her assafedity and hold the hartshorn to her nose. It is a outragous shame that sich walkin scare-crows should be 'lowed to go at large to frighten the wimin and children to death. I wouldn't a had Mary see the ugly cuss not for any thing in the world, for ther aint no tellin yet what may be the consequences.

The next day we went to hear the graduates speak, and to see 'em git ther diplomers. The speeches was all fust rate, but I noticed one thing which I blieve was the case with the junior class too. Them that was the smartest, and made the best speeches didn't have more'n a reasonable quantity of hair on ther heads, which goes to strengthen me in the opinion that it is only uncultivated brains that runs all to hair, as uncultivated lands runs all to weeds. If I had a son and wanted to make any thing out of him, I would keep his hair cut close to his skelp.

After the speeches was over, the President gin each of 'em a piece of paper tied with a blue ribbon, and told 'em to go home and be good boys, to dress like gentlemen, and be gentlemen, and try to git along genteely through the world. Then he called up a whole lot of fellers and made 'em Masters of Arts, and gin 'em a paper tied with blue ribbon. Somebody ax'd me if I wasn't gwine to take the degree, I told him no, for I tuck the "Miscellany." He said he meant the degree of Master of Arts; "Oh, ah," ses I, for I didn't know what else to say, and when he went away I ax'd Mary what it was. She sed it was a title what they give to scholars. Not havin much book larnin myself, I didn't put 'em to the trouble, and we went home to our hotel.

The next mornin we went to hear Mr. Pickens, of South Carolina, make his speech, and sich a thunderin crowd and sich a everlastin gatherin of carriages and horses I never did see. I kep a sharp lookout for the hairy man, for fear he mought give Mary another skeer, but I didn't see him. I spose he got lost durin the night among his whiskers and hair, and couldn't find himself in the mornin in time enough to come to the oration. You heard Mr. Pickens's speech and know how good it was as well as me, so I won't make my long letter any longer by sayin anything about it.

Mary was anxious to git home, and as soon as dinner was over we started, and got home the next day all sound and safe. Mary ses she thinks Franklin College is a fust rate institution, but she ses if she was a professer she would rather belong to the Female College in Macon, for she ses ther wouldn't be half so much danger of gittin walloped now and then as ther is when they have boys to deal with. She ses they didn't whip none of ther professors when she was in College, though they used to make ugly faces at 'em sometimes. But she ses boys is always worse than galls any way you can fix 'em, and I'm very much of her opinion. Georgia boys is monstrous rough customers if they git ther dander up, and it wont do to fool with 'em. No more from

Your friend, till death, JOS. JONES.

P. S. I found a namesake at the Planter's Hotel up in Athens, by the name of Joab Jones. He's a monstrous clever feller, and I wouldn't be astonished if he was a distant relation, for our folks was always monstrous fond of scripter names. They named me after the feller what had the spotted coat, and got sold into Egypt.

LETTER XXIII.

PINEVILLE, *August* 24, 1843.

TO MR. THOMPSON:—*Dear Sir*—My last letter seems to produced a monstrous sensation among the cultivators of hair, and I can't help but feel a little proud of the success of my writins on that subject. Some grate filosofer has said that the man what made two spears of grass grow whar only one growd before, was a bennyfactor. Well, if that's true, the rule ought to work both ways, and I'm of the notion that—in times like these, when things is run into sich bominable extremes—the man what causes only a decent crap of hair to grow whar sich everlastin stacks of it was cultivated before, has a equal claim to the gratitude of all decent people. The way my last letter has cradled off the soap-locks and imperials, and goat-knots and mustyshows is truly alarmin to the vermin what usually inhabits them regions, as the geografy ses. It seems it's made a clean shave of 'em in some parts of the country, and fellers what used to go about in the hot weather sweatin and smokin under their burdens of hair, and stinkin with bar's oil and permatum worse nor a spaniel dog after a shower of rain, is so much altered and look so much decenter that ther friends and relations don't hardly know 'em.

Day before yesterday, I went down to the post-office to git the "Miscellany," and when I ax'd the post-master if ther was any thing for me, ses he, "Well, I reckon you'll think so gin you pay the postage," and he handed me about a dozen letters. I paid him what they come to, and was gwine to start home, when he hollered out, "Stop, stop, Major, here's something else for you," and out he come with a grate big bundle done up in a piece of brown paper.

"Why, what upon yeath is that?" ses I.

"Lord only knows," ses he—"it come in a extra bag this mornin."

I looked at it and hefted it in my hands, but I couldn't make out what it was to save my life—it was $2 postage, and I didn't feel like payin that for noth-

"Maybe it's a bucket," ses the post-master; "you better open it and see, and if it is you won't have to pay no postage."

But I could tell by the feelin it wasn't no bucket letter. I knowed Mary's aunt down in Augusta sed in her last letter she was gwine to send her some little things, and I was fraid to have it opened for fear the post-master would see 'em, and tell every body in Pineville. So I paid the postage and tuck the bundle under my arm, and went home laughin all the way to think what a joke I would have on Mary.

Well, when I got home, Mary and the galls come round me the first thing, wantin to know what was in the bundle.

After foolin 'em a little while I gin Mary a kind of a wink, and ses I,

"Don't you remember what aunt Mahaly writ about in her letter?—them little——"

But Mary's hand was on my mouth in a minit.

"Hush, hush, now Joseph—give it to me," ses she, and she snatched the bundle out of my hands, and she and the galls run off to her room almost tickled to death, to see the little fineries.

I sot down in a chair and begun to open the letters, when all at once I heard a loud scream in Mary's room, and they all come runin out like they was frightened out of ther senses. Mary come screamin to me, as white as a sheet, and I took her in my lap and tried every way I could to quiet her, but she like to faint two or three times. The first word she sed was—

"Oh, Joseph, it's something hairy!"

"Yes," ses all of 'em, "it's some kind of a live varmint, for it stirred as soon as it seed the light."

I couldn't help but cuss a little to myself, it made me so mad to think some dratted thing must all the time be happenin to skeer Mary, and then she's so plagy skary.

As soon as I got her passified a little, I went to see what it was. Miss Carline she got the tongs and Miss Kesiah got the broom-stick and come along as brave as could be, but Mary hung to my cote tail and kep close behind me as she could.

"Take care now, Joseph," ses she, "you don't know what it is, and it mought bite you terrible."

I felt a little sort o' jubus of the dratted thing my-self, and I tuck the broom-handle and poked it two or three times to see what it would do; but it didn't stir, so I went up to it and pulled the paper open, and what *do* you think it was? As shore as I'm settin here it was nothin but a grate big heap of whiskers and hair!

As soon as I seed it I knowed by the color it was the same establishment what skared Mary so up to Athens.

The galls and all of us had a good laugh at the circumstance, and after pullin it about a little with the tongs, we found the followin letter in the bundle, which I send you to print in the "Miscellany:"

"AUGUSTA, *August* 14, 1843.

"TO MAJOR JONES:—*Sir*—I have just heard your letter read in which you seem to have singled my hair and whiskers out as the object of your ridicule. I regret very much that they should have been such a source of terror to your amiable lady, and feeling that some atonement is due for the outrage upon her nervous sensibilities, I have determined to sacrifice those glories of my manhood, and to send them to you to be submitted to such punishment as she may deign to inflict upon them.

"Very respectfully, &c., WHISKERS."

Mary laughed right out. "Well, well," ses she, "if that don't beat any thing! Cut his whiskers off to keep 'em from skarin people. Well, he was a terrible fright, shore enough, and I dare say he's a right Christian lookin sort of a human, now he's tuck all that monstrous heap of hair off his face. I would like to see him now, I would."

"He's a right gallant gentleman, sis," ses Miss Carline, "to send his wiskers to you to be punished for frightenin you so up to Athens, ain't he?"

"He is so," ses Miss Kesiah.

"Well, Mary, what is you gwine to do with 'em?" ses I.

"Why," ses she, "I'll make Cato take 'em out in the old field to-morrow and burn 'em."

"Nonsense, child," ses old Miss Stallins—who's the most economicalist old woman in the world—"let Cato save 'em till next spring to plant Irish taters in; they say hog's hair is the best thing in the world for that, and I don't see why they won't do jest as well."

"That's a fact," ses I; "here, Cato, take 'em out to the barn and be careful of 'em."

"Well," ses Mary, "you can do what you please, but I won't eat a tater."

Cato tuck the things and carried 'em out, and we all sot down and went on readin the letters. Here is the next one what we opened:

"ATHENS, *August* 16, 1843.

"TO MAJOR JOSEPH JONES:—*Sir*—Your letter has caused a most alarming decline of soap-locks and goat-knots, as you very appropriately call them, in this town, and a consequent depreciation of Macassar and bear's oil. The barbers have a perfect harvest of the hair crop, and our community are becoming to look like civilized beings. It would seem that a compromise has been made between the dandys and dandyesses, and that bustles are undergoing a sensible reduction. On last Sunday, at church, I saw twelve young ladies sitting on one bench where but eight could possibly stow themselves on the Sunday previous, and I also observed that fans were not in any thing like such constant requisition as formerly. Having observed these happy, humanizing results, I hail you, sir, as one of the greatest reformers of the age.

"Very respectfully,

"Your ob't serv't,

OBSERVER."

I read the last part over three times to the galls. Mary sed she liked it all very well all but the bustle part. She sed she couldn't see why men need bother themselves about what don't concern 'em.

"But they do concern 'em," ses I, and on I went to read the next letter:

"SAVANNAH, *Aug.* 17, 1843.

"TO MAJOR JONES:—*Sir*—I have just read that ridiculous letter of yours from Athens, in which you have taken the liberty to speak of my whiskers in a most scandalous manner. Sir, you are a fool, sir—a beardless puppy, sir, that aint worth the notice of a gentleman who can raise a pair of whiskers. If you had half sense, you would keep that silly little hysterical wife of yours at home, ('did you ever!' ses Mary, 'the mean old thing,') and not carry her about with you when you go to show yourself. One fool is enough at a time. Besides, you ought to know that the hair indicates the blood, and that some of the greatest heroes of antiquity wore long hair and flowing beards. But who could expect better from a piny-wood's fool?

"Your's, &c., ELFIN."

"Read that over agin, won't you, brother?" ses sister Carline, with a mischievous smile on her pretty face. But one readin of that letter was quite enough. I felt as hot as a pepper-box for about a minit—to think the dratted scoundrel would speak that way about Mary.

"Don't you mind him," ses I to her; "his argyments shows him to be a fool. The hair does show the blood of a horse or a cow, and maybe monkeys, but I never heard anybody say before that human creatures was to be judged by the same rule. And as for the heroes of antiquity wearin long hair, that all may be, but I reckon they was jest as much indebted to ther horses' tails for ther victories as to ther own hair or whiskers. He's a baboon, Mary, and don't less mind him."

Here's another letter:

"EATONTON, *Aug.* 16, 1843.

"To MAJOR JONES:—*Dear Sir*—Go it, old fellow: give the goats a swinging every time you come across them. There is two or three kinds of aristocracy in this country that I want to see put down, and one of them is the 'aristocracy of whiskers.' This is the most annoying of them all, especially in warm weather. Swinge them, Major, till they shed.

"Your's sincerely, A. SHAVER."

I was perfectly willin to read that one over agin, but they all wanted to hear the next, which was the last. It was on pink collor'd paper and in the prettyest hand-writin I ever did see. Here it is:

"ATHENS, *August* 19, 1843.

"To MAJOR JOSEPH JONES:—*Dear Sir*—My excuse for addressing a gentleman must be the irresistible desire I feel to express my gratitude to you for the very great favor you have rendered me. Dear Major, I am indebted to you, words cannot tell how much. To you I owe the preservation of my dear Henry. But for you I would never have enjoyed the bliss of this moment, the rapture of knowing that I possess the undivided affection of the first and only dear, dear object of my heart.

You must know, Major, that an early attachment, when we were yet children, had been formed between us. We grew up in love of each other—I need not say how happy—until about a year since, when the painful conviction was forced upon my mind that Henry was not so ardent in his attachment as formerly. At about this period I perceived a tender growth of little 'pin feathers,' as you have styled them, about his mouth and chin, and I could not fail to observe the assiduity with which he cultivated that tiny growth. At length they became perceptible across the room, and he evidently grew colder and colder, seeming to forget the fond themes of other days in his endless discussion of the fashion of imperials, whiskers, and mustaches; and it was only when I spoke of his beard that he stroked his chin with a degree of complacent satisfaction, and manifested an interest in my society. His beard grew under his constant culture, and he daily became more and more single in his devotion to it, until it assumed the most hideous proportions, and I began to fear that I had lost all place in his affections. One night last week as he sat by the window, the night breeze playing through the great tuft of hair under his chin and filling the room with the odor of rancid oil and absorbed perspiration, he chanced to cast his eye upon the 'Miscellany,'—a paper which I ever keep upon my centre table. It was the number which contained your last letter. He read it. I watched with intensest interest the shade of mortification that played over his once manly features until lost in the mass of hair that deformed them. He read the supplication in my look at parting, and in a tremulous voice bade me a good evening. This morning I received a package neatly enveloped and tied with a blue ribbon, with the following lines:

" 'Dear Julia, receive your discarded rival. *Henceforth my heart is wholly thine.*'

"Dear Major, need I say more? Can words express the deep and lasting gratitude I am bound to feel towards one, who has not only restored to me the affections of my dear Henry, but whose searching ridicule has weaned him from a devotion so unbecoming his noble mind. Please accept my heartfelt thanks, and give my best compliments to your amiable and accomplished wife.

"Yours, with sincere esteem, JULIA.

"P. S. Your remarks upon inordinate bustles were not half severe enough. All modest ladies are either discarding them entirely or reducing them to a size only sufficient to give becoming fullness to the tucks of the skirt; which, I observed, was the extent to which Mrs. Jones indulged in them, and which I believe is approved by good taste."

"Read it agin! read it agin!" ses Mary and all of 'em, and I had to read it over agin to gratify 'em.

Mary ses it's the best letter she ever read, and is worth a dozen of sich things as that old hateful Elfin's, from Savannah. Miss Carline ses I ought to be really proud of it, and ses she wouldn't marry no man in the world that wore big ugly whiskers.

I can't think what upon yeath possessed that feller down in Augusta to send me his whiskers. I spose he thought I meant his whiskers, and was 'termined to give 'em to me, sense I'd made sich a fuss about 'em. Well, I don't care about payin $2 a bundle for potater manure, but I shall see what virtue ther is in hair next spring, and if it *does* make big potaters, then I'll be willin to admit that billy-goats and man-monkeys is some account after all. No more from

Your friend, till death, JOS. JONES.

LETTER XXIV.

PINEVILLE, *September* 27, 1843.

TO MR. THOMPSON:—*Dear Sir*—I ought to writ you a letter last week, jest to let you know how we was all gitin on, but the fact is I had no time for nothing. I've had more than usual to tend to about the plantation, pullin fodder and pickin out a little, over to the new ground, on the side of the hill, whar the cotton's opened considerable; and besides a good deal of my time has been tuck up at home tendin to Mary and the family. So, between overseein the niggers and seein to things about home, I haint had no time to devote to my correspondence.

It's monstrous strange to me how wimin can have so much imagination, and be so dredful skary and notionate. Now, Mary's jest as fat and bloomin as ever she was, her cheeks lookin like roses, and yet she's every now and then imaginin she's sick, and gwine to die, and makin out I don't love her like I used to, and all sich nonsense. And if I go out in the field to look after the niggers a while, or happen to stay down to town more than a hour when I go after my papers and letters, when she's in one of them ways, she's jest as apt as any way to take a cry about it. It makes me feel bad to see her act so, and you can't think how glad I am when she gits over them little streaks of low sperits. Then she's jest as happy as a lark, and if you could see her then, when she's laughin and runin on with the rest of 'em, or plaguein and rompin with me, you wouldn't think her beautiful bright eyes was ever dimmed with a tear, or that her merry little heart ever knew the weight of a sigh. The galls is all the time coaxin and babyin her up so, I don't wonder she acts childish sometimes. But old Miss Stallins, she scolds her one minit and then kisses her the next, and ses I musn't mind her little whims now, and ses she'll outgrow 'em all one of these days. I hope she will, pore gall, more on her account than mine.

The weather has been monstrous hot here for more'n two weeks, and I don't think I ever did see things jest sprawled out and swinged up so with the sun at this season of the year before. It really does seem like ther aint no cool shady place left any more on the face of the yeath. The dogs is all runin about lookin for some cool place, with ther tongues hangin way out, and pantin at the rate of about two hundred and seventy-five breaths a minit, and the hens and turkeys is all got ther feathers pinted tother eend foremost, and if you could hear 'em breath you would be shore they all had the quinsy the worst kind. We have all had pretty good health, except old Miss Stallins, who has had the Tiler Grip for more'n a week. The old woman's had a monstrous bad time of it, and has drunk more yarb tea than enough to kill a hoss. She ses she always did consider old Tiler a cuss sent on the country, for Sabbath-breakin and other badness that's got so common of late years, and now she knows it; she ses she wonders why the people don't petition Congress to send him into Botomy Bay, for all the mischief he's done sense he's been President.

I have received a good many letters sense I wrote to you, about my whisker letters, from fellers all over the country. Some of 'em are terrible mad with me, and some is very much pleased with my stricters on hair. The followin letter was received two or three days ago, and as the writer is a military man and seems anxious to hear my opinion on the subject, I have concluded to give him my views in as few words as possible.

"EATONTON, *Sept.* 6, 1843.

"DEAR MAJOR:—Since your Athens letter made its appearance in the "Miscellany" there has been quite a consternation among the unfortunate disciples of Absalom, and I have no doubt but that as many of these gentry have been shorn of their 'pride,' as suffered damage by the celebrated 'soaplock' order of the *curtailing* Secretary. It is now '*vexata questio*' (as the Lawyers say) with gentlemen of the 'Sword and Plume' whether you intend to extend your prohibition to 'Georgia Majors' and their subalterns—whether there are to be any exceptions to universal smooth faces? Now, I regard the 'Militia' as a kind of privileged class, who have as much right to be hairy as Esau had. But '*nous verrons*," as Mr. Orion used to say, when at a loss for ideas. Now, Sir, as you are a Major yourself, you will perceive the importance of your position, and no doubt in your next letter will give us your views fully on this subject.

"Very respectfully, yours, CORPORAL TRIM."

Now, I wish Corporal Tim and everybody else to understand me on this pint. I haint got no objection to reasonable whiskers in ther right place, on a military man, or anybody else. Decent lookin whiskers is well enough, but what I object to is these bominable grate big outlandish lookin things that kiver a man's face all over, and make it look more like a weasel lookin out of a moss mattrass than the countenance of a human creeter. But all whiskers shouldn't only be of a resonable, decent size, but they should be in ther right place, and not on the upper lip nor on the tip eend of the chin, like a billy-goat's. I have always thought that the great Creator of all things intended, in outside appearances at least, to distinguish between men, monkeys, and goats, though ther does happen sometimes to be a monstrous close resemblance in ther tastes and the order of ther minds. Whenever I see a chap tryin to come the goat by cultivatin a crap of hair on the tip eend of his chin, I can't help but wonder why he don't have his coat tail cut to turn up behind and have it lined on the sides with hair. It would be a decided improvement, and would make him look more like the animal he seems so anxious to imitate.

But the Corporal seems more particularly anxious

to have my opinion about the proper kind of whiskers for militia officers, who, he ses, he thinks has as good a right to be hairy as Esaw. Well, I aint disposed to dispute that, but if ther hair don't do 'em no more good than that chap's did what sold his birth-right for a bowl of red soup, and got fooled out of his father's blessing with a piece of goat-skin, it wouldn't be worth ther while to waste much bear's grease in its cultivation. Besides, if they was to be called into actual service with sich whiskers on as some of 'em wear now-a-days, and had to charge through such hammocks as I did in Florida, ther wouldn't a mother's son of 'em git through, but they would be left hangin by ther whiskers in the bamboo briars, like so many Absaloms of old, for the buzzards to eat at ther leisure.

Ther is some excuse for pretty considerable whiskers on militia officers, in times of danger, because they sort o' hide the signs of skare in a feller's face, where, if he haint got no pluck, he's jest as sure to show the white feather as he's born; and I haint the least doubt in the world but that is the reason why big whiskers is so fashionable in the army. But in times of peace ther aint no excuse for thunderin grate whiskers that look like the man's face growed on them instead of ther growin on his face, specially if they are red or sorrel color. Every man's foot is adapted to a certain sized shoe, and so is every man's face for a certain size and cut of whiskers; some men can go bare-footed, and some can go without whiskers, but ther is no more propriety in wearing a mountain of hair on the face than ther is in stickin one's feet into a pair of leather mail-bags. It's all a matter of taste, and as I blieve the wimin's got more of that article than the men, by a long shot, I think the best plan is for every man to leave it to his wife, and them that haint got no wife to go without whiskers till they git one. When my picter was tuck for my book, the engraver put on a very genteel pair of military whiskers that would do very well for a Major or a Colonel, but sense I got married I've shaved 'em all off, as Mary ses I look a great deal better without 'em, and literary men haint no bisness to encumber ther intellectual faces with sich things. Corporal Trim can git the drummer of his company to drum him up a suitable pair for a Corporal in a few minits, which should always bear about the same proportion to his commandin officer's that a little pompoon in a subaltern's cap does to the flowin feather in that of a Brigadier-General.

But I reckon I've writ enough about whiskers. How do you think Henry Clay Jones would do for a name? I go for Mr. Clay, tooth and toe nail, myself, and 'tween you and me he's jest as good for President next fall as a thrip is for a ginger-cake.

Your friend, till death, Jos. Jones.

LETTER XXV.

PINEVILLE, *December* 29, 1843.

To MR. THOMPSON:—*Dear Sir*—Well, Crismus and New Years is gone, and a heap of fun has gone with 'em. Down here in Pineville we had real times, you may be shore. Every body tuck Crismus, specially the niggers, and sich other carryins on—sich dancin and singin, and shootin poppers and sky-rackets, you never did see.

But the best joke was the way cousin Pete got tuck in 'bout gittin in sister Kesiah's Crismus bag. Pete's had a kind of sneakin notion of her for some time, but the dratted fool don't know no more about courtin nor a hown pup does about 'stronomy. He was over to our house Crismus eve, gwine on with his nonsense, and botherin sister Kiz till she got right tired of him—tellin her how he wanted to git married so bad he didn't know what would come of him, and how he wished somebody would hang up a bag for him, like Mary did for me.

"Oh, yes," ses she, "you want to fool somebody now, don't you—but you'r mighty mistaken."

"No, Miss Kesiah," ses he, "if I ain't in good yearnest, I never was in my life."

"But, now, Doctor, would you give yourself away to any young lady for a Crismus gift like brother Joseph did?"

"That I would," ses he, "and glad of the chance."

"Ah," ses she, "I'm fraid you want to play some

trick—you young doctors is so monstrous hard to please." And then she looked round at me and kind o' winked her pretty black eyes and smiled.

Pete looked in the glass, and sort o' slicked down his whiskers, and then ses he,

"All the galls ses that; but the fact is, Miss Kesiah, we is 'sceptible to female charms jest like common men, I can asshore you. And the fact is, I'm determined to marry the first gall that will have me for a Crismus present."

"Now, you all hear that," ses Kesiah.

"Yes," we all said.

"Now mind," ses she to cousin Pete, "you ain't foolin."

I never seed Pete look so quare.—He looked sort o' skeered and sort o' pleased, and he trembled all ever and his voice was so husky he couldn't hardly speak.

"No, I is in down right yearnest—you see if I aint."

"Well," ses she, "we'll see."

Pete seemed monstrous fidgety, and bimeby he 'lowed it was time to go; and after tellin us all good night, ses he, "Now remember, Miss Kesiah," and away he went with a heart as light as a handfull of chicken feathers.

He hadn't been gone hardly no time before sister Kesiah bust right out a laughin.

"Now," ses she, "if I don't fix Dr. Pomposity good, then I aint Kesiah Stallins, that's all. He's always been cavortin about and makin so much of himself, as who but he! and now I'll take the gentleman down a peg."

"Why, aint you gwine to hang up no bag?" ses sister Carline.

"That I aint," ses she.

"Oh, now, sis, that would be too bad to disappint him so."

"But the doctor shant be disappinted, for I'll make aunt Prissy hang up one for him to take an airin in till mornin if he's a mind to, and then we'll see if he'll be as good as his word."

And shore enough, she called Prissy and made her go up in the loft and empty the feather-bag, and fix a rope in it, and go and hang it on the porch for cousin Pete. Then she told Priss all how she must do in the mornin, and we all went to bed.

I couldn't sleep for thinkin what a bominable fool they was gwine to make out of pore Pete. Mary sed it was a great shame to serve anybody so, but she didn't blieve Kesiah ever would quit bein wild and mischievous.

It wasn't no great time before I heard the gate squeak, and the next minit ther was a monstrous racket among the dogs, and I know'd Pete was come. I could hear the galls a titterin and laughin in ther room, and the next thing bang went something agin the fence, and then one of the dogs sot up a ki-ey! like something had hurt him, and all was still for a few minits. Then I heard Pete steppin about very cautious on the porch, and movin the table and chairs, and then the jice shuck with his weight, as he drapt into the bag. All was still agin for a little while, 'cept the galls gigglin in ther room; then I heard Pete sneeze, and the dogs barked, and I thought the galls would laugh so loud he'd hear 'em; but he kep a sneezin in spite of all he could do.

"Now," ses Mary, "aint that too bad, to fool anybody that way. Jest think how you would feel in that old bag what's been full of stinkin old chicken feathers for ever so long."

"That's a fact," ses I; but I couldn't help laughin all the time.

Pete cleared his throte a time or two, and every now and then he fetched a kind of a smothered up sneeze, and then the dogs would bark. You better keep your mouth shut, old feller, thinks I, if you don't wan't to git your windpipe lined with chicken feathers. Every now and then the jice would shake as Pete kep turnin and twistin round, tryin to git fixed comfortable. But I know'd ther was no comfort in that bag, even if it had no feathers in it; and then when I thought what a terrible disappintment was waitin for him in the mornin, I couldn't help pityin him from the bottom of my heart.

It was a long time before we could go to sleep, but I drapt off after a while, and didn't wake till mornin. I was mighty anxious to see how the thing was gwine to turn out, and got ready long before aunt Prissy come to see what was in her bag. The galls was up by day-light too, to see the fun. Nobody went out till all the niggers from the kitchen had got round the bag.

"Whoop-e-e-e!" ses little nigger Ned, "Mammy see what's dat hangin on de porch."

"Kih!" ses old ant Hetty, "dat mus be ole Santaclaus heself, fell in dar when he was puttin lasses candy for Pris, and can't git out."

Pete never said nothin, waitin for the galls to come.

"Oh! Miss Calline! Miss Kesiah! come and see what I's got in my bag," ses Pris. "I spec its something what uncle Friday fotch from Gusta; he sed he was gwine to give me a Crismus."

By this time the galls was on the porch, and the niggers unswung the bag, and out tumbled Pete, all kivered with feathers from head to foot, so you couldn't see his eyes, mouth, whiskers, nor nothin else.

"Whew!" ses he, as soon as he got his head out and the feathers flew all over the floor, which skeered the little niggers so they split to the kitchen squallin like the very old devil was after 'em.

"Good Lord, massa Pete!" ses aunt Prissy, "dat you in my bag? I thought 'em was something good."

"Your bag!" ses Pete, "drat your infernal picter, who told you to hang up a bag, for white folks to go and git into? Never mind, Miss Kesiah, I was only in fun, anyway," ses he, while they was all laughin fit to die, and he was tryin to brush off the feathers. "Never mind, I was only jokin with you, but I had a better opinion of you than to think you would serve a body so, and ding my feathers if I aint glad I've found you out. Never mind, Miss," ses he, and he gin her a look like he could bite her head off, and then he blowed his nose a time or two and put out.

"But aint you gwine to be as good as your word, doctor?" ses she.

"You jest go to grass," ses he; and that's the last we've seed of cousin Pete sense Crismus mornin.

Mary gave the galls a right good settin down for

servin him so. But for my part I think it aint no great matter, for he is sich a bominable fool, that a few pretty hard lessons won't do him no harm. No more from

Your friend, till death, JOS. JONES.

P. S. Mary's in right good sperits considerin. I expect to write you a letter one of these days, old feller, that'll make your hair stand on eend with joy and gratification. But as the old sayin is, we mustn't count our chickens before they're hatched.

LETTER XXVI.

PINEVILLE, *January* 15, 1844.

To MR. THOMPSON:—*Dear Sir*—News! news! glorious news! Hurra for me!!

—"Let the kettle to the trumpet speak,
The trumpet to the cannoneer without,
The cannon to the heavens, the heaven to earth,"

For Mary's got a baby!!!

And a monstrous fine boy at that! The king of Denmark, you know, wanted to set all heaven and yeath in a uproar, jest because his majesty was gwine to take a drink of licker.—But if ever a man did feel like this world wasn't big enough for him to enjoy his happiness in, I think I ought to on this important occasion.

I never had sich feelins before. When I was 'lected Major of the Georgia Militia I felt a good deal of pride and gratification; and when I married Mary, I thought I was the happiest man in Georgia, but this last bisness has clap'd the climax over every thing that ever happened to me in all my born days. It wouldn't do for people to git much happier in this world than I am, now mind I tell you.

I don't want to brag over other people, and I know it's a old maxim, that "every crow thinks its own young ones the whitest," but I'll tell you what's a fact—mine is one of the most suprisenest children that ever was seed in these parts. It aint but jest four days old this evenin, and it's got plenty of hair on its head, and the prettyest little feet and hands, with toes and fingers, all jest as natural as grown people's; and when it opens its eyes it rolls 'em all round the room jest like it know'd every thing that was gwine on. Mother says she really does blieve the child know'd her the first time she tuck it in her arms, and old Miss Stallins says all she's afraid of is it's too smart to live. The galls is almost crazy about it, and sich another pullin and haulin about it as they do keep! One wants it, and 'tother wants it, and they won't give the little feller no chance to sleep for lookin at it, and showin it to people and talkin to it, and it's all the time "come to its aunty—tweetest little pwecious baby—aunty's little sugar candy, dumpsy diddle—" and every time I take it they're all scared to death for fear I'll hurt it some way.

Jest as I 'spected, the namin has been more trouble than a little. I picked out "Henry Clay" for his name more'n a month ago, but they all wanted to have a say in it, and every one had a name that they liked best of any. Mother said she never liked to have any of her family named after great political characters, for she never know'd a George Washington or a Thommas Jefferson what was any manner of account in her life, except the first ones, and ther names wouldn't been no better than common people's if ther characters wasn't. Old Miss Stallins wanted to call him Aberham Stallins, cause that was her husband's name, and sister Carline wanted him named Theodore Adolfus, cause they were her favorite novel names, and sister Kesiah wanted him named Charles Beverly, cause he was one of the most interestinest characters in "The Children of the Abbey." I wanted 'em all to be satisfied, but it seemed like ther was no fixin the bisness to anybody's likin, until after they all talked themselves down tired about it, we all agreed to leave it to Mary to decide. Pore Mary didn't know what to do, when they all gethered round her beggin her as hard as they could.

"Remember your pore old father that's dead and gone, child," said old Miss Stallins.

"Oh, don't call him Aberham, that's sich a old time name," ses the galls.

"Theodore is *so* pretty," ses sister Carline.

"Oh, that's sich a outlandish French name," ses all of 'em.

"But Charles Beverly was sich a good character in 'The Children of the Abbey,' and sounds so noble," ses sister Kesiah.

"No Christian child ought to be named a novel name," ses old Miss Stallins. "They're all lies from eend to eend."

" Call him what you've a mind to, dear," ses mother, " for you're his mother, and ought to please yourself."

Mary looked up in my face with her pretty blue eyes, and smiled so sweet when sister Carline laid the baby in her arms—and then she sed, as she hugged it to her bosom—

"Tome to its mudder, mudder's tweetest ittle Henry Clay—it *sall* be called Henry Clay, so it sall, mudder's pwecious ittle ring-dove, so it is, and it sall be President too, when it gits a man, so it sall."

" Hurra for Clay," ses I. " Hur——"

" Hush-h-h-h-h, Joseph," ses mother, " aint you shamed to shock Mary's nerves so?"

The fact was, I felt so glad I forgot what I was about. But I went right off and writ down in the family record:

"Henry Clay Jones,

The first son of Joseph and Mary Jones, was born on the 11th day of January, 1844."

I've been so flustrated for the last week that I hardly know what I'm doin half the time, and I don't spose I shall find time to do much else but nurse the baby for some time to come. Mary's right piert, and little Henry Clay is makin a monstrous good begining in the world. No more from

Your friend, till death, Jos. Jones.

LETTER XXVII.

PINEVILLE, GA., *March* 21, 1844.

TO MR. THOMPSON:—*Dear Sir*—You mustn't think hard because I hain't writ you no letter for so long a time. Sense the arrival of the little stranger, my time what I've had to spare from the plantation is been pretty much tuck up with nussin and gwine to town after docter stuff for it.

Babys is wonderful supprisin things, Mr. Thompson, as you know, and when one thinks how much trouble they give a body, we almost wonder what makes us so anxious to have 'em. You mustn't think I'm beginin to git tired of mine. No indeed, not by no means. I wouldn't give my little HARRY CLAY for all the niggers and plantations in Georgy, as much trouble and worryment as he gives me. Aint it curious what store we do set by the little creeters, even before we've had 'em long enough to know any thing about 'em. It seems like a new fountin of happiness is opened in our hearts, a new value given to every thing we've got, and a new purpose to our lives, when for the fust time we look upon a little helpless bein that is born of our love, and is dependent on us for support and protection. How anxious we is to do every thing we can for 'em! What pleasure we find in the pains we take to make 'em happy. But you is a man of experience in these matters, Mr. Thompson, and I needn't tell you nothin about it. I must tell you, though, what a terrible skeer we had t'other night with the baby.

I had been down to Tom Stallinses mill, to see about gittin out some lumber to bild me a new gin-house, and had been ridin and workin hard all day in the wet, and come home monstrous tired, late in the evenin. Mary and the baby was all well, and I went to bed pretty early, thinkin to git a good night's rest for the fust time in a month. Well, how long I'd been sleepin, I can't tell, but the fust thing I know'd was Mary pullin my hair to make me wake up.

"Joseph!—Joseph!" ses she.

"Ha! what's the matter?" ses I, when I seed her leanin over in the bed with the lamp in her hand, and her face as pale as the gown she had on.

"Oh, Joseph, do git up," ses she—"something's the matter with the baby."

That was enough for me, and in a twinklin I was settin up in the bed, as wide awake as if I hadn't been asleep in a week.

"Look at him, Joseph—he acts so curious," ses she, as she tuck the little feller out of the crib, and laid him down in the bed between us.

For about two minits we both sot and looked at the baby, 'thout drawin a breath. Thar it lay on its back, with its little hands down by its side. Fust it would spread its mouth like it was laughin at something—then it would roll its eyes about in its head and wink 'em at us— then it would twitch all over, and ketch its breath—then it would lay right still and stop breathin for a second or two, and then it would twitch its little limbs agin, and roll its eyes about the strangest I ever seed any thing in my life; and then it would coo, so pitiful, like a little dove, two or three times till it would kind of smother like, and stop breathin agin.

I could hear Mary's heart beat plain, and I felt the cold blood runnin back to mine like a mill-tail. I looked at Mary, and she looked at me, and sich a expression as she had in her eyes I never seed in any human.

"Joseph!" ses she.

"Mary!" ses I.

"Oh, dear!" ses she, the big tears fillin her butiful eyes. "Oh, dear! the baby is dyin—I know it is. Oh what *shall* we do?"

"Oh, no, Mary, don't git skeered," ses I, with what little breth I could summons up for the effort.

"Oh, yes, I know it is. I know'd something was gwine to happen, I had sich a dreadful dream last night. Git up, Joseph, and call mother and the galls, quick as you can. Oh, dear me, my pore little baby."

"Don't take on, Mary—maybe it aint nothin bad," ses I, tryin to compose her all I could, though I was skeered as bad as she was, and put my trowses on wrong side before in my hurryment.

In a minit I had all the famly up, and by the time I got the fire kindled, here come old Miss Stallins and the galls, all in ther night clothes, skeered almost out of ther senses.

"Dear me, what upon yeath's the matter?" ses old Miss Stallins.

"Oh, the baby! my pore little baby!" cried Mary.

"What is happened?" ses all of 'em, getherin round the bed.

"I don't know what ails it," ses Mary, "but it acts so strange—like it was gwine to die."

"Mercy on us!" ses the galls.

"Don't take on so, my child," ses old Miss Stallins. "It mought be very bad for you."

But pore Mary didn't think of any thing but the baby.

"What's good for it, mother? what'll cure it?" ses she.

The old woman put on her specticles, and looked at it, and felt it all over, while Mary was holdin it in her lap by the fire.

"Don't be skeered," ses she. "Don't be skeered, my child, maybe its nothin but the hives, or the yaller thrash, or some other baby ailment, what won't hurt it."

"Oh, it'll die—I know it will," ses Mary.

"Maybe its only sick at its little stummick, mother," ses sister Carline, "and some sut tea is the best thing in the world for that, they say."

"And if its the thrash, some catnip tea will drive it out in half a ower," ses the old woman. "Prissy, make some catnip tea, quick as you can."

"And have some water warmed to bathe its little feet in," ses sister Kesiah,—"for maybe its spasomy."

"Oh, dear, see how it winks its eyes!" ses Mary.

"That aint nothin uncommon, dear," ses her mother.

"Now its twitchin its little limbs agin. Oh, it will die, I know it will."

"Wouldn't some saffron tea be good for it?" ses Miss Carline. "Pore little dear."

"Yes, and a musterd poultice for its little bowels," ses the old woman.

By this time all the niggers on the place was up gettin hot-baths, and yarb teas, and musterd poultices, and ingun-juice, and lord knows what all, for the baby. Mother and the galls was flyin about like they was crazy, and I was so tarrified myself that I didn't know which eend I stood on. In the hurryment and confusion, aunt Katy upsot the tea-kittle and scalded little Moses, and he sot up a yell in the kitchin loud enough to be heard a mile, and I knocked the lamp off the table, and spilled the oil all over every thing, tryin to turn round three ways at the same time. After breakin two or three cups and sassers, and settin Mary's night cap afire with the candle, old Miss Stallins made out to git a teaspoonful of sut tea in the baby's mouth, hot enough to scald its life out, and then ther was sich another to-do as nobody ever did hear before.

"Wa!—wa-ya!—ke-wa!—ke-wa-ah!" went the baby.

"Good gracious! mother, the tea's bilin hot," ses sister Carline.

"My lord! Prissy, haint you got no better sense? What upon yeath did you give it to me so hot for?" ses the old woman, when she put her finger in the cup.

"Miss Kesiah tell me to pour bilin water on it," ses Prissy, with her eyes as big as sassers.

"Wa-ya! ke-wa-ah! ke-wa!" ses the baby, kickin and fistin away like all rath.

"Miss Stallins made out to git a teaspoonful of sut tea in the baby's mouth, hot enough to scald its life out."

p. 180.

"Whar's the draps, Joseph? Git the draps, it must be colicky," ses old Miss Stallins.

I got the parrygorick as quick as I could, and tried to pour out five draps, as she told me. But my hand trimbled so I could't drap it to save me.

"Give it to me, Joseph," ses she—"you's too agitated."

And she tuck the vial and poured half of it on her lap, tryin to hit the spoon—the pore old woman's eyes is so bad. Then she told sister Carline to drap it—but both the galls was fraid they mought pour too much. So Mary had to do it herself. Then the next difficulty was to git it in the baby's mouth, and when they did git it thar, it liked to choke it to death before it could swaller it.

Pretty soon after that it got quiet and went sound to sleep in Mary's lap, and we all begun to feel a good deal better. Old Miss Stallins sed she know'd what it wanted as soon as she had time to think, and she wondered she didn't think of it before. Lord only knows what mought happened if we hadn't had the parrygorick in the house. We all felt so good after we got over our skeer, that we sot thar and congratulated one another a little while before gwine to bed agin.

While we was all chattin and old Miss Stallins was beginnin to nod, I noticed Mary was watchin the baby monstrous close, and her eyes was beginnin to git bigger and bigger, as she looked at its face. Bimeby it groaned one of the longest kind of groans.

"Oh, dear!" ses Mary, "I do blieve its dyin agin!"

We all jumped up and run to her, and shore enough, it looked a heap worse than it did before, and kep all the time a moanin like it was breathin its last gasp.

"Oh, mother its gwine! Its jest as limber as a rag, and its got sich a terrible death look. Send for the doctor, quick," ses Mary, trimblin all over, and lookin as if she was gwine to faint in her cheer.

Miss Carline tuck hold of its little hands, and moved 'em, but they was jest like a dead baby's, and staid anywhar she put 'em.

Ned was sent to town for Doctor Gaiter, as hard as the hoss could go.—Mary and the galls all fell a cryin like they was at a funerel, and I felt so fainty myself that I couldn't hardly stand on my feet. Old Miss Stallins would give it some ingin-juice, and have it put in a warm bath all over; but nothin we could do for it done it any good, and we jest had to wait in a agony of suspense till the doctor come.

It aint only two miles to town, and Selim's one of the fastest hosses in Georgia, but it seemed like the doctor would never come.

"Pore little thing!" ses Mary, "I know'd my heart was sot on him too much,—I know'd it was too pretty and sweet to live. Oh, dear!"

"How it does suffer—pore little angel," ses Miss Carline.—"What kin ail the child?"

"I wish the doctor would come," ses all of 'em.

Sich thoughts as I had in that ower, I never want to have agin, as long as I live. A coffin, with a little baby in its shroud, was all the time before my eyes, and a whole funeral procession was passin through my head.

The sermon was ringin in my ears, and I could almost hear the rumblin of the fust shovelful of yeath on the grave boards of my little boy, as I walked round and round the room, stoppin now and then to take a look at the pore little thing, and to speak a word of incouragement to Mary. It was a dredful feelin, Mr. Thompson, and I do believe I've felt ten years older ever sense.

Bimeby we heard the hosses feet—all of us drawed a long breath, and every face brightened up at the sound. In a minit more the doctor laid his saddle-bags on the table :—

"Good evenin, ladies," ses he, jest as pleasin and perlite as if nothing wasn't the matter. "Good evenin, Majer, how are you this——"

"The baby! The baby!" ses all of 'em. "Doctor, can't you cure the baby?"

"Yes, doctor," ses Mary, "our only hope is in you, doctor."

"And Providence, my child," ses old Miss Stallins.

It seemed like the doctor would never git all his grate-coats, and gloves, and hankerchers off, though the wimmin was hurryin him and helpin him all they could. Bimeby, he drawed a cheer up to whar Mary was sittin, to look at the baby.

"What's the matter with yer child, Mrs. Jones?" ses he, pullin away its gown and feelin its pulse.

"I don't know, doctor—but its dredful sick," ses Mary.

"When was it tuck sick, and what was its simptoms?" ses the doctor.

All of 'em begun to tell at once, till the doctor told 'em he could understand 'em better if they'd only talk one at a time, and then Mary told him all about it.

"And how much parrygorick did you give it?" ses Doctor Gaiter.

"Five draps," ses old Miss Stallins; "I wanted to give it more, but the children was all so skeery."

"Let me see your parrygorick," ses the doctor.

He tuck it and smelled it, and tasted it, and then, says he, "You're sure you didn't give it only five draps, madam."

"No, no more'n five," ses Mary, "for I poured it out myself."

Then the doctor looked monstrous wise at the baby, for about a minit, and if you could jest seed the wimmin lookin at him. None of us breathed a single breath, and pore Mary looked right in the doctor's face, as if she wanted to see his very thoughts.

"Doc——"

"Is——"

"Don't be allarmed, madam," ses he, "ther aint no danger!"

Sich a change as come over the whole of us! The room seemed to git lighter in a instant. It was like the sunlight breakin through a midnight sky.

Mary cried like a child, and hugged her baby to her bussum, and kissed it a dozen times, and talked baby talk to it; and the galls begun puttin the room to rights, so it would be fit for the doctor to see it.

"Is you shore ther aint no danger, doctor?" ses old Miss Stallins.

"None in the least, madam," ses he. "Ther's

nothing in the world the matter of the child, only it had a little touch of the hives, what made it laugh and roll its eyes about in its sleep. In your fright you burnt its mouth with your hot teas, till it cried a little, and then you've doctored it with hot baths, onion-juice, and parrygorick, till you've stupyfied it a little. That's all, madam. By mornin it'll be well as ever it was, if you don't give it no more big doses of parry-gorrick."

"I sed so," ses old Miss Stallins. "I told Mary ther was no use takin on so 'bout the baby. But young people is so easily skeered, you know, doctor."

"Yes, and old grandmothers too, sometimes," ses he, laughin.

The baby soon quit moanin so bad, and Mary laid it in the bed and kiver'd it over with kisses.

"Bless it, mudder's tweetest 'ittle darlin baby—its dittin well, so it is—and dey sant dive it no more natty fisics, and burn its tweet 'ittle mouf no more, so dey sant," ses she; and the galls got round, and sich a everlastin gabblement as they did keep up.

By this time it was most daylight, and after drinkin a cup of strong coffee what old Miss Stallins had made for him, and laughin at us for bein so skeered at nothing, the good old doctor bundled on his overcoat, and went home to charge me five dollars for routin him out of his bed and makin him ride four miles in the cold. But I aint sorry we sent for him, for I do believe if he hadn't come, we would have dosed pore little Harry dead as a door nail before mornin.

The little feller is doin prime now, and if he was to have another attack of the hives, I'll take monstrous good care they don't give him no more dratted parrygorick. So no more from

Your friend, till death, Jos. Jones.

LETTER XXVIII.

Pineville, Ga., *April* 10, 1844.

To Mr. Thompson:—*Dear Sir*—Ever sense I read that piece in the Spirit of the Times whar the editer sed he would walk a hundred miles jest to shake hands with me, I've been monstrous anxious to git acquainted with him. But it's sich a terrible long ways to New York, and cotton's down so low, I'm 'fraid I wont never have the pleasure of seein him in this world. But if I shouldn't there's one consolation we literary men's got over other people, and that is we can form 'quaintances and friendships by our writins, without ever seein one another; and, bein as some of us aint no great beauties, perhaps it's as good a way as enny. They say he's a monstrous grate, long, gander-legged feller, and he may be 'bomination ugly for all I know; but ther's one thing I'm certain of—he must be a smart man, and a man of fust rate taste, or he wouldnt like my writins so much. I've been thinkin about writin him a letter one of these days, but the fact is, sense last Febuary, I haint had much time for nothing. The baby's been cross as the mischief, most all the time sense it had the hives, and Mary, she's been ailin a good deal, ever sense she got that terrible skare last month,—and then you know this time of year we planters is all as bissy as we can be, fixin for the crap.

Nothin very uncommon haint tuck place down here sense I writ my last letter to you, only t'other day a catasterfy happened in our family that come monstrous nigh puttin a eend to the whole generation of us. I was never so near skeered out of my senses in all my born days, and I don't b'lieve old Miss Stallins ever will git over it, if she was to live a thousand years. But I'll tell you all about it.

Last Monday mornin all of us got up well and hearty as could be, and I sot in our room with Mary, and played with the baby till breckfast time, little thinkin what was gwine to happen so soon. The little feller was jumpin and crowin so I couldn't hardly hold him in my arms, and spreadin his little mouth, and laughin jest like he know'd every thing we sed to him.

Bimeby, aunt Prissy come to tell us breckfast was ready, and we all went into tother room to eat, 'cept sister Kesiah, who sed she would stay and take care of little Henry Clay, till we was done. Mary's so careful she wont trust the baby with none of the niggers, not a single minit, and she's always dredful oneasy when Kesiah's got it, she's so wild and so careless.

Well, we sot down to breckfast, and Kesiah she scampered up stairs to her room with the baby, jumpin it up, and kissin it, and talkin to it as hard as she could.

"Now, sis, do be careful of my precious little darlin," ses Mary, loud as she could to her, when she was gwine up stairs.

"Oh, eat your breckfast, child, and don't be so tarrified about the baby," ses old Miss Stallins—" you don't allow yourself a minit's peace when it's out of yer sight."

" That's a fact," ses sister Carline, " she wont let nobody do nothin for little Henry but herself. I know I wouldn't be so crazy about no child of mine."

" Well, but you know sister Kiz is so careless. I'm always afraid she'll let it swaller something, or git a fall some way," ses Mary.

" Tut, tut," ses the old woman, " ther aint no sense in bein all the time skeered to death about nothing. People's got enough to do in this world to bear ther trouble when it comes, without studdyin it up all the time. Take some of them good hot-corn muffins," ses she, " they's mighty nice."

We was all eatin along—the old woman was talkin about her garden and the frost, how it had nipped her Inglish peas, and I was jest raisin my coffee cup to my mouth when I heard Kesiah scream out—" Oh, my lord! the baby! the baby!" and kerslash! it come right down stairs on to the floor.

Lightnin couldn't knocked me off my seat quicker! Down went the coffee, and over went the table and all the vittles. Mary screamed, and old Miss Stallins fainted right away in her cheer. I was so blind I couldn't hardly see, but I never breathed a breth till I grab'd it up in my arms and run round the house two or three times, before I had the heart to look at the pore little thing, to see if it was dead.

By this time the galls was holt of my coat tail, hollerin " April Fool! April Fool!" as hard as they could—and when I come to look, I had nothing in

" By this time the galls was holt of my coat tail, hollerin 'April Fool April Fool!'" p. 188.

my arms but a bundle of rags with little Henry Clay's clothes on. I shuck all over like I had the ager, and felt a monstrous sight more like cussin than laughin.

"April Fool, dingnation!" ses I.—"Fun's fun; but I'm dad blamed if there's any fun in any sich doins,"—and I was jest gwine to blow out a little, when I heard Mary screamin for me to come to her mother.

When we got in the dinin room, thar the old woman was, keeled over in her cheer, with her eyes sot in her head and a corn muffin stickin in her mouth. Mary was takin on at a terrible rate, and all she could do was to jest clap her hands and holler.

"Oh, mother's dyin! mother's dyin! whar's the baby? Oh, my pore mother! Oh, my darlin baby!"

I tuck Mary, and splained it all to her, and tried to quiet the pore gall, and the galls got at the old woman. But it tuck all sorts of rubbin, and ever so much assafedity, and campfire and hartshorn, and burnt hen's feathers, to bring her too; and then she wouldn't stay brung too more'n a minit before she'd keel over agin, and I do b'lieve if they hadn't brung little Henry Clay to her, so she could see him and feel him, and hear him squall, she never would got her senses agin. She aint more'n half at herself yit. All the galls kin do they cant make her understand the April Fool bisiness, and she won't let nobody else but herself nuss the baby ever sense.

As soon as I had time to think a little, I was so monstrous glad it wasn't no worse, that I couldn't stay mad with the galls. But I tell you what, I was terrible rathy for a few minits. I don't b'lieve in this

April foolin. Last year the galls deviled me almost to death with ther bominable nonsense, sowin up the legs of my trowses, punchin holes in the water gourd, so I wet my shirt bosom all over when I went to drink, and heatin the handle of the tongs, and cuttin the cowhide bottoms of the cheers loose, so I'd fall through 'em when I went to set down, and all sich devilment. I know the Bible ses there's a time for all things; but I think the least a body has to do with fool bisiness at any time the better it is for 'em. I'm monstrous tired of sich doins myself, and if I didn't think the galls had got ther fill of April foolin this time, I'd try to git a almynack next year what didn't have no fust day of April in it.

No more from your friend, till death,

Jos. Jones.

SUPPOSING A CASE;

OR,

THE LONG AND SHORT OF RANCY COTTEM'S COURTSHIP.

Perhaps ther aint no character in the world so much to be pitied as a old bacheler what wants to get married. It seems like ther's a certain period in sich a man's life when his matrimonial prospects becomes perfectly hopeless, and when the more he wants to change his condition from single to double blessedness, the more he can't do it to save him. Beside all the embarrassin circumstances that has conspired all his life to keep his neck out of the noose, a new one arises in the fact that the galls all knows he's anxious to get married, and then the very ones that has been settin ther caps for him all ther lives, runs from him like a flock of partridges from a weasel. The more he sets at 'em the more they shies off, and every woman of his acquaintance, from fourteen to forty-five, takin it into ther heads that he wants to marry 'em right off, he aint allowed to come within gun-shot of the uglyest of 'em.

Them's tryin times, and ought to be a warnin to all young men what don't want to mend ther own stockins while they live, and be nursed by the charity of the community in ther last sickness.

Rancy Cottem was one of the melancholyest examples of this deplorable condition that I ever seed, and the way his heart was broke at last ought to be recorded as a example to all future generations of men, and a reproach to the female sex forever. Rancy Cottem was a extremely bashful young man, and from the time he was old enough to know one gall from another, he had always had a idee that they was beins of a more exalted natur than men, and though he loved the whole generation of 'em, it was more'n he could do to look one of 'em right straight in the face, let alone talkin to one of 'em or tetchin 'em. He was a long way out of his teens, and though he mought been a tolerable lookin chap some twenty years ago, his countenance had been so long exposed to the weather that he had become very dilapidated in his personal appearance. Perhaps it was his consciousness of this fact, and that he wasn't improvin with age, that made him more determined than ever to get married; or perhaps the bright, mischievous eyes and rosy cheeks of Becky Wigfall, over the Runs, gave a new and sudden impulse to his desperate resolution. Some people sed it was the smart chance of property that Becky had that made him sich a regular visiter to old Mrs. Wigfall's. Whatever it was that actuated him, one thing is certain, he laid regular siege to the house, and as he was pretty well to do in the world himself, Becky's mother didn't make no objections, and used to give him all the chance she could to git ahead in her daughter's affections.

Becky was one of the teariest, wildest galls in

the settlement, and as she hadn't no lack of admirers, she hung out a bold flag of defiance, 'specially to Rancy Cottem, who bein so monstrous faint-hearted, was at a perfect nonplus how to make the attack, notwithstandin he had come to the desperate resolution to court her if it cost him his life.

Regular every Saturday night he used to ride over to old Mrs. Wigfall's and take tea with the family; and regular every time he tuck a seat in the parlor by the door, and thar he sot and sot, till all the family went to bed, lookin all sorts of love at Becky, but without ever venturin to open his mouth to her on the subject. Sometimes he sed it was gwine to rain, or the weather was very warm, or cold, and as he generally told the truth about it, Becky never disputed the pint with him. After settin thar listenin to the crickets in the fire-place until Becky had a fit of gaping and the chickens begun to crow for daylight, he would get up and take his hat and go to the door; then he would turn round and look for a minute, and drawin in his breath, he would break out with "Well, good evenin to you all, Miss Becky!" loud enough to wake up the whole family, though he didn't mean his partin salutation for nobody but her.

This sort of courtship didn't amount to much. He was satisfied that it was no use to try to capture the fortress by sich approaches, and he would have gin the world if he could only pluck up courage enough to throw a bombshell right into the very heart of the citadel; but every time he looked into Becky Wigfall's face he felt a sort of faintyness come over him, and he was ready to give up the siege in despair.

It was a desperate case. He felt that something must be done; and in the spirit of a forlorn hope, he determined to make an assault at all hazards.

The next time he came he found Becky and the rest of the galls cardin and knittin. After settin and talkin about the craps and the weather for a while, little by little he worked his chair up pretty close to Becky, determined to make a bold beginin, when the old woman was thar to stand by him. But when he found himself within arm's length of the object of his adoration, he was tuck all of a sudden with sich a terrible chokin that for more'n a minit he couldn't say a word to save him.

Becky was cardin away as hard as she could, makin bats of cotton for a quiltin they was gwine to have, and lookin as mischievous as she could be. Bimeby ses Rancy, after clearing his throat two or three times—

"What's them things for, Miss Becky?" ses he.

"Them's bats for a quilt," ses she.

Rancy like to fall off his chair, but after composin himself a little, ses he—

"Then you's gwine to make a quilt, is you?"

"To be shore we is," ses Becky.

Then ther was a dead pause, and Rancy twisted about in his seat, and breathed so loud you could hear him all over the room. He would give his horse, saddle, and bridle for another question to ax her. Jest then old Mrs. Wigfall helped him out by axin him if he wouldn't come to the quiltin.

"To be shore I will," ses he, lookin sideways at Becky, "if *she'll* let me come."

"Oh, certainly, you must come," ses Becky.

By this time the sweat begun to pour off Rancy's face in a stream, and the young galls run off to ther room to laugh, leavin nobody with him but Becky and ther mother.

Things had come to a stand-still agin, and Rancy was in another dilemmy. Bimeby a bright idee struck him, and he tuck up a bunch of the cotton what Becky had been cardin and mussed it all up.

"Thar," ses he, "I spilt yer bats, Miss Becky. Now you got to make 'em over agin."

"Why, Mr. Cottem, what did you do that for?" ses she.

"Jest for fun," ses he, "I love to spile things."

And then he laughed like he had the highstericks, but his face looked solemn as a tombstone all the time.

Becky was so full of laugh herself that she could hardly set on her chair; but she carded the bats over agin and put 'em on the chair by her side, and then set 'em out of his reach, for fear he mought spile 'em agin. Then she tuck her needles to finish a piece of lace what one of the galls had been knittin, and old Mrs. Wigfall went to her room, jest to give 'em a fair chance to court.

Rancy had made more headway, he thought, in a single hour than he had made in the last six months; and as he was a little over his skeer, he was determined to make the most of his opportunity. So he jest pulled his chair up a little closer and looked at Becky a bit, while her pretty little fingers was flyin about her needles so fast that a body couldn't hardly tell which hand they belonged to—and catchin hold of the thread a few inches from her hand, held on to it with his fingers while she went on knittin.

"Thar," ses he, "Miss Becky, you shan't have no more'n so much, now. Only jest so much—jest up to thar," ses he, while she was knittin away, her face gittin reder and reder the nearer her fingers come to his.

"It's most all gone—only a little bit more," ses he, holdin on to the thread till his fingers come agin her little white hand, when he jumped like he was 'lectrified, drap'd the thread, and begun to squirm round in his seat like a yeath-worm on the pint of a fish-hook.

After gittin over it a little he tuck hold agin and went through the same interestin operation two or three times, tellin Becky that he loved to bother pretty girls, they always looked so interestin when they was bothered; and how she shouldn't have another bit after she knit that bit up, and a whole heap of sich nonsense, until Becky put away her knittin.

"Thar," sed he, "I knowd I'd make you quit workin, and I know you'r mad at me for botherin you so much—aint you, Miss Becky?"

"Oh, no, Mr. Cottem," ses she, "I'm not mad in the least."

But what was to be done now? Every minit he sot thar sayin nothin he was growin more and more faint-hearted; no time was to be lost, and after screwin his courage up to the very highest notch agin, and clearin his throat two or three times, ses he in a low husky voice:

"—— and catchin hold of the thread a few inches from her hand, held on to it with his fingers while she went on knittin." p. 196.

"Miss Becky!"

"What?" ses she.

"Spose now, a young man was to fall desperately in love with you?"

"Oh, I'd like that very much!" ses she.

"—And was to love you almost to death?"

"That would be very delightful."

"—And sposin he wanted to marry you and nobody else?"

"That, of course," ses she.

"—And sposin he had plenty of property to make you comfortable?"

"That would be all the better."

"—And sposin," ses Rancy, drawin his chair a little closer—"sposin he was to court you?"

"I'd like that first rate!" ses Becky.

"—And sposin, Miss Becky, your family didn't have no objections to the match?"

"All the better," ses Becky.

"—and that young man was a man of good character?"

"I wouldn't have no other," ses she.

"—And a man of sense and experience?" ses Rancy, lookin as dignified as he could.

"That's the sort."

"And sposin," ses Rancy, nervously feelin for her hand—"sposin he was willin to die for you, he loved you so much?"

"Dear me," sighed Becky.

"And sposin he was to tell you how he couldn't be happy in this world without you, and how he often come near droundin himself in the branch about you?"

Becky put her hankerchef up to her face and shuck all over.

"Don't cry, Miss Becky," ses Rancy, in a very affectionate voice.

"Oh, Mr. Cottem," ses she.

"Ah, Miss Becky," ses he, kind o' chokin—"sposin then, he, that young man, what loved you so much—sposin he was to ax you to have him right off, Miss Becky—what would you say to him?"

"That depends on who he was," ses Becky.

"Well, Miss Becky," ses he, gaspin for breath, and grabin hold of her with both hands—"sposin it was me?"

"*Then I'd tell him to go along about his business, for a silly old fool!*" ses she, with a loud laugh, as she pulled away from him and scampered off to the room whar the galls, who had been listenin all the time, was laughin like they would die.

Pore Cottem never got over the shock he received that night. His heart was broke outright, and from that day until the day of his death, when it may be said he jest naturally dried away, nobody ever seed him smile. He used to read the marriages in the papers with tears in his eyes, and whenever a weddin tuck place in the settlement, he was shore to have a serious time for a month, when he would git so bad off that the neighbors used to have to set up with him every night.

WHAT MADE THE BABY CRY;

OR,

HOW THE CHAVERSES COULDN'T GO TO AUGUSTA.

Jimmy Chavers was a grate politician, and nothin would do but he must go down to Augusty to see Mr. Clay when he was thar in 1843. But his wife wouldn't hear to no sich arrangement 'thout she could go too; so all Jimmy had to do was jest to pack up the whole family, consistin of himself, his wife Nancy, and her baby, and the baby's puppy-dog, a travelin bag and a bandbox, and be ready for the stage when it come along. He 'spected nothin else but the stage would be cram'd full, as everybody was gwine to the city; and shore enough when it come the people's heads was stickin out of its sides like chicken's heads from a market wagon.

Everybody but the driver sed there wasn't no room for any more passengers. But, as Mrs. Chavers had been to so much trouble to get ready, and had walked half a mile to the road, she was determined to go, if she could squeeze in any way. Mr. Chavers would been monstrous glad if she and the baby would stay home; but go she would, and after two or three passengers had crawled out and got on top with the driver, the Chavers family bundled in, and squeezed down into the middle seat.

"You don't want that infernal dog along, do you, Mr. Chavers?" sed the driver, when he was handin in the travlin bag full of provisions for the journey.

"Oh, no, cuss the dog!—leave that to home," ses one of the passengers.

Chavers didn't say nothing, but looked at his wife as much as to say ther wasn't really no room for little Tip.

"Yes, but he must go," ses Mrs. Chavers. "I couldn't never think of leavin pore little Tip home, the baby's so much attached to the little feller."

It tuck 'em some time to git stowed away, the stage was so crowded. The travlin bag was jammed down between the passenger's legs, and Chavers tuck the dog in his lap, while Mrs. Chavers held the baby in hers. When they was all ready the driver started his team, and away they went, but not very fast you may depend.

Little Gustus was about ten months old, as fat as a pig, and one of the best-natured baby's in the world, and for a while he tugged away at the ginger-cake what he had in his hand as quiet and contented as could be.

Mrs. Chavers kep talkin to him all the time, showin him the cows and the horses and the trees, tellin him whose place that was, and whar they was gwine, and who they was gwine to see, jest as if the little feller could understand a single word she sed. Bimeby dab went his ginger-cake, right on one of the gentlemen's clean, white trouses.

"Before the cake was found the baby got hold of one of the passenger's hats."

p. 201.

"Hity tity!" ses Mrs. Chavers—"jest see what mamy's naughty baby is done!"

Then she told Chavers to git the ginger-cake, for it was too much to waste. In stoopin over and lookin for it, Tip's tail got cramped up some how, and he sot up a yell, like his neck was broke, and snapped another gentleman's leg; and before the cake was found the baby got hold of one of the passenger's hats, and was crumplin it all into a mush before his mother could get it away from him.

The little feller wanted something to play with, so she let him have her parasol. That tickled him monstrous, and sot him to jumpin and caperin so she couldn't hardly hold him in the stage. Then he begun to crow and lay about him like he was gwine to break the heads of everybody in the stage, and the first thing his mother know'd, whack he tuck a old gentleman with specticles on, right on his nose, in spite of all his winkin and dodgin. The old man snapped his eyes and worked his jaws, but he didn't say nothin.

"Oh, oh!" ses Mrs. Chavers—"mudder's baby mustn't hurt the gentleman—dat's naughty tricks, so it is," ses she, grabin hold of the parasol, and settin Gustus down in her lap.

Chavers looked over to the baby and shook his head, and said:

"Little Gussy mustn't be a bad boy."

Then the younger Chavers pulled at Tip's tail awhile, and between grabin hold of his mother's bonnet-strings, and kickin his feet in the gentlemens' laps, and puttin everything he could git hold of into his mouth, he kep his father and mother both as busy as they could be to take care of him.

By this time the passengers begun to wish the Chavers family to the mischief, and one crusty old bacheler begun to show signs of hydrafoby very plain. He was one of the alfiredest uglyest men any time, that ever was seed in Georgy; but when he was in a bad humor, he was enough to skeer the very old Harry himself, jest to look at him. With the exception of his nose, what was about two sizes too large, ther wasn't nothin very remarkable about his features, but ther was a sort of freezin, northeaster look about him that was enough to stop the grass from growin whar his shadder fell; and what was the most singular thing in the world, he looked like he'd been dead about twenty years, and had jest lately been dug up.

The old bacheler never sed a word after the Chaverses come in the stage, but jest sot and watched the motions of the baby, like he would go into fits if it was to touch him.

Little Gussy begun to git monstrous restless, and kep his mother busyer than ever to keep him out of mischief. Bimeby, all of a sudden, the baby squalled out like he was snake bit.

"Whush-h-h, whush-h-h," ses its mother, gatherin it up in her arms and tryin to quiet it, while its father looked over to it and shuck the puppy at it, and coaxed it and talked baby-talk to it too.

But it was all no use—"Wah, wah!" went the baby—"wah, wah!—ke-wah ah!"

"Oh my!—what ails mama's little darlin baby?

Dony ki so, tweetest ittle pweshus," ses its mother, dancing it as well as she could on her knee, and hoverin over it and kissin it with all her might.

"Wah, wah-ah!—ke-wah—ke-wah!" went the baby.

"Jeems," ses its mother, "what upon yeath can ail the baby? I never heer'd it cry so before!"

"Let me take it," ses Chavers, and then they swaped the baby for the dog, and for a minit little Gussy seem'd to get better. But before they got done wonderin what made it do so, away it went agin worse than ever.

"My lord, Nancy, what can ail the child?" ses Chavers, after trying his best to pasify it. "Some pin or something must hurt it."

"Let me have the child," ses Mrs. Chavers, lookin monstrous allarmed.

She overhauled all its clothes, but didn't find no pins, and then she tuck it and jumped it up and talked to it agin.

"Looky, looky," ses she, holdin it up to the winder of the stage, and drummin on it with her hand—"Looky, see de pretty green treeses and de green grasses."

"Wah-wah," squalled the baby.

"Oh, de pretty cow! See de wheely rolly roundy, roundy, and de horsy go trotty, trotty—oh, de pretty. Look, mama's baby!" says Mrs. Chavers.

After a little while Gustus begun to lower his key a little. But he was no sooner down in his mother's lap than away he went agin, as loud as he could squall.

"Goodness gracious," ses Mrs. Chavers, the tears comin into her eyes—"what does ail the child? It must have the cholic dreadful."

Then Chavers had to take it till she got out the draps. In the botherment Tip got into a tight place and got his tail mashed agin, what made him set up another terrible ki-eye; Chavers slapped Tip aside of his head, and Mrs. Chavers spilled the parrygoric all over the man with the white trouses, tryin to pour some out for the baby.

"Dear me!" ses Mrs. Chavers, "the baby must be sick, or it wouldn't take on so. If we can jest git to Betsy Radkinses, I won't go another step."

By this time little Gustus had got quiet agin.

"How far is it, driver, to Radkinses?" axed the old bacheler.

"'Bout a mile," ses the driver.

"Thank Heaven!" ses the man with the white trouses; then, after waitin a while, "that the baby is better."

"Pore ittle one—what was de matter wid mudder's ittle tweety baby?" sed Mrs. Chavers, kissin and hugin it up.

Little Gustus looked up in his mother's face, through his tears, as pleasant and bright as a flower-garden after a shower of rain, but he couldn't tell her what was the matter with him.

"Do it feel better now, mudder's ittle pweshus?—pore ittle one," ses Mrs. Chavers; and then she gin it a great big piece of 'lasses candy, and went on talkin to it about gwine to see Mr. Clay.

Every time the stage would jolt, and sometimes

when it didn't jolt, down would go the candy on somebody's knee, and all of the passengers on the front seat would screw and twist themselves about to keep out of the way.

By changin him about, and standin him up, and rollin him over and swapin him every now and then for the dog, and lettin him pull the puppy's ears and tail, they had managed to git him in a pretty good humor agin, and had made up ther minds to go on to Augusty. But jest as they got in sight of Radkin's house, down went the 'lasses candy, and away went little Gustus agin, as hard as he could squall.

"My lord! Jeems, I really do blieve the baby is spasomy. Mercy on me! it jumps and twitches like it is fitty. Dear me, what shall we do?" ses she—the baby rippin and kickin and squallin liker ath all the time.

Chavers took it, an talked to it and jumped it, and his wife talked to it, and showed it the wheels "rollin roundy roundy" agin, but it was all no use. It would stop for a minute or so, till it could git its breath, and then away it would go agin, worse'n ever.

By the time they got to Radkinses, Mrs. Chavers was almost skeered out of her senses, and as soon as the stage could be stopped, she got out with the baby and run to the house, leavin Chavers to bring the dog, and the band-box, and the travellin bag.

Pore Chavers was terribly skeer'd himself, and seein the passengers tuck so much interest in his family afflictions, advisin him to stop and send for a doctor for the baby—with his heart in his mouth, and his eyes swimmin in tears, he ax'd 'em if anybody know'd what was the matter with it, and what was best to do for it.

One sed it mought be one thing, and one sed another, all agreein that the best way was to git a doctor right off. Chavers had Tip under one arm and the bandbox and carpet-bag under the other, and the stage was drivin off when the old bacheler stuck his head out of the winder and ses to him:

"I say, mister, do you want to see what made the baby cry?" and with that he giv Chavers one look right full in the face, that made him feel like he had the nightmare, and drap bandbox, carpet-bag, and all on the ground.

As soon as he got over the shock he gethered up his traps and run to the house and told his wife all about it. He ses to this day he only wonders that his child wasn't ruined for life.

The baby was no more trouble after it got out of the stage, but the Chaverses were mortally put out because they couldn't go to Augusty to see Mr. Clay. Mrs. Chavers ses she 'spicioned something was the matter all the time, but Lord knows, she ses, it never entered her head that any human man was ugly enough to skeer her baby into fits.

BEGINNING TO PRACTICE;

OR,

COUSIN PETE'S FIRST CASE OF CHOLERA.

Cousin Pete had jest come home from his first course in college, and he was monstrous anxious to make everybody believe he was a great doctor. Uncle Josh put him with old Dr. Gaiter to learn the practice of medicine, for though he had been to college a whole winter, and had ever so many lecters from the professors, and know'd all about the theory, as he called it, he hadn't got his hand in yet, and didn't know much about mixin fisic and sich like. Dr. Gaiter tuck him into his office, and used to take him round with him to see his patients and examine ther simptems, and sometimes he used to send him by himself to give the perscriptions what he made for 'em, and see how his fisic operated.

Pete soon begun to put on professional airs, and anybody to see him ridin Uncle Josh's horses to death, or to hear him talkin and swellin about the despert cases he had on hand, would tuck him to be one of the greatest doctors in Georgy. If he only had to go five hundred yards to give a nigger-baby a dose of parrygoric, he always went on horseback, as hard as he could gallop, and when he had no cases to doctor he would git onto his horse with his saddle-bags, and go tearin out into the country, as if somebody's life depended on his motions. He was all the time talkin about surgical operations, and toptical examinations, and cuttin up dead bodys, so more'n half of Uncle Josh's niggers was afraid to go to sleep nights, for fear he'd cut 'em up and bile the meat off ther bones before mornin. The fact is, Pete was about as perfect a specimen of a journeyman man-killer in the first stage of his profession as was to be seed anywhere.

One day, while Dr. Gaiter was gone to Milledgeville, and Uncle Josh was away from home, the overseer sent in word that some of the niggers was sick. That was jest into Pete's hands. His saddle-bags was on his horse in no time, and away he went dashin out to the plantation to see what was the matter. In about a ower he come back agin, at full gallop, jumped off his horse at the office door, run in and got some medicine, and away he dashed agin as hard as he could go. Several persons ax'd him what was the matter, but Pete only looked wise, and sed nothing. He hadn't time to say a word, and away he galloped, like ther wasn't a minit to spare. All night he staid to the plantation, and everybody was wonderin what upon yeath was the matter out thar to keep him so long, when a little nigger come into Mr. Perkins' drug store to git some more medicine.

"What's broke loose among you all out to the plantation?" ax'd Mr. Perkins.

"Oh," ses he, "daddy and Uncle Abram, and Bill and Aunt Sukey, and two or three more of the people, is dreadful sick."

"What's the matter with 'em?"

"Done-no, sar. Massa Pete says um got de easy-atic collery, and he tole me to give you dis letter."

Mr. Perkins tuck the letter, and after putin on his specks he made it out.

"PLANTATION, *July 15th.*

"TO MR. PERKINS:

"SIR—The dredful scourge is ragin here, the Asy-atic cholery. Six of the niggers is got it in the most malignant tipe. Send the follerin perscription as quick as possible:

R. Callumy ozj
Morfeene gr. xxxiv M
ft. 6 powders

"Make powders for six patients, and send' em im-megitly, as ther aint no time to be lost.

"In haste, PETER JONES, M. D."

The old man flew rouna like a house afire till he got the powders all made up; then he gin 'em to little Sampson and told him to take 'em to the doctor as quick as his mule could carry him.

No news was heard from the plantation all day. Everybody was in a state of dredful excitement about the cholery, and they was afraid to go within a mile of the place for fear of ketchin the eppydemmick.

The next day was Sunday, and everybody in Pine-ville was gwine to church, they was skared so dred-ful. The panick was spread all over the town, and Mr. Perkins sold more campfire and alcohol than he had sold in six months. Everybody sed somebody ought to go out to the plantation to help Dr. Jones, but nobody didn't volunteer to go.

The excitement was getin worse and worse every hour, when, about noon, Cousin Pete come ridin into town on Uncle Josh's old ball-faced hoss, in a slow walk, with his head hangin down and a sort of a wild look out of his eyes. Instead of chargin up the middle street, and racin round the court-house like he always did, he tuck the privatest way he could find as if he didn't want nobody to see him.

Something terrible had tuck place on Uncle Josh's plantation, certain as the world, and everybody was anxious to know all about it. In a minute ther was a rush to the Doctor's office, and all begun at once axin Cousin Pete about the cholery.

"How is the niggers?—how is your patients, Dr. Jones?" axed half a dozen voices of Pete, who was stretched out on the sofa, breathin very hard and rollin his eyes about like he was half out of his senses.

"How's the sick niggers, Doctor?"

"They's dead," says Pete! "all the medicine in Georgy couldn't saved 'em."

"What?" ses Mr. Perkins, "Dead! How many is dead?"

"Five of 'em," ses Pete.

Then the panick was worse than ever. The news went through the town like wild fire, more'n half the people was for 'packin up and movin right off, to escape sich a dreadful fatal disease. No doubt Pete had done his best. Pore feller, he was so overcome with exertin himself, that he couldn't hardly stand, and didn't go out of the house all afternoon.

About five o'clock in the afternoon Dr. Gaiter come home, and hearin the dreadful accounts about the cholery, the first thing he done was to ride right out to the plantation with Cousin Pete, to see into the matter. After lookin about a little and questionin the overseer and the niggers what had been sick, he pronounced the eppidemmick nothing but a common cholery-morbus, brung on by eatin too much green corn and water-melons; and after lookin at Pete's perscription he wasn't at no loss to account for the uncommon fatality of the disease. Only two niggers out of the lot that was sick had escaped, and one was old Abraham, who never would take nobody's fisick as long as he had strength enough in his jaws to keep 'em shut, and the other was Aunt Sukey, who was most well before the medicine come.

Pore Pete! When the Doctor explained it all to him, and told him how so much callamel and morfeen was enough to kill all the niggers on the plantation, he tuck it monstrous hard. Uncle Josh was as mad as a hornit, and come monstrous nigh givin Pete a lickin, big as he is. But old Mr. Mountgomery told him that wouldn't bring the niggers to life, nor save the lives of anybody else that mought have the bad luck to fall into Pete's hands. He's a monstrous plain spoken old man, Mr. Mountgomery is, and goes his death agin quacks and pretenders of all kinds. He told Uncle Josh it was a great pity for the pore niggers, but so far as he was consarned, it served him jest right, for settin his son up for a Doctor before he knowed the first principles of the science of medicine. He said it was a great pity that them who was turnin loose on the country as doctors, ignorant, young upstarts, who's jest got knowledge enough of medicine to make 'em dangerous to the lives of the community, couldn't always be treated by the fisicians of ther own manufacture. He sed ther was a great responsibility restin on a parent in the selection of a profession for his son, and that in adoptin a pursuit as much regard should be paid to the ability of the young man to discharge his duty to the public, as to his taste or preferences. If that matter was always taken into consideration, many a chap that is now fillin the grave-yards of the country, with dead victims to their ignorance and vanity, would be better employed in plowin and hoein, and makin corn for the livin.

Mr. Mountgomery's remarks was not, under the circumstances, perticularly agreeable to Uncle Josh, but he knowed what he sed was true as gospel, and he never sed a word out of the way to his old friend.

Pete's been monstrous thoughtful and quiet ever sense his encounter with the Asyatic cholery. Some of the boys plagues him a good deal, but some of his friends is more tender of his feelins. Bob Moreland had a long talk with him, tryin to persuade him that sich cases often happens with the best of doctors.

"Why," ses Bob, "you aint the first Doctor that ever met with sich a accident. Sich things happens every now and then, if they was only found out. Why, thar was Dr. Barker, you know, killed himself by mistake; and everybody knows that Dr. Sansum, down on the Runs, killed his own wife and child, by givin 'em the wrong kind of medicine."

"I know that," ses Pete, with a long sigh, "I know that."

"Well, aint that consolin to you? You is only a young doctor, and they was old ones. One killed himself and the other killed his wife and child."

"Yes," ses Pete, shakin his head with a heavy groan. "Yes, Bob, *but that wasn't like killin ther own niggers, worth seven hundred dollars apiece.*"

Bob didn't try to console him no more after that. Sich grief was too sacred to be disturbed by words of condolence, and must be left to time to heal.

THE RUNAWAY MATCH;

OR,

HOW THE SCHOOLMASTER MARRIED A FORTUNE.

It's about ten years ago sense the incident what I'm gwine to tell tuck place. It caused a great sensation in Pineville at the time, and had the effect to make fellers monstrous careful how they run away with other people's daughters without ther consent ever sense.

Mr. Ebenezer Doolittle was the bominablest man after rich galls that ever was. He hadn't been keepin' school in Pineville more'n six months before he had found out every gall in the settlement whose father had twenty niggers, and had courted all of 'em within a day's ride. He was rather old to be poplar with the galls, and somehow they didn't like his ways, and the way they did bluff him off was enough to discourage anybody but a Yankee schoolmaster, what wanted to git married, and hadn't many years of grace left. But it didn't seem to make no sort of difference to him. He undertook 'em by the job. He was bound to have a rich wife out of some of 'em, and if he failed in one case, it only made him more perseverin' in the next. His motto was—"never say die."

Nettie Darling, as they used to call her—old Mr. Darling's daughter, what used to live out on the

Runs—was about the torndownest mischief of a gall in all Georgia. Nettie was rich, and handsome and smart, and had more admirers than she could shake a stick at, but she was sich a tormentin' little coquet that the boys was all afraid to court her in downright yearnest. When Mr. Doolittle found her out he went for her like a house-a-fire. She was jest the gall for him, and he was determined to have her at the risk of his life.

Well, he laid siege to old Darling's house day and night, and when he couldn't leave his school to go and see her, he rit letters to her that was enough to throw any other gall but Nettie Darling into a fit of the highstericks to read 'em. Jest as everybody expected, after encouragin the feller long enough to make him believe he had the thing dead, she kicked him flat. But, 'shaw! he was perfectly used to that, and he was too much of a filosofer to be discouraged by such treatment, when the game was worth pursuin. He didn't lose no time, but jest brushed up and went right at her agin. Everybody was perfectly surprised to see him gwine back to old Mr. Darling's after the way he had been snubbed by Nettie, but they was a good deal more surprised and the boys was terribly allarmed, in about a month, at the headway he was makin. All at once Miss Nettie's conduct seemed changed towards him, and though her father and mother was desperately opposed to the match, anybody could see that she was beginnin to like the schoolmaster very much.

Things went on in this way for a while, till bimeby old Mr. Darling begun to git so uneasy about it, that he told Mr. Doolittle one day, that he mustn't come to his house no more; and that if he ketched him sendin any more love letters and kiss verses to his daughter by his nigger galls, he'd make one of his boys give him a alfired cowhidin.

But Mr. Doolittle didn't care for that neither. He could see Miss Nettie when she come a shopin in the stores in town, and ther was more'n one way to git a letter to her. What did he care for old Darling? His daughter was head and heart in love with him, and was jest the gall to run away with him too, if the old folks opposed the match. And as for the property, he was certain to get that when once he married the gall.

One Saturday, when ther was no school, Mr. Doolittle went to old Squire Rogers and told him he must be ready to marry a couple that night at exactly ten o'clock, at his office.

"Mum," says Doolittle. "You mustn't say a word about it to nobody, squire. The license is all ready, and the party wants to be very private."

Squire Rogers was one of the most accommodatin old cusses in the world, on sich occasions. Mrs. Rogers was a monstrous cranky, cross old woman, and nothing done the old squire so much good as to marry other people, it didn't make no odds who they was. Besides, Mr. Doolittle was a injured man and a great scholar, in his opinion, and belonged to his church.

Mr. Doolittle had arranged the whole business in first-rate order. Miss Nettie was to meet him at the eend of her father's lane, disguised in a ridin dress borrowed for the occasion, when he was to take her in a close one-horse barouche, and "fly with her on the wings of love," as he said he would, to Squire Rogers' office, whar they would be united in the bands of wedlock before anybody in the village know'd anything about it. He had made arrangements at the hotel for a room, which he seed fixed up himself for the auspicious occasion, and he had rit a letter to a friend of his down in Augusty to come to Pineville the next week to take charge of his school, as he thought it mought be necessary for him to keep out of the way of old Darling for a few weeks, till the old feller could have time to cool down.

All day Mr. Doolittle was bustlin about as if he wasn't certain which eend he stood on, while the sunshine in his heart beamed from his taller-colored face in a way to let everybody know that something extraordinary was gwine to happen

Jest after dark he mought been seen drivin out by himself in a barouche, towards old Mr. Darling's plantation. Everybody suspicioned something, and all hands was on the lookout. It was plain to see that Squire Rogers' importance was swelled up considerable with something, but nobody couldn't git a word out of him.

Mr. Doolittle didn't spare the lash after he got out of sight of town, and with strainin eyes and palpitatin heart he soon reached the place appinted to meet the object of his consumin affections.

Was she thar? No! Yes! Is it? Yes, thar she is!—the dear creetur! the skirt of her nankeen ridin dress, what fits close to her angelic form,

10

flutterin in the breeze. She stands timidly crouchin in the corner of the fense, holdin her thick vale over her lovely face, tremblin in every jint, for fear she mought be discovered and tore away from the arms of her dear Ebenezer!

"Dearest angel," ses he, in a low voice.

"Oh, Ebenezer!" and she kind o' fell in his arms.

"Compose yourself, my love," ses he.

"Oh, if father should—"

"Don't fear, dearest creeter. My arm shall protect you," ses Doolittle.

And then he was jest gwine to put away her vale to kiss her—

"Oh!" ses she, "didn't I hear somebody comin?"

"Eh?" ses Doolittle lookin quickly round. "Let's git in, my dear."

And with that he helped her into the barouche, and contented himself with imprintin a burnin kiss, that almost singed the kid glove on her dear little hand, as he closed the door. Then jumpin onto the front seat and seizin the lines, he drove as fast as he could to town, encouragin her all the way and swearin to her how he would love her and make her happy, and tellin her how her father and mother would forgive her when it was all over, and think jest as much of her as ever.

Pore gall! she was so terribly agitated that she couldn't do nothing but sob and cry, which made her dear Ebenezer love her the more and swear the harder.

When they got to the squire's office, and the boys, who was on the watch, seed him help her out of the barouche, everybody know'd her at once in spite of her disguise, and sich another excitement was never seed in Pineville. Some of the fellers was half out of their senses, and it was necessary to hurry the ceremony over as quick as possible for fear of bein interrupted by the row that was bruin.

"Be quick, Squire," ses Doolittle, handin out the license, and shakin like he had a ager—"for Miss Darling is very much agitated."

The Squire hardly waited to wipe his spectacles, and didn't take time to enjoy himself in readin the ceremony slow and solem, like he always did. The noise was gettin louder and louder out of doors, and somebody was knockin to get in.

"Oh, me!" ses Nettie, leanin on Mr. Doolittle's arm for support.

"Go on!" gasped Doolittle, pressin the almost faintin Nettie to his side, with his eyes on the Squire and his face as white as a sheet.

"Open the door, Rogers!" ses a hoarse voice outside.

But the Squire didn't hear nothin till he pronounced the last words of the ceremony, and Ebeneezer Doolittle and Nettie Darling was pronounced man and wife.

Jest then the door opened. In rushed old Mr. Darling and Bill and Sam Darling, followed by a whole heap of fellers.

The bride screamed and fell into the arms of the triumphant Doolittle.

"Take hold of her!" ses old Darling flourishin his cane over his head. "Take hold of the huzzy!"

"Stand off!" ses Doolittle, throwin himself into a real stage attitude, and supportin his faintin bride with one arm. "Stand off, old man! She is my lawful wife, and I claim the protection of the law!"

"Knock him down! Take hold of him!" hollered out half a dozen, and Bill Darling grabbed the bridegroom by the neck, while Squire Rogers jumped upon the table and called out—

"I command the peace! I command the peace, in the name of the State of Georgia!"

"She's my wife! my lawful wife!" shouted Doolittle. "I call upon the law!"

By this time the bride got over her fainting fit and raised her drooping head—the vale fell off and—oh, cruel fate! Mr. Ebeneezer Doolittle stood petrified with horror, holdin in his arms, not Miss Nettie Darling, but Miss Nettie Darling's waiting-gall, one of the blackest nigger wenches in Georgia, who at that interestin crisis, rolled her eyes upon him like two peeled onions, and throwin her arms around his neck, exclaimed—

"Shore dis is my husband, what Miss Netty done give me her own self."

Sich a shout as the boys did raise!

"Go to the devil, you black —— " screamed Doolittle, tryin to take her arms from his neck."

"Hold on to him, Silla," shouted all the fellers, "he's your husband according to law."

Old Squire Rogers looked like he'd married his last couple, pore old man, and hadn't a word to say for himself. The boys and the young Darlings liked to laugh themselves to death, while old Mr. Darling

"—— and throwin her arms around his neck, exclaimed—"

p. 220.

who was mad as a hornit, was gwine to have Doolittle arrested for nigger stealin, right off.

Pore Doolittle! He made out at last to git loose from his wife, and to find the back door. He haint never been heard of in Pineville from that day to this.

FLYING NELLY;

OR,

HOW COUSIN PETE GOT CURED OF HORSE RACING.

I DON'T believe ther ever was sich a bominable fool about horses as Cousin Pete used to be. You know ther's some people what don't know anything else but horse-knowledge, and don't know any other kind of history but horse-history. Well, that's jest the way with Cousin Pete. Uncle Josh sent him down to Augusty to the Medical College, to try to make a doctor of him. But it was all no use. When he come back the only kind of anatomy he know'd anything about was to tell the good pints in a horse, and his fisiology only enabled him to tell one horse from another. He was a monstrous sight nearer a horse-doctor than a man-doctor, and understood curin the distemper, the bots and sich horse ailments a great deal better than he did prescribin for the fever 'n ager. He never would read any other book but the Turf Register, and didn't take no other paper but the Spirit of the Times, and when he went to see the galls all he had to talk about was horses, and if he could get 'em to listen to him, he'd give 'em the peddygrees of all the great race-horses in the country, from ther dams clear back to ther everlastin great, great, great, great grand-dams.

He always had two or three of Uncle Josh's horses in trainin, and every now and then he was tradin one of 'em off for a racer to some Yankee pedler or other, when he never missed gettin cheated all to pieces. Uncle Josh used to kick up a muss about his horse trades sometimes, but Pete was determined to have a "crack nag" as he called 'em, and every man what passed through town with a horse was shore to get a banter for a trade, if his creeter had any pints about him, which Pete was always the first one to discover.

One day, shore enough, he jumped up a real full-blooded Eclipse, a regular "crack nag." The man was takin her to New Orleans and didn't want to part with her as he was gwine to enter her for the great fall sweepstakes. He had a Spirit of the Times with a full description of Flyin Nelly in it, her age and a great long peddygree, what Pete understood as soon as he read it. Flyin Nelly was jest the thing he'd been lookin for, and he was bound to own her if it cost all the money and horses he could raise. One of Uncle Josh's best horses and three hundred dollars in cash, was the man's lowest notch, and Pete closed the bargain. The man left Pineville the next day, and Pete was the owner of Flyin Nelly, a real Eclipse racer, with a string of dams long enough to dam all the horse-flesh in Christendom. He was so completely tuck up with his bargain that he didn't talk of nothin else but his thorough-bred, crack nag, for more'n a month, and two or three times a day Old Saul had to carry Flyin Nelly all around town to exercise her. Pete had two or three of Aunt Mahaly's best blankets and sheets cut up to make kivers for his racer, and, you may depend, Flyin Nelly cut a swell around Pineville, kivered all over up to the very ears, and its eyes lookin out through two holes bound round with red flannel.

Everybody was quizin Pete about his racer, but he didn't care much what most of 'em sed, because he know'd they wasn't no judge of horses.

"What upon yeath is you gwine to do with that creeter, Doctor?" ses Mr. Mountgomery to Pete one day.

"Why, Mr. Mountgomery," ses Pete, "that's one of the finest blooded horses in all Georgy—a real genewine Eclipse, by a Timoleon colt, whose dam was a —"

"Well, well," ses the old gentleman, "what of all that? what's the animal good for, Doctor, that's the question?"

"Why, she's—I can tell you—she can beat any horse in Georgy!"

"At what?" axed Mr. Mountgomery.

"Runin mile heats," ses Pete.

"Well, what's heats good for?" ses the old man.

"Why," ses Pete, "to show the blood of the horse."

"Well, what's the good of her blood, if she aint good for nothing but to run heats?"

"A heap of good," ses Pete. "The fact is, Mr. Mountgomery, I see you don't know much about horses. 'Spose, now, I was to have a patient three miles in the country, what was gwine to die if I didn't git to him in ten minits—wouldn't my racer be worth something then?"

"Indeed I don't think it or its master either would be worth much to a man in that situation," ses Mr. Mountgomery. "One would do him about as much good as the other, if you fool away so much of your time with horses instead of studyin your profession. This keepin of race horses is a monstrous pore bisness, Doctor Jones. I have always considered horse-racin more demoralisin to the characters of men than it is improvin to the blood of horses; and whenever I see a young man gettin sich foolish notions into his head, I can't help but think of a piece of poetry about a horse-racer, what I read in a newspaper when I was a boy:

'John ran so long, and ran so fast,
No wonder he ran out at last;
He ran in debt, and then, to pay,
He distanced all and ran away.'

If you'll take my advice, doctor, you'll—"

But Pete was so oudaceous mad that he didn't stop to hear the old man out. Away he went down to Mr. Harley's store, whar ther was a lot of the boys lookin at Flyin Nelly what Saul was leadin about in her blanket.

"Do you call that a race horse?" ax'd Bob Moreland.

"A genewine Eclipse," ses Cousin Pete—"jest a leetle bit ahead of anything in these parts."

"Well, I can tell you what, doctor, I think you is most bominably tuck in in that critter, if you bought her for a racer," ses one.

"It looks to me like it haint had a good feed of corn in a month," ses another.

"I wouldn't give my mule Blaze not for two sich tackeys as that," ses Billy Wilder.

"I'll bet old Ball can beat it to death," ses Bob Moreland. "It aint no racer."

"Maby you'd like to bet something," ses Cousin Pete, lookin as wise as if he was feelin somebody's pulse.

"I don't care about bettin much, but I'll go you a few bits that I can beat your racer with any creeter standin at that rack yonder," ses Bob.

By this time Cousin Pete begun to git monstrous hot.

"I'll bet you five hundred dollars," ses he, "that ther aint no piece of horseflesh in the county that can beat my mare, and if any of you want to back yer judgment agin her, there's a chance for you," ses he.

"Why, doctor," ses Tom Stallins, "I can beat that thing of your'n myself, with my boots on."

"Ha! ha! ha!" ses Pete, tryin his best to laugh, mad as he was. "Well, that's the best thing yit."

"Well," ses Tom, "you was banterin for a race for your tackey in the blanket thar, and I've offered you a chance. If you want to back out you kin do so."

"Oh, yes," ses all of 'em, "it's a clean back out."

"Take home yer Flyin Nellie, Saul, and save her feelins," ses Bob Moreland.

"Well, gentlemen," ses Pete, "if you really want to make a race, I'm your man, and I'll bet you what you please, from five dollars up, agin anything you can bring, any distance, any time, any way, and any whar. Now let's see who'll back out."

"Nuff sed, doctor!" ses Tom Stallins, "I take that banter myself. Now, jest peel your creeter, and trot her up here, if you want to see her beat clean out of countenance."

"But," ses Pete, takin out his pocketbook, "you must understand, gentlemen, I don't run my mare for nothin. How much is the stakes?"

"I don't want to win yer money," ses Tom, "but I'll go a dollar or two to make it interestin."

"Well," ses Pete, "the more you bet the more interestin to me. Put up yer money, gentlemen, and you can have yer fun at yer own expense."

"Stand up to him, Tom," ses all of 'em, "we'll back you."

"Twenty dollars," ses Pete, "on Flyin Nelly agin any horse, mare, or geldin!"

"Mule or man?" ses Tom.

"Yes," ses Pete. "Put up yer money and name your distance."

"Good," ses Tom. "Here comes Mr. Mountgomery. Let him hold the stakes."

"All right," ses Pete. "Now whar's yer nag?"

"Here's yer mule!" ses Tom, slappin himself on his breast.

"What!" ses Pete, lookin at Tom as scornful as he could, "is you a fool, Tom Stallins?"

"I tuck you at your own banter," ses Tom. "Thar's the twenty dollars, and now I'm gwine to beat yer Flyin Nelly myself, a single heat of five hundred yards, two hundred and fifty yards and double.

"That's fair, that's fair, docter," ses all of 'em.

"You said any horse, mare, geldin, mule, or man, yer know."

"But I didn't say jackass," ses Pete.

Tom thought that remark was a leetle personal, and for a minit the prospect looked about as good for a fight as a horse-race. But the fellers was all high up for the race, and they soon talked Tom out of gettin mad.

"Never mind, Tom," ses Bob Moreland, "we'll see who's the jackass when the race is over."

By this time the horse-race had got noised all over Pineville, and everybody come out to see the fun. Pete seed thar was no way for him to git out of the scrape. So the money was put up and the terms of the race all fixed. A stake was to be druv in the ground two hundred and fifty yards down the road—they was to start at the word "Go," run to the stake and pass round it, and the one what got back to the startin pint first was to take the money. Pete told old Saul to go and take the blanket off of Flyin Nelly and put her saddle on, and Tom shucked off his coat and jacket and shoes, and tied a hankerchief round his waist. While Pete and Tom was gettin ready, Bob Moreland and Billy Wilder stepped off the ground and druv down the stake.

The excitement was gettin greater and greater all the time. All the men and boys in town was on the ground, and the wimmin and children at the doors and winders to see the race. Everybody wanted to bet. Pete was bettin three to one on Flyin Nelly whenever he could git anybody to take his bets, and some of his friends, who laughed at the idee of Tom

Stallins runnin agin a full-blooded Eclipse racer, was given all sorts of odds and takin all the bets they could git. Even the niggers wanted to bet, but all except some old fool niggers, what didn't know no better, wanted to bet on Flyin Nelly.

When everything was all ready, and Cousin Pete was mounted, Bob Moreland told everybody to clear the track, and called the racers up to the judge's stand to hear the charge.

"Now, gentlemen," ses he, "ther aint to be no hunkerslidin nor jockeyin in this business. It's to be a fair race and the one that beats is to take the money and treat the crowd. This line here is the startin pint. You are to start at the word "Go," and run to that stake, and go round it, and the one that gits back to the startin place first wins the stakes. Now, you all understand?"

"Yes," ses both of 'em.

Flyin Nelly was very fractious, so Cousin Pete could hardly manage her, and Tom reared and cavorted about so Billy Wilder had to hold him till they both came up to the scratch together.

"Go!" ses Bob, and away went Tom like a shot off of a shovel, the crowd yellin and shoutin as if the old Harry was broke loose. Flyin Nelly squat like she was skeered, and then made three or four jumps before she know'd which way she was gwine, and by the time Pete got her started Tom was a long ways ahead.

"Hurra! Go it, Tom!" shouted the crowd.

But Pete laid on the whip—Flying Nelly come down to her work—and before Tom was much more'n half way to the post, the mare was ahead.

"Thar she goes! Hurra for Flyin Nelly!" shouted her backers.

"Pull up, Tom! Spread yourself, old feller," yelled his friends.

Pete was excited, and gin Nelly the rein and whip, and on she went, at a full run, 'way beyond the post; while Tom reached it with one hand, swung round it, and come streakin it back like a quarter horse.

"Hurra, Tom! now's yer time. Go it, old feller!"

While Tom was on the home stretch, Flyin Nelly was makin good time the other way. The excitement was at a terrible pitch.

"Hold in, Doctor! Stop her! Whar upon yeath is you gwine?"

But Flyin Nelly had too much headway, and was too hard in the mouth for Pete, and before he got her turned round, Tom was more'n half way back, and by the time the mare was fairly started on the back track, Tom Stallins, with a loud horse neigh, jumped over the line.

Sich another yell as the crowd sot up was never heard in Pineville. But Flyin Nelly was down to her work agin. Pete was so blind mad that he didn't seem to see nobody. He jest cussed and laid on the whip, and away flew Flyin Nelly right through the crowd. Down the street she went a tearin, Pete pullin and sawin at the reins—round Uncle Josh's house, with half a dozen dogs barkin at her heels, through the horse-lot, settin the ducks and geese a squallin and flyin in every direction—and never stopped til she fetched up agin the garden fence.

"Pete was excited, and gin Nelly the rein and whip, and on she went, at a full run, 'way beyond the post; while Tom reached it with one hand, swung round it, and come streakin it back like a quarter horse."

p. 230.

Lucky Pete wasn't hurt, but he was so mad that he was almost beside himself. He told Saul to take Flyin Nelly to the stable, and when he come back with his friends what had gone to look after him, he was the sorryest lookin man on the ground. He didn't make no dispute about givin up the stakes, but he sed he was completely disgusted, and cussed himself for disgracin his mare in sich a race.

Tom Stallins was shakin hands with all the boys and strutin round as proud as a peacock, and when Bob Moreland made his speech and handed him the money, he turned round to Pete, and ses he, "Cousin Pete, who is the jackass now?"—and then he axed the crowd to come down to the grocery and take some peach and honey.

Cousin Pete tried to take his defeat as good-naturedly as possible, but he was terrible sore about that horse race for a long time. Mr. Mountgomery told him that it was a good lesson to him, and that it ought to satisfy him that he'd never make a fortin at horse racin. Uncle Josh and Aunt Mahaly's lectures, and the ridicule of the boys, helped him to come to that conclusion himself. Flyin Nelly was sent out to the plantation with the other stock, and Pete was never afterwards known to have anything to do or say about throroughbred horses and "crack nags."

SOLD AT THE FAIR;

OR,

THE WAY BILL HICKSON COME TO BE A OLD BACHELLOR.

MR. SHAKSPEARE says ther's a tide in the affairs of men which when it is taken at the flood leads on to fortune, but which if it catches a feller in the ebb plays the mischief with his calculations. Well, Mr. Shakspeare was a filosifer and know'd a heap about human natur, and I wouldn't be afraid to venture something, if I was a bettin man, that ther aint a real hopeless, confirmed old bachellor in the world what haint experienced the truth of his remarks on the tide. Ther aint one of 'em but what can look back and pint out the very time he missed the flood, and can tell you the very circumstance that knocked all his fat in the fire. The catastrofy of Bill Hickson's love affair was a very remarkable one, and I must tell my readers about it.

Ther was a grate excitement in Pineville. The ladys was gwine to have a fair to raise money to build a new church. It was the first thing of the kind that ever tuck place in Pineville, and of course it caused a grate sensation. For more'n a month all the galls in town had been busy with ther needles, and the niggers was to be seen runin from house to house, with patterns and little bundles of things, and all the remnants of silks and little pieces of ribbons had been bought out of the stores to make fineries for the fair. The whole business was under the management of old Mrs. Rogers, who made it a pint to keep everything as secret as possible, till the night when the fair was to be opened to the public. Some of the boys was monstrously put too to make out what the fair meant, but it was generally understood that it was to be a very splendid affair, and everybody was to pay half a dollar to go in, and no gentleman wasn't expected to come to it without bringin a lady with him and a pocket full of money.

At length the auspicious night ariv, and the fair, with all its brilliant display of fancy fixins, bust upon the astonished Pinevillians. The old church was all in a blaze of taller candles. The walls was hung round with green bushes and flowers, and on little tables, all round the room, was all sorts of fineries and gigamarees, more'n anybody know'd what to do with. At every table was a young lady dressed as killin as she could be, so that nobody couldn't refuse to buy anything she offered 'em without ever thinkin of the price. Everybody in town was thar, and the prettyest galls had jest as much as they could do to wait on the gentlemen, sellin 'em everything, from a pair of baby-stockins to a cup of coffee, sweeten'd with ther own fingers, or a love letter from ther sweethearts, what they had in a little post-office in one corner of the room.

Bill Hickson was thar of course splurgin round with Jenny Turner, buyin everything for her that she tuck a fancy to. Bill was one of the stingyest fellers in the world, and was jest the man to sell his heart for a plantation and niggers, and as old Mrs. Turner was rich as cream, he was dead set after her daughter Jenny. All the galls in town know'd how Bill had courted all the rich galls in the county, and they hadn't much mercy on him in the price, whenever Jenny wanted him to buy anything at their tables. It was like pullin Bill's eye teeth every time they got a dollar out of him, but he couldn't help himself, and that was the only revenge they could have on him.

Jenny had a good deal more dollars than she had sense, and was jest vain and silly enough to make Bill buy all the baby toys ther was in the room, and by the time the fair was near over she had drained his pockets of his last dollar. It went monstrous hard with him, and he cussed the fair in his heart; but ther was no sich thing as backin out, if he expected to git Jenny's fortin, which was the main chance with him.

It was gettin most one o'clock, and most of the things was sold, when Bill allowed they mought as well go home, but Jenny wanted to see it out. Jest then old Mr. Mountgomery went up into the pulpit and told the company, that on the part of the ladys who had given the fair, he thanked them very much for ther liberal patronage, and as ther was a few things left he would offer 'em at auction to close the consarn. He sed he hoped the gentlemen would stay and bid for the articles.

All the plunder was gathered up from the tables

and carried to the old gentleman, who begun cryin 'em off to the crowd what gathered round the pulpit, every gall holdin a gentlemen by the arm to make 'em bid for the things they tuck a fancy to.

Bill stuck monstrous close to Miss Jenny, for fear some other chap mought git to buy something for her, or, what would be worse, go home with her.

Mr. Mountgomery went on cryin off doll-babys, and pin-cushions, and work-bags, and watch-papers, and baby-clothes, and all sorts of things, till bimeby he come to a basket what tuck Miss Jenny's fancy monstrous.

"Ah, ladys and gentlemen," ses Mr. Mountgomery, "here's a gem! How much for this beautiful christal basket? Jest look at it," ses he, holdin it up to the light, what made it shine like diamonds in all the colors of the rainbow.

"Oh, my!" ses Jenny, "what a beautiful thing! Now, you *must* buy that for me, Mr. Hickson."

"Jest look at it, ladys and gentlemen," ses Mr. Mountgomery.

"Oh, dear!" ses Jenny. "Won't you buy it for me, Mr. Hickson?"

"To be sure, I will," ses Bill.

"How much for this beautiful christal basket?" ses Mr. Mountgomery.

Before anybody had time to bid for it, Sally Dawson, the prettyest gall in the room, who had been standin with her mother near enough to Jenny to hear what she sed, run up to Tom Culpepper and tuck hold of his arm and whispered something to him.

"One dollar!" ses Tom.

Jenny pinched Bill's arm.

"One dollar, I'm offered for this beautiful basket," ses Mr. Mountgomery. "One dollar—one—"

"One dollar and a quarter," ses Bill.

"One dollar and twenty-five cents—one dollar and twenty-fi—"

"Two dollars," ses Tom.

"Two dollars—two dolllars—"

"Two twenty-five," ses Bill.

"Three dollars," ses Tom.

"Three—three—"

"Twenty-five," ses Bill.

"Four dollars," ses Tom.

"Four dollars—four dollars!" ses Mr. Mountgomery, holdin up the basket and lookin right at Bill.

"Five dollars," ses he, in a husky sort of voice.

"Six dollars," ses Tom.

"Six dollars—six—six," ses Mr. Mountgomery.

Bill looked kind of implorinly at Jenny.

"Oh," ses she, "I wouldn't begrudge any thing in the world for that beautiful basket."

"Is you all done at six dollars?" ses Mr. Mountgomery.

"Six and a quarter," ses Bill, with jest breath enough to make himself heard.

"Seven dollars," ses Tom, bold as a brigadier, with Sally Dawson hold of his arm, and lookin up into his face with her beautiful bright eyes.

"Seven dollars—seven dollars—gwine at seven dollars," ses Mr. Mountgomery, lookin round to Bill and holdin up his hand and his breath at the same time.

Bill giv Jenny another look.

"Seven—seven—gwine at seven dollars—"

Jenny nudged Bill, keepin her eyes fixed on the basket.

"And a quarter," gasped Bill.

"Seven and a quarter, jest in time," ses Mr. Mountgomery.

"Eight dollars," ses Tom.

By this time everybody was beginnin to laugh and buz to one another about the contest between Bill and Tom, so Mr. Mountgomery had to speak very loud.

"Eight dollars!—eight dollars!—gwine at eight dollars!" ses he, lookin right at Bill.

The sweat was beginnin to start out of Bill's face in a stream—his eyes was sot in his head, and he chaw'd his tobacker like he didn't know what he was doin. He was too far gone to speak—but Jenny giv him a nudge, and he noded his head at Mr. Mountgomery.

"And a quarter," ses the old man.

"Nine dollars," ses Tom.

"Nine—nine—nine!" ses Mr. Mountgomery, lookin at Bill—"gwine at—"

Bill noded agin,

"And a quarter—"

"Ten," ses Tom.

"Ten—ten—ten dollars—"

Bill noded agin.

"'Leven dollars," ses Tom.

Bill noded agin, while Jenny supported him to keep him from drapin on the floor.

"Twelve dollars," ses his opponent.

By this time Bill was so far gone that he jest kep nodin all the time, without knowin whose bid it was, or hearin a word that was sed.

"Thirteen," ses Tom.

"Thirteen—thirteen— "

"Fourteen!"

"Fifteen!"

"Sixteen!"

By this time the laughin was so loud that nobody couldn't hear nothin, and Mr. Mountgomery knocked off the christal basket to Mr. William Hickson for sixteen dollars.

Then they all got round Bill, congratulatin him for his spunk, and Tom Culpepper said he giv him joy with his bargin.

Mr. Mountgomery sed the gentlemen could call in the mornin for ther purchases, when the ladys would have their bills ready for 'em, and the fair broke up. Jenny went home with her little brother, tickled to death with her triumph over Sally Dawson, and Bill went home by himself, cussin the fair, the christal basket and Tom Culpepper, from the bottom of his heart.

When Bill got home he counted up the damage, and when he found out that he was out more'n thirty dollars, he wasn't able to sleep a wink all night.

He didn't have no appetite for his breckfast, and as soon as it was time he went to see Mrs. Rogers. He found his basket ready for him with his bill for sixteen dollars in it. He looked at it awhile and breathed monstrous hard.

"Don't you think that's a little too digin, Mrs. Rogers, to make me pay sixteen dollars for a basket what aint no bigger than my fist."

"Well," ses she, "bein as you was sich a liberal patron of the fair, Mr. Hickson, I think we *ought* to make a deduction. We'll receit the bill for ten dollars."

"My conscience!" ses Bill, "couldn't you take off more'n that, Mrs. Rogers? I'll give you five dollars and say quits."

"Very well," ses she, "if you insist on it, Mr. Hickson.

So the bill was receited, and the basket with the bill for the full price, was sent home that afternoon "to Miss Jenny Turner, with the compliments of her friend, William Hickson." But what was his mortification, when the nigger brung it back to him with the followin letter from Miss Jenny's mother:

"*To Mr. William Hickson:*

"SIR:—This is to inform you, sir, that I don't allow my daughter to receive no presents from no young gentlemen whatsumever, bein as I think it's highly improper. And furthermore, Mr. Hickson, I think it is a very ridiculous shame for anybody to go and giv sixteen dollars for a basket made out allum and cotton-yarn, what aint worth a cent no how, and didn't cost a thing to make it. Sich kind of extravagance aint gwine to git no child of mine, so no more from

"Your very respectful

"NANCY TURNER."

Bill was terribly tuck aback. The very thing

what he thought was gwine to make his fortin had knocked the whole business in the head. To explain to Jenny's mother how he only giv five dollars for the cussed basket, if it made matters any better with the old woman, would only make 'em worse with the gall, who had been all over town braggin to the other galls how he paid sixteen dollars for it jest for her. But when he found out that the whole thing was a trick played off on him by Tom Culpepper and Sally Dawson, who put Jenny Turner up to beg him to buy the basket for her, and how Sally made it herself, and didn't want it no how, and how all the galls was laughin at him for beggin off from the price, and then sendin the full bill home with it, he cum monstrous nigh hangin himself for shame.

The way Bill Hickson was sold at the fair was the town-talk for more'n a month, and everybody enjoyed the joke but Bill, who said it was a ding'd mean trick. It completely cured him of courtin rich galls, and as he had always held his head above the pore ones, they now turned up their noses at him, and he couldn't find a gall in a day's ride of Pineville that would have any thing to do with him. Is it any wonder, then, that Bill Hickson remained a old bacheler the balance of his days?

"In about a minit here come Fanny with a mahogany box in her hands."

p. 241.

THE MYSTERIOUS BOX;

OR,

HOW THE STEAM DOCTOR LIKED TO GIT BLOWED UP WITH A INFERNAL MACHINE.

It was about half-past seven o'clock, and terrible dark—jest the kind of night for doin a diabolical deed. The family of Gabriel Pepper, the steam doctor, was settin round the tea table, enjoyin ther supper and never dreamin what was gwine to happen. Mrs. Pepper was axin Mr. Brown if his tea was to suit him, and makin apologies to Miss Patience Pepper, her husband's maiden aunt, about the cake bein heavy; the galls was a gabblin to one another, and Dr. Pepper was tellin little Jimmy how he mustn't eat no more cake to make him sick agin.

Everything was gwine on in a harmonious, sociable way, when all of a sudden ther was a loud knock at the door. Thinkin nothing of that all went on eatin and talkin to one another, while Fanny, the servant gall, went to see who was at the door.

In about a minit here come Fanny back into the room, with her mouth wide open and her eyes startin out of her head, and a mahogany box in her hands, which she held out before her by the brass handles on each eend, as far from her as she could.

"Oh! my goodness gracious! Take it, Massa Gable, quick, fore I let it drap," ses Fanny, lookin like she was gwine to faint, shore enough.

If a dead ghost, with its own coffin in its arms, had come right into the room it couldn't have made a worse panic among the Peppers. Every one seem'd to be instantly putrified with horror. Them that had ther mouths open hadn't time to shut 'em, and them that had ther mouths shut seemed to have the lock-jaw simultaneously. Miss Patience made out to git both her hands up, and as her mouth was open the cake she was eatin jest naturally drapped onto her plate. Miss Susan Pepper was the first to scream, and that seemed to relieve 'em all a little, for the next instant the whole party exclaimed:

"What upon earth is that?"

Everybody jumped up from the table at once.

"Name o' sense!" ses Dr. Pepper, "what does this mean?"

"Whar did you git that box, Fanny?" axed Mrs. Pepper, upsettin the tea-pot onto Mr. Brown's legs in her excitement. But Mr. Brown was so scared that he never felt it.

"Take it out, Fanny! Don't touch it, for your lives!" ses Miss Patience, as she grabed Dr. Pepper's coat tail.

"Ugh, ugh!" groaned Fanny, as she sot it down in the middle of the floor, and run into the corner.

It was a mahogany box, about three feet long by eighteen inches wide and six deep. It was varnished as bright as a dollar, and had a key stickin in the lock. Nobody dared to go near it.

"Whar did you git that box, Fanny?" ses all of 'em.

Fanny told how she went to the door to see who was a knockin, and how a man was standin on the steps with the box in his hands, and how he told her to take it to Dr. Pepper, and to be careful how she handled it; and how, as soon as he put it into her hands, he went off as fast as he could.

"What kind of a lookin man was he?" axed Dr. Pepper.

"I don't know," ses Fanny, "only he had on a cloak, and a cap way down over his eyes."

"Are you shore it was a real man?" axed Miss Patience, lookin very mysterious.

"Didn't he say what was in it?" ses Dr. Pepper.

"No; he jest told me to take it to you, and be careful not to let it fall."

"Oh, Pepper! Pepper!" sed Miss Patience, lookin more mysterious than ever. "Is it possible that you, a man of family—oh, for shame, Pepper!"

Pepper looked wild as buck rabbit.

Mrs. Pepper begun to feel more and more interested, after the remark of Miss Patience.

"What in the name of sense *can* it mean?" ses she.

"Listen," ses Miss Patience, "if you can hear any thing move in it."

"I'll soon see what's inside of that box," ses Pepper, gittin sort o' desperate at his aunt's insinuations.

And with that he went up to it, and was jest gwine to take hold of the lock, when Mr. Brown tuck hold of his arm and told him to stop.

"Stop, Pepper," ses he, "don't be so rash. How do you know but what it's a infernal machine, sent here by some of your enemys to blow up your whole family?"

"My lord!" gasped Miss Patience, as she backed into the farthest corner of the room, and all the rest of the wimmen tried to git behind her.

—"Sich things is gittin very common now-a-days," sed Mr. Brown. "A whole family was killed by one tother day in France, and jest as like as not some of your enemys has laid a scheme to blow you up and your whole family."

"Oh, goodness gracious!" ses all of 'em at once.

Little Jimmy, thinkin something terrible was gwine to happen, grab'd hold of his mammy's skirt and sot up a squall like forty thousand cats. Pepper's eyes showed the white all round 'em, and Mrs. Pepper put her arm round him and pulled him further away from the box.

"Who could do sich a thing, my dear?" she axed.

It was impossible to tell that; ther was no knowin what wicked men mought do; and it was very certain that the medical doctors was very hostile to the botanicals; and who could tell but this was a plan of the medicals to blow up the man what they couldn't put down no other way.

Mr. Brown's diabolical idee seemed to take possession of the minds of the whole party, and though Pepper felt relieved in one respect, he was still in a terrible perplexity what to do with the box. He had a great mind to call in the police or some of his neighbors, but as he wasn't exactly certain what *mought* be inside of the thing, he didn't wish to run the risk of making himself ridiculous. For his own part he would been perfectly willin to let the matter drap whar it was for the present; but the wimmin was dyin to know what was in that box, and he know'd they wouldn't rest till it was opened somehow or other.

Brown was a brave man under ordinary circumstances. He come monstrous nigh volunteerin to go to Mexico as a quarter-master's clerk, before he fell in love with Miss Susan Pepper, but he had a mortal aversion to bein blow'd up by a infernal machine. If it wasn't for that he'd open the box in a minit. Pepper himself ventured to touch it with his cane, but the thing had sich a combustible look about it, and sich a decided gun-powder smell, that the ladys wouldn't consent that either of the gentlemen should risk ther precious lives by openin it with the key tied to the eend of a pole ten feet long. After consultin a long time about it, it was finally agreed that Fanny should take it up careful and carry it out in the back yard and set it down on the ground, and then they would throw rocks on it from the upper story winders, and then if it went off it couldn't hurt nobody.

Accordingly, with fear and tremblin, pore Fanny tuck up the box, and carried it out doors and sot it in the right place, with a candle on the back porch so they could see it. Then, after all the family was safe into the second story, the winder was histed, and Mr. Brown made the first heave with a big rock weighin about twenty pounds. Whang went the rock, and in dodged Brown's head like a snappin-turtle's. They all held their breath for the terrible explosion—but the box wasn't touched. After three or four trials he hit the box and smashed it into forty thousand flinders, but no explosion followed.

After waitin till they was satisfied ther was no danger of the thing goin off, they all run down stairs to see what was in the box shore enough.

The box was smashed to pieces, and the mahogany strewed in every direction. And horrible to relate—thar on the ground, in the midst of the wreck, laid a beautiful—yes, reader, a beautiful little white billy-dux. With trembling hands Dr. Pepper tuck it up, opened it, and read as follows:

"*Dr. Pepper:*

"DEAR SIR—That medicine what you give me for my old woman done the business first rate, and I want you to send me the medicine what I spoke to you about tother day. I've had this medicine chest fixed up for the purpose, and I want you to send me some of your medicines for all kinds of ailments, in separate vials, with the names of the diseases rit on 'em, so I won't make no mistake. Put in a box of life linament, as Peter's got the rumatiz dreadful, and I'll send you a jug for the number six to-morrow. The baby didn't take the lobelia no how, but I reckon we got enough down it with a spoon to stop its simptems. It's looked terrible blue round the mouth ever sense. But it don't seem so frisky and restless sense we give it the last steamin. Betsey ses she wishes you would come and see it in the mornin.

"Very respectfully,

"JOHN DOSER."

"Well, now," ses Pepper, drapin the letter on the ground, and getin as red in the face as a pepper pod, "if that aint a devlish nice piece of bisness!"

The wimmen was greatly relieved by the demolishin of Mr. Doser's medicine chest. Brown didn't have another word to say about infernal machines, and Pepper's mind was tuck up for the balance of the night planin out how he should meet his patient in the mornin, and how he should explain the catastrofy to him.

The fact is, Doser never ought to put his letter inside of his medicine chest.

INTO A HORNET'S NEST;

OR,

HOW ABSOLEM NIPPERS COME TO LEAVE THE SETTLEMENT.

Absolem Nippers was a widower, and one of the perticklerest men perhaps that ever lived, though some people sed that when his wife was alive he used to dress as common as a field hand, and didn't use to take no pains with himself at all. In his own settlement he had a monstrous bad name, specially among wimmin, who used to say that he didn't allow his wife more'n one dress a year, and as for a new shawl or bonnet, the pore woman didn't know nothin about sich things. Everybody noticed how he spruced up about three weeks after Mrs. Nippers died, and how he went to church regular every Sunday; but they didn't have no confidence in his religion, and used to say that he only went to show his new suit of mournin, and to ogle the galls. Old Mrs. Rogers hated him like pisen, and sed she didn't wonder his pore wife died broken-hearted; and as for his pretendin to be sorry about it, that was all sham, for she could see plain enough at the funeral that he had one eye in the grave and the other on the galls that was thar, tryin to pick one of 'em out for his second wife.

With sich a reputation among the wimmin, it

aint to be supposed that he stood any sort of a chance of gettin another Mrs. Nippers near home, and whether he was as bad to his first wife as they sed he was, or not, one thing was certain, he had to look abroad for some one to fill her place.

Mr. Nippers was very lucky in findin a gall jest to his mind, what lived in Hardscrabble district, about seven miles from his plantation. Judy Parker was tolerable well off, and though she wasn't very young nor very handsome, she belonged to Mr. Nippers's church, was a industrious, economical woman, and filled his eye exactly; so he sot to courtin her with all his might.

Seven miles was a good long ride, and as he was a very economical man, he used to ride over to old Mrs. Parker's plantation every Sunday mornin, go to church with the family, take dinner with 'em, court Miss Judy in the afternoon, and ride home in the cool of the evenin. In that way he managed to kill two birds with one stone, that is, to advance the prospects of his happiness on this earth, and in the world to come, at the same time, without losing any of the week-day from his business.

A ride of seven miles on horseback, on a hot Sunday mornin, on a dusty road, is monstrous apt to soil a gentleman's dry-goods, as well as to make himself and his horse very tired. Mr. Nippers didn't mind the fatigue so much as his horse, but in a matter sich as he had in hand, it was very necessary that he should make as good a appearance as possible; so he hit upon a plan by which he was able to present himself before the object of his affections in apple-pie order, with his new Sunday coat as clean, and his bloomin ruffles as fresh and neat as if they had jest come out of a band-box. This was a happy idee of Nippers, and one what nobody but a widower-lover would ever dreamed of. He used to start from home with his new coat and a clean shirt tied up in a pocket handkerchef, and after ridin within about a quarter of a mile of Mrs. Parkers's plantation, he would turn out into a thicket of chinkapin bushes, whar nobody couldn't see him, and thar make his toilet.

One bright Sunday mornin Mr. Nippers had ariv at his dressing-ground. It was a important occasion. Everything was promisin, and he had made up his mind to pop the question that very day. Ther was no doubt in his mind that he would return home a engaged man, and he was reckonin over to himself the value of Miss Judy's plantation and niggers, while he was settin on his horse, makin his change of dress.

He had draped the reins on the neck of his horse, what was browsin about, makin up for the last night's scanty feed from the bushes in his reach, and kickin and stompin at sich flies as was feedin on him in turn.

Mr. Nippers was sanguine and happy. "I'll fix the business this time," ses he to himself. "I'll bring things to the pint before I go home this night, or my name aint Nippers," ses he, as he untied the handkerchef with his clean clothes, and spread them out on the saddle-bow before him.

"Who, Ball!" ses he. "Ther's no use of foolin away any more time. I've only jest got to say the word, and—who!" says he to his horse, what was kickin and reachin about—"who! you dratted fool! —and the thing is fixed jest as slick as fallin off a log."

He was drawin his shirt over his head and had it most off, when old Ball giv a sudden spring what like to make him lose his balance.—"Who!" ses he—but before he could git his arms out of the sleeves, Ball was wheelin and kickin like wrath at something that seemed to trouble him from behind. Down went the clean clothes on the ground.—"Who! blast your infernal picter!" ses Nippers, drapin his shirt and grabin at the bridle reins. But before he could git hold of them, Ball was off like a streak of lightnin, with a whole swarm of yaller-jackets at his tail.

Nippers grab'd hold of his horse's mane, and tried his best to stop him, but he mought as well tried to stop a locomotive by pullin at the cow-catcher. Away went the infuriated Ball, and takin the road that he was used to travellin, another moment brung him to the house. The yard gate was open, and in dashed the horse with the almost naked Nippers hangin to his neck, hollerin "Stop him!—hornets! hornets!" as loud as he could scream.

Out come the dogs, and after Ball they went—round and round the house—scatterin the ducks and chickens, and terrifyin the little niggers out of their senses. The noise brung the wimmen to the door.

"Don't look, Miss Judy! Hornets!—Who, Ball! —Hornets!" shouted Nippers, hangin on to his horse's mane with both hands, as he went dashin out of the gate agin with the dogs still after him, and his tail switchin about in every direction like a harry-cane.

Miss Judy got but one glimps of her forlorn lover, and before she could git her apron to her eyes, she fainted at the awful sight, while his fast-receding voice, above the clamor of the dogs and niggers, crying "Hornets!—Who!—Stop him!—Hornets!—Hornets!—Hornets!" still rung in her ears.

She never seed her devoted Nippers agin. The Hardscrabble settlement was too full of hornets for him after that. He recovered his garments, but he hadn't the courage ever to look Miss Judy in the face after that luckless adventure.

"Stop him!—Hornets!—Hornets!" p. 252.

A NIGHT IN A GRAVE-YARD;

OR,

BILLY WILSON'S TERRIBLE ENCOUNTER WITH A GHOST.

About two years ago the people in Pineville was almost alarmed out of ther senses by a ghost what made its appearance every night in the grave-yard. The niggers seed it first, and they told sich terrible tales about it that the wimmen and children was afraid to go to bed in the dark for a month, and you couldn't git a nigger to go a hundred yards from the house after dark not for all Georgy. It made a monstrous talk for more'n ten miles round the settlement, and everybody was anxious to find out whose ghost it was, and what it wanted. Old Mr. Walker, what had been cheated out of all his property by the lawyers, hadn't been dead a great while, and as he was a monstrous curious old chap any how, the general opinion was that the old man had come back for something.

Sammy Stonestreet seed the ghost, and Bob Moreland seed it, and old Miss Curloo seed it, when she was comin to town to see her daughter Nancy, the night she had her baby, and they all gave the same account the niggers did, about its bein dressed in white, and talkin to itself, and cryin and walkin about among the toombstones. Bob Moreland said he heard it sneeze two or three times, jest as natural as any human, and cry ever so pitiful.

A good many of the boys sed they was gwine to watch for it some night and speak to it; but somehow their hearts always failed 'em about dark, and nobody didn't go.

One day Bill Wilson come to town, and was about half corned down to Mr. Harley's store, when the boys got to banterin him about the ghost.

"Ding'd if I don't see who it is," ses Bill; "I aint afraid of no ghost that ever walked on the face of the yeath."

With that some of 'em offered to bet him five dollars that he dassent go inside the grave-yard after dark.

"Done!" ses Bill, "jest plank up yer money. But I'm to go jest as I've a mind to?"

"Yes," ses the boys.

—"And shoot the ghost if I see it?" ses he.

"To be shore."

"And I'm to have a bottle of old Jimmaky, to keep me company?"

"Yes," ses all of 'em.

"Nuf sed," ses Bill. "Put up the stakes in Mr. Harley's hands.

The money was staked and the bisness all fixed in no time.

"Now," ses Bill, "giv me a pair of pistols and let me load 'em good myself, and I'll show you whether I'm afraid of ghosts."

Captain Skinner's big brass horse-pistols was sent

for, and Bill loaded one of 'em up to the muzzle, and after gettin a bottle of licker in his pocket, and takin two or three more good stout horns to raise his courage, he waited till it was dark. Everybody in town was wide awake to see how the thing would turn out, and some of the wimmin was monstrous consarned for Bill, for fear he'd git carried off by the ghost shore enough.

Jest about dark Bill sot out for the grave-yard, with a whole heap of fellers, who went to see him to the gate, so he couldn't give 'em no dodge.

"Look out now, Bill; you know ghosts is monstrous dangerous things to fool with. Keep yer eyes skined, Bill, or you're a goner," sed the boys as they was leavin him at the gate.

"Never you mind," ses Bill. "But remember, I'm to shoot, and—"

"To be shore," ses all of 'em.

Bill marched into the middle of the grave-yard, brave as a lyon, singin "Shiny night" as loud as he could—but monstrous out of tune—and tuck a seat on one of the grave-stones.

The grave-yard in Pineville stands on the side of a hill about half a mile from town. The fence is a monstrous high post and rail fence, and the lot is a tolerable big one, extendin a good ways down in the holler on tother side, whar ther is a pine thicket of about a acre, in which ther aint no graves.

The night was pretty dark, and Bill thought it was monstrous cold, so he kept takin drinks every now and then to keep himself warm, and singin all the songs and salm tunes he know'd to keep awake.

Sometimes he thought he heard something down in the bushes, and then his hair would sort o' crawl up, and he would hold his breath and grab hold of his pistol, what he held cocked in his lap, ready to shoot. But it was so dark that he could see nothin ten steps off. Two or three times he felt like backin out and goin home; but he know'd that wouldn't never do; so he'd take another drink and strike up another tune. Bimeby he got so sleepy that he couldn't tell whether he was singin "Up in a balloon, boys," or "I'm bound for the promised land;" and bimeby he only sung a word here and thar, without bein very pertickler what song it belonged to.

He was so bominable sleepy and corned together, that he couldn't keep awake, and in spite of his fears, he begun to nod a little.

Jest then something sneezed.

"Ugh!" ses Bill; "what's that?"

But he soon come to the conclusion that he must been sneezin in his sleep; and after seein that his pistol was safe and takin another drink, he was soon in the land of Nod agin.

About this time old Mr. Jenkins's gang of goats come out of the thicket, whar they had got through the gap in the grave-yard fence, and with old white Bellshazer in the lead, come smellin about whar Bill was watchin for the ghost.

Old Bellshazer is a monstrous big goat, and one of the oudaciousest old cusses to butt in all Georgy, and the old rascal, seein Bill settin thar all alone by himself, he goes up and smells at him. Bill noded to him in his sleep. The goat stepped back a step

"Bill noded to him in his sleep." p. 256.

or two and Bill noded agin. The old feller tuck it for a banter shore enough, and comin forward and raisin up on his hind legs a little, he tuck deliberate aim, and spang! he tuck Bill, right between the eyes, knockin him and his horse-pistol off at the same time.

Bang! goes the .pistol, roarin out on the still night air, like a young five-pounder, so everybody in town heard it, and the next minit you mought heard Bill hollerin "Murder! murder!" for more'n a mile.

The whole town was roused in no time, and everybody that could go was out to the grave-yard as quick as they could git thar.

Thar was Bill Wilson layin sprawled out on the ground, with his nose knocked as flat as a pancake, and both his eyes bunged up so he couldn't tell daylight from dark.

The goats was skeered as bad as Bill was at the pistol, and was gone before he fairly touched the ground. Bob Moreland and Tom Stallins, who had gone out to the grave-yard to skeer Bill, havin tuck care to change the pistol what he loaded for one that had no bullets in it, got thar jest in time to see his encounter with old Bellshazer. They was the first ones to git to him, but it was so dark and they was rapped up in white sheets so Bill didn't know 'em. The more they talked to him and shuck him, the louder he hollered till they thought he would go into a fit.

After a while he kind o' come to his senses. Somebody struck a light, and Bill seed whar he was. He swore he was wide awake all the time, and that when the ghost come up to him he tuck a fair crack at it, when all of a sudden a clap of thunder and lightnin knocked him clean out of his senses.

Bob Moreland tried to explain to him how it was. But it was all no use. He swore the ghost was six foot high, and that he smelled the brimstone and seed the lightnin jest as plain as he ever seed lightnin in his life.

The next day Bill claimed the stakes, and everybody said he ought to have the money, which was give up to him. But you may depend Bill Wilson wouldn't have sich another ghost-fight, not for all the money in Georgy.

The fence was mended whar it was broke in the thicket, and ther has never been any more ghosts seed in that grave-yard ever sense.

THE HOOSIER AND THE HARDSHELL;

OR,

HOW THE INDIANY DROVER SPOILED A SERMON ON LOTT'S WIFE.*

It is very refreshin in these days of progress, after rattlin over the country for days and nights, at the rate of twenty miles a ower in a railroad car—with your mouth full of dust and smoke, and with sich a everlastin clatter in your ears that you can't hear yourself think—to git into a good, old-fashioned stage-coach. Ther's something sociable and cosey in stage-coach travelin, so different from the bustle and confusion of a railroad, whar people are whirled along "slam bang to eternal smash," like they wer so many bales and boxes of dry-goods and groceries, without so much as a chance of seein whar they're gwine, or of takin any interest in ther feller sufferers. I love to hear the pop of the whip and the interestin conversation between the driver and his horses; and I like the constant variation in the motion of the stage, the rattle of the wheels over the stones, the stillness of the drag through the heavy sand, the lunging and pitching into the ruts and gullies, the slow pull

* This sketch was first published in the Baltimore *Western Continent* in 1848. Some four or five years afterward Carey & Hart issued a volume of humorous sketches by Danforth Marble, which contained the same sketch, slightly altered, under the title of "The Hoosier and the Salt Pile." In 1858 William E. Burton compiled his "Encyclopædia of Wit and Humor," published by D. Appleton & Co., giving "The Hoosier and the Salt Pile" as an extract, and the only one from Mr. Marble's book. I make this explanation simply that I may not be charged with appropriating what is not my own. W. T. T.

up the steep hills, the rush down agin, and the splashin of the horses' feet and the wheels in the water and mud. And then one has time to see the country he's passin through, to count the rails in the panels of the fences, and the wimen and children in the doors of the houses, to notice the appearance of the craps and the condition of the stock on the farms, and now and then to say a word to the people on the roadside. All these things is pleasant, after a long voyage on the railroad. But what's still more agreeable about stage-coach travelin, is that we have a oppertunity of makin the acquaintance of our feller passengers, of conversin with 'em and studdyin ther traits of character, which from the strikin contrast they often present, never fail to amuse if they don't interest our mind.

Some years ago I had a tolerably fair specimen of a stage-coach ride from Warrenton to Milledgeville. The road wasn't the best in the world, and didn't run through the most interestin part of Georgia, but we had a good team, a good stage, and a first-rate driver, what could sing like a camp-meetin and whistle like a locomotive, and the company was jest about as good a one as could be jumped up for sich a occasion. Ther was nine of us besides the driver, and I dont blieve ther ever was a crowd of the same number that presented a greater variety of characters. Ther was a old gentleman in black, with big round spectacles, and a gold headed cane; a dandy gambler, with a big dimond breast-pin and more gold chains hangin round him than would hang him; a old hardshell preacher, as they call 'em in Georgia, with the biggest mouth and the ugliest teeth I ever seed;

a circus clown, whose breath smelled strong enough of whiskey to upset the stage; a cross old maid, as ugly as a tar-bucket; a butiful young school-gall, with rosy cheeks and mischievous bright eyes; a cattle-drover from Indiany, who was gwine to New Orleans to git a army contract for beef, and myself.

For a while after we started from Warrenton nobody didn't have much to say. The young lady put her green vail over her face and leaned her head back in the corner; the old maid, after a row with the driver about her band-boxes, sot up straight in her seat and looked as sharp as a steel-trap; the old gentleman with the spectacles drummed his fingers on his cane and looked out of the coach-winder; the circus-man tried to look interestin; the gambler went to sleep; the preacher looked solemn, and the hoosier stuck his head out of the winder on his side to look at the cattle what we passed every now and then.

"This aint no great stock country," ses he to the old gentleman with the specs.

"No, sir," ses the old gentleman. "There's very little grazing here. The range in these parts is pretty much worn out."

Then ther was nothing said for some time. Bimeby the hoosier opened agin.

"It's the d—st place for 'simmon-trees and turkey-buzzards I ever did see."

The old gentleman didn't say nothin, and the preacher fetched a long groan. The young lady smiled through her vail, and the old maid snapped her eyes and looked sideways at the speaker.

"Don't make much beef down here, I reckon," ses the hoosier.

"No," ses the old gentleman.

"Well, I don't see how in the h—l they all manage to live in a country whar ther aint no ranges, and they don't make no beef. A man aint considered worth a cuss in Indiany what hasn't got his brand on a hundred head or so of cattle."

"Your's is a great beef country, I blieve," ses the old gentleman.

"Well, sir, it aint nothing else. A man that's got sense enough to foller his own cow-bell, with us, aint in no danger of starvin. I'm gwine down to Orleans to see if I cant git a contract out of Uncle Sam, to feed the boys what's been lickin them infernal Mexicans so bad. I spose you've seed them cussed lies what's been in the newspapers about the Indiany boys at Bona Vista?"

"I've read some accounts of the battle," ses the old gentleman, "that didn't give a very flattering account of the conduct of some of our troops."

With that, the Indiany man went into a full explanation of the affair, and gittin warmed up as he went along, begun to cuss and swear like he'd been through a dozen campaigns himself.

The old preacher listened to him with evident signs of displeasure, twistin and groanin every time he uttered a big oath, until he couldn't stand it no longer.

"My friend," ses he, "you must excuse me, but your conversation would be a great deal more interestin to me, and I'm sure it would please the company much better, if you wouldn't swear so terribly. It's very wicked to swear so, and I hope you'll have respect for our religious feelins, if you hain't got no respect for your Maker."

If the hoosier had been struck with a clap of thunder and lightning he couldn't been more completely tuck aback. He shut his mouth right in the middle of what he was sayin, and looked at the preacher, while his face got as red as fire.

"Swearin," continued the old hardshell, "is a terrible bad practice, and ther aint no use in it no how. The Bible says 'swear not at all,' and I spose you know the commandments about taking the Lord's name in vain."

The hoosier didn't open his mouth.

"I know," ses the old preacher, "a great many people swear without thinkin, and that some people don't blieve in the Bible."

And then he went on to preach a regular sermon agin, and to quote the Scripture like he knowed the whole Bible by heart. In the course of his argyments he undertook to prove the Scriptures to be true, and told us all about the miracles and prophecies and their fulfillment. The old gentleman with the cane tuck a part in the conversation, and the hoosier listened without ever once openin his head.

"I've jest heard of a gentleman," sed the preacher, "what has been to the Holy Land, and went all over the Bible country. It's astonishin what wonderful things he seed thar. He was at Soddom and Gomorrow, and seed the place whar Lot's wife fell!"

"Ah?" ses the old gentleman with the specs.

"Yes," ses the preacher. "He went to the very spot, and what's the most remarkablest thing of all, he seed the pillar of salt what she was turned into."

"Is it possible?" ses the old gentleman.

The hoosier's countenance all at once brightened up, and he opened his mouth wide.

"Yes, sir; he seed the salt standin thar to this day."

The hoosier's curiosity was raised to a pint beyond endurance.

"What!" ses he, "real genewine good salt?"

"Yes, sir, a pillar of salt jest as it was when that wicked woman was punished for her disobedience."

All but the gambler, who was snoozin in the corner of the coach, looked at the preacher—the hoosier with an expression of countenance that plainly told that his mind was powerfully convicted of a important fact.

"Standin right out in the open air?" he axed.

"Yes, sir,—right out in the open field where she fell."

"Well," ses the hoosier, "all I've got to say is, *if she'd drap'd in Indiany, the cattle would lick'd her up long ago!*"

The preacher raised both hands at sich a irreverent remark, and the old gentleman with the specs laughed himself into a fit of the asmetics what he didn't git over till we got to the next change of horses. The hoosier had played the mischief with the gravity of the whole party; even the old maid had to put her handkerchef up to her face, and the young lady's eyes was filled with tears for half a hour afterwards.

The old preacher looked very grum and hadn't another word to say on the subject, but whenever we come to any place or passed anybody on the road, the circus-man was certain to inquire the price of salt.

THE BABY'S GHOST;

OR,

HOW LITTLE TOMMY'S MOTHER BECOME RECONCILED.

I KNOW ther's a heap of people what don't blieve in ghosts, and I've seed the time when I didn't put much faith in 'em myself; but the followin circumstance, which tuck place in the famly of one of my nearest friends, convinced me that ther is, as Mr. Shakspear ses, "more things in heaven and earth than is dreamed of in our filosophy."

I don't wish to be understood as blievin in common ghost stories—not by no means. I don't blieve in no vagabone ghosts what go about hantin people's houses, makin noises, and rapin on tables, and cuttin up all sorts of foolish anticks. But I aint so certain that mortal attachments do not sometimes exist in sich strength, of sich a etherial natur, that death itself can't dissolve 'em, and that even after one of the persons is dead, his sperit can come back to this earth and hold communion with the object of his affections. If anybody who doubts my theory of ghosts axes me why no more husbands don't see the ghosts of ther dead wives, or more wives don't see ther dead husbands, my answer is that they aint always the best subjects for the illustration of my argyment. In order to preserve a spiritual intercourse sich as I speak of, the attachment must be of the strongest and purest natur, so that the livin feels unwillin to give up the dead, and longs and yearns to have 'em come back to 'em.

But I haint got room here to discuss my theory of ghosts. The circumstance what I'm about to relate, and which may be relied on for a positive fact, will explain my idee of sich things better than any essay what I could write.

Dick Ramsay and his wife Nancy was about as affectionate a couple as ever lived on the face of the earth. Nancy was an only daughter, and was a great pet in the famly before she was married. She was very handsome, and one of the sweetest, best natured creeters in the world, so that everybody loved her that know'd her; and when Dick Ramsay led her up before Squire Rogers to marry her, ther wasn't a young feller in the settlement what didn't feel like he couldn't help breakin the tenth commandment. Nancy was so much attached to her mother that she couldn't make up her mind to leave her for a long time, and it wasn't till after ther first child was two years old that Dick could git her consent to move onto the plantation. It was a great trial for Nancy to leave her home and go out and live on that lonesome plantation, but she know'd it was better for her husband's interests to be on the place, whar he could see to things himself, without trustin everything to a overseer, and she made up her mind to be happy with him and her boy, sense she couldn't expect always to be with her mother.

Dick was a first-rate farmer, and had everything comfortable about him, and Nancy was a smart, managin wife. She soon got satisfied with her new home, and devoted herself cheerfully to the care of her baby and the comfort of her husband. All went on pleasant enough for about six months, when her little boy tuck sick. It was his first sickness, and pore Nancy was most out of her senses. Her mother was sick at the same time, so she couldn't come out to the plantation to help her nurse the baby. Pore little Tommy got worse and worse in spite of all the doctor could do, and after sufferin for most a month, he died.

The shock was most too much for pore Nancy. For some time everybody thought she would go distracted, if she didn't foller her baby to the grave herself. For more'n a week she had to have the doctor with her, and when she got able to set up, she done nothin but cry all the time, and talk of her little boy. She would not blieve he was dead—she sed she could not give him up, and that she never could be satisfied till she seed him once more.

Her husband tuck the loss of his little son very hard too, but he tried to hide his feelins and done all he could to passify his wife, tellin her it was wrong to grieve so, and that little Tommy was a great deal better off in the good place whar he was gone to. He got the preacher to talk to her too; but it all seemed no use. She cried from mornin till night about her little Tommy that was dead.

It was 'way in September before she was able to be about much, and though Dick staid home with her all he could, he had to leave her sometimes to look after the niggers that was pickin out his cotton, and when he come home in the evening, he was shore to find her out in the orchard, whar little Tommy was buried under the trees, sometimes walkin up and down, ringin her hands, and sometimes sittin down on the grass by little Tommy's grave, cryin like her heart would brake.

It troubled Dick very much to see her take on so about the baby, but all he could do, he couldn't git her to give up grievin after it. One evenin he had been to town rather later than usual, and when he come home Nancy was not in the house. After lookin about for her every whar, he went to little Tommy's grave, and thar she was, lyin on the ground, sobbin in her sleep, while her hair, what was hangin loose over her pale face and shoulders, was wet with the evenin due. Dick raised her gently in his arms.

"Nancy," ses he, as he led her to the house, "why will you grieve yourself to death? Don't you care nothin for me, that you expose yourself to the damp night air, as if you wanted to git sick and die?"

"Oh, dear Richard," ses she, "you know I love you; but how can I give up my pore, dear little baby?"

"But, Nancy," ses Dick, "grievin so much won't do no good. Besides, its wrong to do so. You know we can't have him back."

"I know he can't be alive agin, pore little angel —I know he can't be ower little baby agin, in this world. But it seems to me like he was near to me when I'm at his grave. If he would only come back to me once more, and I could see his dear, sweet, little face, I know I would feel better."

"Dear Nancy," ses her husband, "don't you know

that can't be; and if it could, you oughtn't to wish for sich a thing. It's wicked."

Pore Nancy only cried. And all the reasonin in the world couldn't convince her that it was wrong to grieve about her baby, or to wish to see him agin. She was one of those who instead of tryin to shake off a heart-sorrow takes pleasure in givin way to ther grief, and finds consolation in the sacrifice of feelin they make to the memory of them they love.

Weeks and months passed, and still Nancy grieved for her baby, and every night her piller was wet with her tears. Dick loved her too much and was too tender to her to scold her, but he tried his best to make her forgit her sorrow, by every argyment he could think of. But it was all no use, and six months after little Tommy's death he was as fresh in the mind of his mother as he was the day of his death.

One night they had gone to bed as usual talking about little Tommy. Nancy had been tellin her husband how glad she would be to see him once more, and Dick had been tryin to convince her how wrong it was to make sich wishes, when he fell asleep, leavin Nancy cryin and sobin as usual. How long pore Nancy had indulged her grief before she went to sleep, nobody knows, but the first thing Dick know'd, he was waked up by his wife grabin hold of him by the arm and shakin him.

"What's the matter, Nancy?" ses he, as he tried to git bright awake.

"Oh, Richard, Richard, don't you hear him?" ses Nancy, settin up in the bed, and cryin like a child.

"Hear what?" ses Dick, risin up on his elbow, and openin his ears as wide as he could.

"Oh, Richard, he's come back—he's come back to see us once more!" ses she, grabin hold of her husband's arm, and tremblin all over.

"Why, Nancy," ses Dick, "what upon yeath ails you? Who's come back?"

"Our little baby. Listen, Richard!" ses she, clinging closer to him. "Listen!"

Dick begun to breathe monstrous short, thinkin that his pore wife was really gwine crazy. Jest then he heard a noise at the door.

"Don't you hear it?" ses Nancy, in a faint whisper.

Shore enough, he heard a baby voice say "Momy—momy!"

Dick's hair stood right upon eend, and a cold chill run all over him.

"Git up, Richard, and open the door," ses Nancy. "Pore little dear, it's come back to see its mother once more."

"Why, my lord, Nancy! you don't spose that's little Tommy, do you?"

"I know it's him! Do git up, Richard, and let him in."

"Momy—momy—oh, momy—tum to your pore little Tommy.

"Thar," ses she, "it's callin to us agin. Do git up, Richard."

"But, Nancy—you wouldn't let a ghost in the house, would you?" ses he, shakin all over like he had a ager.

"To be shore," ses she. "I know my dear little Tommy wouldn't hurt its mother. I know he wouldn't. Listen agin. Do git up, Richard!"

"But, Nancy," ses Dick, "spose it was to be some other ghost?"

"No, Richard! I know my dear baby's voice. It's nobody else's ghost but his, and we must let it in."

Agin the voice called, so pitiful.

Nancy could stand it no longer, and was gwine herself, when Dick got up and they both went side and side, holdin each other tight by ther night-clothes, towards the door, to let in the ghost of ther dead baby. The tears was pourin down Nancy's face, and her hands was cold as ice, while Dick shuck so he couldn't hardly walk straight. It was a moonlight night, and a strong shadow lay on the side of the house on which the door was. Before the door was a little portico, and near it stood several rose-bushes and other shrubbery. As they got near the door they stopped. Agin the voice sent forth its pittiful cry.

"Oh!" sighed Nancy.

"Let's look out of the winder first," whispered Dick.

They both stepped softly to the winder, that was open near the door. Cautiously they looked out, when, shore enough, what should they see, standin under the portico, close by the door, but little Tommy, with his white shroud on, jest as he was buried!

"Oh!" breathed pore Nancy.

But Dick was too much skeered to say a word.

"There he is!" whispered Nancy. "Pore, dear, little creetur. I know'd it would come back to see its mother once more."

"Momy—momy!" ses the little ghost, very slow and pitiful.

"Pore dear," sighed Nancy, leanin on her tremblin husband for support.

"Tommy—Tommy!" ses another baby voice a little ways off.

"Thar's another one!" gasped Dick—"a black one!"

"Whar is it?" whispered Nancy.

"Why, over thar, by the rose-bush."

"Shore enough!" ses Nancy.

"What is it?" ses Dick. "Whose ghost is that?"

"Why, that's little Abe's ghost. Don't you remember little Abe died jest a week after little Tommy, and you know how fond they was of one another, and how they used to always play together. Little Abe's come back with his little mas' Tommy, for company."

"Shore enough!" ses Dick.

"Shan't we open the door for 'em, Richard?" ax'd Nancy, holdin tight to him.

Dick hesitated. He didn't know what to do. He didn't want to let a ghost in the house, and yet he couldn't bear the idee of turning his own child away from the door. They both stood in breathless suspense for a minit, lookin each other in the face. The ghost called for its mother agin, in a tone so pittiful that it went to ther very hearts.

"Tommy—Tommy!" ses the black ghost under the rose-bush.

Jest then Dick sneezed in spite of all he could do

"Whaw!—fit—fit—whaw, yuh!" went both ghosts at once, as they vanished quicker'n lightning over the gardin fence.

"His cats! you d—ls!" yelled Dick, almost startled out of his skin, and grabin Nancy in his arms to keep her from drapin on the floor.

Dick had been too bad skeered to laugh, and he felt too sorry for his pore wife to say much to her about the ghosts. Jumpin into bed agin, they nestled themselves together under the kiver, and managed to keep from ketchin any more cold during the rest of the night.

Nancy's got two or three boys and galls now, and though she often thinks of little Tommy, she don't grieve to have his ghost come back to her any more.

MAN-WITH-THE-POKER;

OR,

HOW SAM ODUM COME TO JOIN THE TEMPERANCE SOCIETY.

SAM ODUM was the father of all the tailors in Pineville; or, in other words, he was the first man that ever sot up in the tailorin business in our town. He was a monstrous good workman, and used to give his customers fits whenever he made any thing for 'em. He was a very industrious man, and one of the cleverest little fellers that ever lived. Every body liked him first rate; and even after Mr. Shears, the "fashionable tailor from New York," sot up his emporium on the opposite side of the street, Sam got as much to do as he could attend to. But Sam Odum did have one fault. He had fits himself sometimes—drunken fits—when he wasn't fit for nothing for weeks together. He didn't have no wife; and used to keep a sort of bachellor's hall, as he called it, in the back room of his shop, whar he always had a bottle of good licker, and a half dozen split-bottom chairs, for the accommodation of his friends, and a soft-plank floor for them to sleep on if they happened to be overcome with his hospitality.

Sam wasn't drunk all the time. He used to touch his bottle lightly, as a common practice; but every now and then he used to have a regular blow-out, as he called it, when he wouldn't do nothing else but drink whiskey for whole weeks. On sich occasions he was very quiet and good-natured, and never disturbed anybody; but sometimes he used to keep it up so long, and drink so much licker, that his head-works would git out of order, and then he used to have the devlishest notions that ever entered the brains of any human white man. Sometimes he would git so bad off that he would have to have the doctor to him for several days; and when he would git over his crazy spell, it would be a week before he could do any thing, and before he would look natural out of his eyes. After drinkin to a certain notch he seemed to have a idee that the devil was gwine to carry him off; and sometimes, when he got in one of these tantrums, he used to see all sorts of sights, and it tuck three or four of his friends to hold him in his bed, and all they could do they couldn't persuade him out of the notion that the old gentleman with the horns and the cow's foot was after him with a three-pronged pitch-fork.

One time, jest after the October election, when Sam's candidate for Governor got beat (he was a great politician, and used to bet strong sometimes), he tuck one of his regular blow-outs. He had been full as a tick for more'n a week, and had got to that pint when it was necessary for him to taper off. That was always a difficult matter with Sam, and had to be managed with a great deal of caution. His friends had been settin up with him, and watchin him for a couple of nights, and he was jest beginin to come to his senses a little, when a circumstance happened that like to been the eend of him.

It was about daylight on a cold, frosty morning, and Sam was lyin on his bed tryin to collect his senses, which had been wanderin all over creation, while his friends, what was watchin him, had draped off into a doze. He had seed "the man with the poker," as he called him, two or three times durin the night, and had managed to give him the dodge; and he was wonderin whether the old cuss had gin up the chase, or was jest skulkin about watchin for a good chance to git hold of him. Bimeby he heard a noise out of doors like the trampin of feet. Springin up on his elbow he listened for a minit. The noise growed louder, and a voice said, "We must have him along this time!" and the next minit ther was a loud blast from about five hundred horns, and more'n a thousand dogs sot up a most unearthly howl all round the house.

The thought flashed on Sam's mind that the devil was after him with his hounds. Quicker'n lightning he sprung from his bed with eyes startin from ther sockets, and every hair on eend—he rushed to the door and away he went. His friends, aroused by the noise, waked up jest in time to see him clear the garden fence.

"Odum! stop Odum!" shouted one.

"Ketch him!" hollered the other, both of them given chase with all ther might.

The street and yard was full of men and horses and dogs, and in a minit all hands was in hot pursuit of the flyin Odum, who, with his night-shirt streamin in the wind, was makin for the woods over fences and ditches, brush and briars, with the speed of a race-horse.

The horses couldn't follow, and the men couldn't keep up, and the dogs wasn't allowed to give chase. Men and horses went tearin about in every direction. The horsemen tuck the road to the woods, to try to nead him, and them on foot was climbin the fences and racin over the cornfields, and through the brush and briars all hollerin to Sam to stop. But they mought as well hollered to the winds. Away he went, never stopin for any thing, till he got to the woods, in which he soon disappeared, screamin and yellin like a maniac all the time.

After runnin about half a mile in the woods, he tuck a sweet-gum, and, climbin into the very top limbs, sot thar when his pursuers come up, tremblin and shakin like he had a ager, with his shirt all tore to ribbons, and his legs and feet bleedin whar they was cut and scratched all to pieces with the brush and briars.

His friends tried to coax him down from the tree, but all they could do they couldn't git him to move a peg.

"Come down, Samy," ses Joe Enderman, "what upon yeath has got into you to cut sich a antic this mornin? Come down, old feller."

Sam tuck no notice, but jest kep on groanin and screamin and holdin tight to the tree.

"Come down, Samy—we's yer friends—nobody shan't hurt you."

"Oh, let me off this time, Mr. Devil," ses Odum,

clingin to the limb he was on, and lookin down as wild as a loon.

"Nonsense!" ses Bob Moreland. "Ther ain't no devil here. Don't you know me, Sam? Come down and less go home before you catch yer death of cold."

"Ow!—ow!—oo—oo—oo!" ses Odum.

"Oh, don't be a dinged fool, Samy!" ses old John Hendricks, who was a partickeler chum of Odum's and had had the "man with the poker" after him a time or two himself. "Come down, out of that. Nobody aint gwine to hurt you."

But all the scoldin and coaxin in creation couldn't move Sam. He know'd the old devil was after him with all the hounds in the infernal regions, and he was determined not to let 'em catch him if he could help it.

His friends findin that they couldn't do nothin by reasonin with him, they all agreed to go away and hide themselves, and see if he wouldn't come down by himself. But thar he sot and sot, makin the ugliest noise through his rattlin teeth that ever mortal heard, lookin round all the time as wild as a buck rabit, but without movin to come down.

"I'll bring him, boys," ses John Hendricks; and with that he sent a nigger to town to bring him a bottle of whiskey.

As soon as the whiskey come, Hendricks tuck a drink himself, and then went to the tree and axed Sam if he wouldn't have some.

"Come, Samy," ses he, "it'll do you good this cold mornin. Come down, old feller, and try some."

"Shore enough, the first thing they know'd, Sam come slidin down the old sweet gum."

p. 279.

"Ow!—ow!—oo—oo—oo!" was all that Sam could say.

After tryin in vain to convince him that ther wasn't no devil about, Hendricks tuck another drink, and sot the bottle on a stump a little ways from the tree, so Samy could see it, and then went and hid himself again, to watch.

By this time the sun was up several hours and the frost was off the ground. Sam begun to calm down. He gradually got over his skeer. Lookin round to satisfy himself that the devil and his hounds was all gone, he spied the bottle of whiskey what Hendricks left.

"Now you watch him," ses Hendricks; "he's beginnin to come too, and he's monstrous dry by this time, and if that bottle don't bring him, then he ain't Sam Odum no more.

Shore enough, the first thing they know'd, Sam come slidin down the old sweet gum, and gwine straight to the stump, tuck a good long swig. Before he tuck the bottle from his head his friends had him surrounded. The whiskey had the effect to bring him to his senses, and after putin on some clothes what they had brought for him, he went along quietly enough with 'em to his home, whar every thing was explained to his satisfaction.

The whole circumstance grow'd out of a fox-hunt what the boys was gwine to have that mornin. They had come after Bob Moreland, who lived next door to Odum. Not knowin that Sam was jest gittin over one of his blow-outs, they blow'd ther horns to wake Bob, which sot the hounds to howlin, and made pore

Odum think the devil was come for him shore enough.

The doctor was sent for, and Odum was put to bed agin. He was scratched and bruised considrable, and wasn't able to be about agin for some time. But that was his last blow-out. The dreadful bad cold he got liked to kill him, and skeered him so bad, that he swore off drinkin any more whiskey as long as he lived, and jined the temperance society the first thing when he got well.

A COON HUNT IN A FENCY COUNTRY.

It is really astonishin what a monstrous sight of mischief ther is in a bottle of rum. If one of 'em was to be submitted to a analization as the doctors calls it, it would be found to contain all manner of devilment that ever entered the head of man, from cussin and stealin up to murder and whippin his own mother, and nonsense enough to turn all the men in the world out of ther senses. If a man's got any badness in him, let him drink whiskey, and it will bring it out jest as sassafras tea does the measles; and if he's a good-for-nothin sort of a feller, without no bad traits in partickeler, it'll bring out all his foolishness. It affects different people in different ways—it makes some men monstrous brave and full of fight, and some it makes cowards—some it makes rich and happy and some pore and miserable. And it has different effects on different people's eyes—some it makes see double, and some it makes so blind that they can't tell themselves from a side of bacon. One of the worst cases of rum-foolery that I've heard of for a long time tuck place in Pineville last fall.

Bill Sweeney and Tom Culpepper is the two greatest old coveys in our settlement for coon-huntin. The fact is, they don't do much of any thing else, and when *they* can't catch coons, it's a shore sign that coons is scarce. Well, one night they had every thing ready for a reglar hunt, but owin to some extra good fortin, Tom had got a pocket-pistol, as he called it, of genewine old Jimmaky rum. After takin a good startin horn, they went out on ther hunt, with ther lightwood torch a blazin, and the dogs a barkin and yelpin like they was crazy. They struck out into the woods, gwine in the direction of old Starlin Jones's new ground, a great place for coons. Every now and then they would stop to wait for the dogs, and then they would drink one another's health, until they begun to feel first-rate. On they went, chattin away about one thing and another, takin a nip now and then from Tom's bottle, not mindin much whar they was gwine. Bimeby they come to a fence. Well, over they got without much difficulty.

"Who's fence is this?" ses Bill.

"Taint no matter," ses Tom, "let's take a drink."

After takin a pull at the bottle, they went on agin, wonderin what upon yeath had come of the dogs. The next thing they come to was a terrible muddy branch. After gropin ther way through the bushes and briers and gittin on tother side, they tuck another drink. Fixin up ther torch and startin on agin, they didn't go but a little ways before they come to another branch, as bad as the first one, and a little further they come to another fence—a monstrous high one this time.

"Whar upon yeath is we got to, Culpepper?" ses Bill; "I never seed sich a heap of fences and branches in these parts."

"Why," ses Tom, "it's old Starlin's doins; you know he's always bildin fences and makin infernal improvements, as he calls 'em. But never mind; we's through 'em now."

"The devil we is," ses Bill; "why, here's the alfiredest high fence yit."

Shore enough, thar they was right agin another fence. By this time they begun to be considerable tired and limber in ther jints; and it was sich a terrible high fence. Tom drapped the last piece of the torch, and thar they was in the dark.

"Now you *is* done it!" ses Bill.

Tom knowd he had, but he thought it was no use to grieve over what couldn't be helped, so, ses he,

"Never mind, old hoss—come ahead, and I'll take you out," and the next minit, kerslash! he went into the water up to his neck.

Bill heard the splash, and he clung to the fence with both hands like he thought it was slewin round to throw him off.

"Hellow, Tom!" ses he, "whar in creation has you got to?"

"Here I is!" ses Tom, spittin the water out of his mouth, and coughin like he'd swallered something. "Look out, ther's another dratted branch here."

"Name o' sense, whar is we?" ses Bill. "If this isn't a fency country, dad fetch my buttons!"

"Yes, and a branchy one, too!" ses Tom, "and they is the thickest and the highest and the deepest that I ever seed in all my born days."

After a good deal of cussin and gruntin Bill got himself loose from the fence.

"Which way is you?" ses he.

"Here, right over the branch," ses Tom.

The next minit in Bill went, up to his middle in the branch.

"Come ahead," ses Tom, "and let's go home."

"Come thunder!" ses Bill, "in sich a place as this, whar a feller hain't more'n got his coat-tail unhitched from a fence before he's over head and ears in a cussed branch."

Bill made a terrible job of gittin across the branch, which he swore was the deepest one yit. They managed to git together agin after feelin about in the dark a while, and, takin another drink, they sot out for home, cussin the fences and the branches, and helpin one another up now and then when they got ther legs tangled in the brush; but they hadn't gone more'n twenty yards before they found themselves in the middle of another branch. After gittin through the branch and gwine about twenty yards they was brung up all standin agin by another everlastin fence.

"Dad blame my picter," ses Bill, "if I don't think we's bewitched. Who upon yeath would go and build fences all over outdoors this way?"

It tuck 'em a long time to climb this fence, but when they got on top of it they found the ground on tother side without much trouble. This time the bottle was broke, and they come monstrous nigh havin a fight about the catastrofy. But it was a very good thing the licker was spilt, for after crossin three or four more branches and climbin as many more fences, it got to be daylight, when to ther great astonishment they found out that they had been climbin the same fence and wadin the same branch all night, not more'n a hundred yards from the place whar they first come to 'em.

Bill Sweeney ses he can't account for it no other way but that the licker sort o' turned ther heads; and he ses he really does believe if it hadn't gin out, they'd been climbin that same fence and wadin that same branch till now.

THE END.

www.ingramcontent.com/pod-product-compliance
Lightning Source LLC
La Vergne TN
LVHW020225110826
845151LV00003B/827

* 9 7 8 1 4 2 5 5 3 1 9 1 1 *